MERCURY'S CROSSING

CAMERON DREAMSHARE

ISBN: 978-0-9959557-8-3
Copyright 2018 by Cameron Montgomery
Author website: www.CameronDreamshare.com

Studio Dreamshare Press
Pembroke, Ontario
www.StudioDreamshare.com
For information and permissions contact:
studiodreamshare@gmail.com

The ego plays the role of guardian until the master returns.

CONTENTS

PART ONE: HER SMALL GREAT ACT

CHAPTER ONE

The beat dropped and Mercury Elmahdy spun on her heel, the sound of a chainsaw rising and falling as the lights throbbed faster with the music. The energy of the crowd rose in a collective wave as pink smoke puffed out of machines along the walls of the old theatre. Illaria shrieked with joy, pumping harder to the music. Mercury raised her arm in the air, her handful of rings sparkling under the club lights. Samar and Allison wove around them, dancing, twirling, glittering with sequins and pops of neon.

Mercury loved to dance. She loved the pulse of uncomplicated techno-house channeling through the thud of her heart and making her body move.

I'm bloody glad we came here, said Illaria through Virtual Reality Connect.

Of course, thought Mercury back. *How could we go anywhere else on my last night in town?* The girls squeezed each other in a hug and kept dancing.

Merc loved it here. Camden Palace was an old refurbished opera house painted matte gold. It was retro and real. Most of the clubs in London these days had hologram girls to get the guys in the door. Last month Merc went to a club that felt packed, and when she realized that most of the women were fake, she felt like she was living inside a gif cycling on repeat. The crowd at Camden Palace was always good.

The beat melted into ambient progressive break like clouds floating across the sky and the girls moved slowly with expansive gestures, bending and folding until the beat built back up and they were twisting and grinding again.

"Mercury!" shouted a voice from high above them on a balcony. They looked up. It was Asma. She waved. Mercury grinned and gestured her to come down and dance with them.

"I found you," said the girl, squeezing through the crowd to get to them on the main floor.

Mercury hugged her and kissed her cheek.

"Thanks for coming," she said.

Asma closed her eyes and started to dance. It was her first time in a club—she came out for Mercury's last night in London. She closed her eyes because somewhere in her mind she couldn't stop thinking that her father's-auntie's-friend's-son could somehow be in the crowd and blow her cover. She also felt like everyone was looking at her in her hijab.

Mercury grabbed her hands and they danced together. It wasn't long before Asma relaxed and let the music flow through her. As long as she didn't meet anyone's gaze she felt okay.

Mercury threw herself into the music, willing this night to be epically memorable, but it just felt surreal. She kept drawing her friends into her arms while she danced. Tomorrow, her life would change forever.

Boom. A cannon went off on stage and glitter rained down on the revellers' outstretched hands. The girls danced harder, shrieking with delight. Mercury caught Asma's eyes, startled open by the cannon, and they smiled at one another in a shower of gold.

The girls danced on and on. The bartender announced last call and Allison, Samar and Illaria made their way over to get a last round of shots.

Mercury laughed and shook her head. The girls didn't pressure her; they knew she rarely drank.

"Go ahead, I don't mind," said Asma.

Mercury pulled her in close, wrapping her arms tight around Asma's waist. Asma squeezed her back. She sighed.

"I'll miss you," she said into Mercury's ear.

They danced like that, holding one another, Mercury's head on Asma's shoulder, until the other girls came back. Mercury kissed her on the neck and pulled away. She smiled at Asma and they all danced until the club closed.

Finally the night was over and they hugged and kissed outside Camden Palace as partygoers streamed past them to catch the night tube home.

"I can't believe you're going tomorrow," said Samar. "It came so fast."

"Don't you have a plane to catch in the morning, you crazy bitch?" said Illaria.

"I'll be fine," said Mercury. She kissed them all fiercely.

"You have to come visit," she said.

"I will for sure," said Illaria.

They made their way to the station and then went their separate ways to get home. Mercury gave Asma's hand one last squeeze as she disappeared into the underground.

Mercury Elmahdy decided that tonight she would walk home. It would take her less than an hour to walk to her house by Bryanston Square from here, and this was the last time she would get the chance in a long time.

Maybe ever, she thought. She shivered. She knew she would come back to London someday, but it would never be quite like this: twenty-one years old without a care in the world.

It was a hot night and Mercury was sticky from dancing for hours. Her skin sparkled under the streetlights from the glitter cannon. She looked at her arm and smiled.

I wonder what my new friends in Washington will be like, she thought. She tried to imagine them. It was impossible.

It was after four am, but she wasn't tired at all.

I could walk all night, she thought.

She looked from side to side, taking in the familiar streets she had known all her life. She was excited for this adventure, starting the next chapter of her life.

She passed Park Square West. The usually busy roadway was the quietest she had ever seen it. She breathed in the air.

Night air? Morning air? The June sky was light enough now to see the street signs and the sun would soon break against the horizon.

Two figures slithered out of the darkness of the trees.

"Nice whaps," hissed one menacingly. They both chuckled.

They were quintessential white trash chavs complete with bad teeth and ball caps.

Mercury rolled her eyes and kept walking.

They followed.

So much for my last walk in Marylebone, she thought. She quickened her step.

The thugs kept pace behind her, whistling and hooting. One reached out and ran his fingers under the hem of her shorts. She spun around.

"Leave me alone!" she screamed, pushing him, and turning to run.

"Ugly cunt!" he shouted.

"Go back to Pakistan!" hollered the other.

Mercury was long gone. Her lean legs carried her down the B524 in record time and she only slowed down when she got to George Street. She paused on the corner to catch her breath, wiping an angry tear out of her eye. The fuckers had ruined her night.

The sun was up. Mercury walked the last few blocks briskly, let herself in, and crashed into bed to get a few hours of sleep before she had to be up to catch her flight.

"Wake up habibti." Mercury's grandmother shook her awake.

Mercury sat up slowly, and her grandma clucked at the imprint of glitter on the pillow.

"How will you take care of yourself," she laughed.

Mercury kissed her on the cheek on her way to the shower. She scrubbed off the glitter and let the hot water wake her up slowly. It would be a long day.

Mercury was raised by her grandparents in London. Her parents died in the Egyptian Revolution of 2021 when she was just seven years old. She remembered nothing of Egypt but her grandparents talked about it enough that she felt connected to it through stories. She loved it for its history and beauty but she hated it for taking her parents.

When Mercury finished in the shower, her hand lingered on her shampoo and conditioner bottles. She decided weeks ago that she wouldn't take them with her; they took up too much room in her suitcase, they could explode in the belly of the plane, and it would be fun to shop for new products in her new home. Today though, she suddenly felt attached, like she wished she could bring the familiar objects to an unfamiliar place. She sighed and pushed her jitters aside. Her suitcases were packed. No time for regrets now.

Mercury put on a comfy cotton t-shirt and high-waisted black silk shorts. She put on her favourite jacket, a green, yellow and red tie-dye oversized quilted bomber jacket. It was cozy, like a blanket. She pushed up the sleeves because it was hot outside. There would be air conditioning at the airport. The pockets were deep, and she plunged her wallet and passport inside. She put on a wide Mayan choker and completed her look with pastel blue lipstick. She was ready for adventure.

"Come eat," said grandma Neena. Grandpa Giddy was already at the table having his coffee. The silence was tense. Mercury sat down to eat.

"Do you have your passport?" asked Neena finally, fingering the tablecloth.

"I have it," said Mercury, finishing her breakfast and pouring one last cup of coffee before she had to leave.

"Good. You will be fine."

Neena's lips were set in a tight line. She was trying not to cry.

"I'll call you as soon as I land," said Mercury.

She felt strangely numb. If she thought about it too much she would cry herself. She stood up quickly. Her grandfather's hands were shaking as he stood to take hers.

"Stay away from foolish people," he said, kissing her forehead.

"I will," laughed Mercury. She squeezed him tight.

"I love you," she said to her grandmother, holding her. She pulled away and looked down quickly, grabbing her bags and heading to the door.

"She has an adventurous soul," said Neena, watching her go. "Eqlib al-qidra ala fummaha, titlaa el bint li Ummaha[1]" said Giddy, his eyes sparkling with tears.

Just like that, Mercury was gone.

The ride to the airport was faster than she expected. Mercury looked up at the soft grey skies over London one last time, the muted and insistent buzz of drones filling the air. There were more here at

[1] Like mother, like daughter.

the airport than there were downtown. It always amazed her that they didn't collide into one another more often.

"Smile," said a chirpy man passing her by.

She frowned at him and said nothing.

Time to go, she thought.

She rolled her two massive suitcases into the departures area. She checked them in, relieved to be rid of them. Everything she needed for the flight was in her backpack.

"So you're going to America for school," asked the attendant. "How much time did you spend in Britain?"

"My entire life so far," said Mercury Elmahdy.

"Oh. But... you're Egyptian right?" said the attendant, glancing at her passport.

"As you can see by my passport, I'm British," said Merc.

"But you were born in Egypt."

"Yes I was born in Egypt. London is all I remember."

In the last few years Britain had implemented a policy of including country of birth on the passports of non-Caucasians. Since then Mercury found travelling more difficult.

"I see. Well good luck to you miss," said the attendant with a smile, returning her passport with a boarding pass inside.

Mercury made her way to the security check queue. She was immediately flagged and transferred to a special line. She always gave herself an extra hour to get through security when she travelled. Her name, Elmahdy, and now the Egyptian note on her file aroused the suspicions of the National Aviation Authority.

In a special room, two agents went through every item in her backpack, carefully checking the lining, dusting each surface for trace amounts of chemicals. They inspected her shoes, her jacket, and reviewed her files.

"All clear," said one. "You can clean up your things."

Mercury repacked her bag.

"So you're going to America for school, are you?" asked the other. "Are you excited?"

"I am, but I'll miss home, to be honest," she said.

"Well you can always go back to Egypt when you're done," said the agent.

Mercury did not bother to explain to him that London was home and had always been home. She zipped up her backpack.

"Can I go now?"
"Yes."

The flight was eight hours direct from London to Washington. Mercury stayed awake as long as she could. She was exhausted from the night before, but she knew that when she arrived it would be late evening and if she slept now her whole sense of time would be messed up for days. She watched a few films and avoided talking to the man sitting beside her.

When the plane landed, Mercury picked up her bags without incident. Before she left the airport, she queued up at Customs and Border Control to get cleared to enter the country.

"Mercury Elmahdy," drawled the agent at the kiosk, looking over her passport. "That you?"

She nodded.

"Can you speak English?" he asked slowly.

"The Queen's, mate."

"Good. Why are you entering the You-nited States of America?"

"I'm going to Georgetown University in the fall."

"What will you be studying?"

"Computer programming."

"Are you a Muslim?" he asked.

Mercury's relationship with Islam was complicated. She was raised Muslim and had many friends in the community. She refused to believe in a man in the sky. Everyone else had an opinion about whether or not that made her Muslim. Today it was easier not to be.

She looked him straight in the eyes. "No."

"Well go on ahead then."

Mercury dragged her bags out of Customs to find a cab to Georgetown.

It was already evening. Mercury went straight to her guest house and checked in. She would be staying there for two months and then moving into university residence. She was hoping to get a feel for the city and the neighbourhood before school took up all of her time.

Mercury pushed her suitcases into the corner and jumped up onto the bed. She sank into its softness with a sigh. It had been a long day. She wanted to go out and explore the neighbourhood but now that she was nestled into her room she changed her mind.

Fuck it, she thought.

It was dark outside anyway. Tomorrow she would get an early start.

The ceilings in the suite were soaring, like her grandparents' flat in London. This row house had a kind of old-world charm, but it was different than Britain. She tried to put her finger on it.

Rustling dried flowers and dusty books reeking of dark dirt and ink. Stained brown wallpaper and amber glass. Faded carpets and family portraits...

London was a different kind of old. *Grey lions, cobblestones, a narrow street, Victorian china, crumbling ancient walls glassed in beside a trendy café in an old barber shop. Books reeking of musty perfume.*

There was a sepia-toned picture of a man with mutton chops and a severe expression on the wall opposite the bed. Mercury fell asleep dreaming he would come home soon and demand his room back.

Mercury woke up in the big bed. Yesterday she was exhausted and anxious but today a little fire of excitement burned inside her heart the moment her eyes fluttered open.

I made it. I'm here, she thought. *I can't believe it.*

She got out of bed and peeled off her travel clothes. They smelled like the airplane. She went to the shower. Before she did anything today she would have to call her grandparents. London was five hours ahead so they were probably panicking already.

She lathered up her body with unfamiliar soap and washed away her past.

My new life begins today, she thought.

She put on a comfortable t-shirt and connected to the guest house internet. She called her grandparents on Zype. After a few rings, their faces appeared on her screen.

"Hai! Ez-ai-yek habibti!" They waved to her from the kitchen table.

"Hai! I'm safe and sound," laughed Mercury.

She showed them her room.

"What will you do today?" asked Neena.

"I'm just going to walk around the neighbourhood and see what it's like."

"Go and see the university. Make sure you're ready for school. Get your books."

"I have lots of time," said Mercury. "School doesn't start until September."

"Don't wait until September," said Neena with a worried look.

Giddy and Mercury laughed. Giddy rubbed Neena's shoulders. "Go explore. Call us tomorrow," he said.

"Love you!"

"Love you."

Mercury grabbed her purse and went down to the lobby. The halls of the guest house were lined with faded pictures of bygone times labelled with description tags. She would check them out in more detail later. She passed by the breakfast room quickly so she wouldn't have to make small talk with the owner. She was excited to get out and see the city.

The street was quiet. It was very early and the shops would not be open for an hour yet. Merc was glad to be out before the other people crowded the street. She sometimes felt overwhelmed when there were too many people around in the day time.

As she walked quickly up and down the hills of Georgetown, Mercury fell in love. This was it. She was in the right place. She could feel it.

She walked until she was hungry. She stopped for lunch at a little Mexican restaurant.

"I've never had Mexican," she said to the waitress without looking at the menu. "Just give me whatever you like best."

The waitress brought her a big bowl of ceviche.

"How do you like it?" she asked after Mercury had taken a few bites.

"It's tasty. Perfect for a hot day," said Mercury. "Thank you."

"I love your accent," said the waitress.

"Just got in from London yesterday," said Merc.

"Welcome to Washington."

Mercury left the restaurant feeling very satisfied. The sun was high in the sky and painfully bright. She walked on, popping in and out of local shops.

Mercury came across a charming limestone building.

Old Stone House, she read. It was some kind of museum. She went inside.

The house was the oldest in Georgetown, built in the early Colonial era before the United States was a country. The massive hearth fire reminded Mercury of cottages in the English countryside. She read the pamphlets explaining the history of the home.

Oh yes, she thought. *Slavery.* It was that very particularly American institution that coloured every aspect of American history. When *Old Stone House* was built by slaves, the white family lived upstairs, the black one below. Mercury suspected that reminders of slavery were everywhere in this city for locals, from side doors where "coloureds" entered, to faded spaces on walls where signs like "whites only" had been taken down. Immigrants and tourists visiting the shops would have no idea that these streets and walls were laid by slaves' hands. Mercury took a pamphlet for her scrapbook and left the house.

Over the next week, Mercury wandered the neighbourhood, settling into the rhythm of the city. Everything here was a bit old-fashioned. She got a pass card at the local library; in London everything was high-tech. She found a small café called Marley's where there were lots of cozy corners to curl up with a book, and some evenings there was live music. Merc was starting to feel lonely, but she wasn't sure how to make friends. It wasn't something she ever had trouble with before. She thought of all her closest friends back home. How had they connected? She didn't really remember. The thought of her friends made her feel a pang of homesickness.

There was a young man sitting near her with a coffee, engrossed in something on his computer screen. She didn't want to interrupt him. He felt her gaze and his eyes flicked up, locking with hers. She smiled awkwardly. He pulled out his headphones.

"Sorry did you say something?" he asked.

"Oh, no. Just... wondering what you're watching that is so interesting," she stammered.

He looked at her with curiosity.

Is she a religious nut trying to recruit me? he thought. He realized that he had never seen her here before, and he came here a lot. *She's got an accent though... that's strange...*

"It's a music video," he said carefully.

"Oh wicked. I'm Merc, by the way," she said, holding out her hand. "Mercury Elmahdy."

"Raif Jones," he said, deciding she seemed nice. He shook her hand. "So... are you a tourist in Georgetown?"

Mercury laughed. "Is it obvious?"

"Yea." Raif grinned.

"I'm starting school at GU in the fall actually," she said.

"Oh, cool." Raif relaxed. She was just new in town.

There was a silent pause.

"Let's see the video, then," said Merc.

Raif turned the computer sideways on the table so Mercury could see the screen. He pulled out the headphone cord.

"Play," he said.

The video picked up where he left off. It was a live show. The singer was a young man with longish hair. He was holding the microphone with both hands and singing with his eyes closed. His voice was pleading with the audience from a small stage.

"This is good," said Merc. "I actually really like this."

"I just found them online. They don't have a lot of followers but I think they'll blow up soon."

They listened to the end of the song.

"Great voice," said Merc. "What's his name?"

"I can't remember, but the band is called the Waves."

Mercury and Raif chatted all afternoon. Raif was a second-year student (the Americans called it 'sophomore') at Georgetown studying International Affairs.

"I have to head out soon, I'm meeting some friends for dinner, but you're welcome to come if you like."

"Really? That sounds great."

Mercury went with Raif to meet up with his friends. They all seemed nice enough; they were dressed in khaki pants and polo shirts and they talked about politics the entire dinner. They stared at her blue-green lipstick and cornrows with a kind of blank curiosity. She liked Raif, but his friends were not really her scene.

"Thanks for inviting me to dinner," she said to Raif at the end of the night. "It was really nice to sit down with some humans finally."

"No problem. Add me on Virtual and we can meet up again

some time."

They tapped devices, exchanging information.

"See you at Marley's."

"Goodnight."

Mercury knew that there must be a fun hub tucked away in the city somewhere. She would find it. She decided that she would hop on the bus and take it anywhere until she found what she was looking for. As the bus passed through what she assumed was downtown, she realized that there was a large section of the city dedicated to parks for large monuments. From a distance, it reminded her vaguely of Pyongyang. She passed it by. Mercury Elmahdy was from London; aspirational empire statuary anywhere else was not going to impress her.

She got off the bus and onto a streetcar. The driver gave her a wide welcoming grin.

"How do?" she said cheerfully.

He laughed. "Where you headed?"

"Don't rightly know, just exploring really."

"I got you."

The streetcar trundled along for a while, eventually passing a massive mural painted on the side of a crumbling brick building.

Now this is more like it, thought Mercury.

"You hungry?" asked the driver.

"Now that you mention it..."

The streetcar groaned to a stop.

"Try that place," he said, pointing to an unassuming hole in the wall with a faded Art Deco sign.

"Thanks!"

Mercury got off the tram and went into the building.

"I've come for a bite," she said to the bartender. "What's good here?"

"Try the ramen upstairs. You won't be disappointed."

Mercury followed the delicious sour smell of kimchi up to a small restaurant with colourful walls and a rough arched wood ceiling that felt like a lobster trap. She was seated in a lone chair at the bar between two groups of chatting diners. Although she was sitting shoulder to shoulder with the people beside her, she felt lonely.

"What can I get you?"

"First time," smiled Merc. "Give me what's popular tonight."

"Kimchi ramen?" asked the server.

"Perfect."

Mercury's bowl looked delicious. It was a cloudy yellow broth dolloped with richly coloured pastes, a healthy portion of kimchi, and raw grated vegetables and sesame seeds on top. She listened to snippets of conversations as she sipped her drink and waited for her soup to cool. The sun was starting to set and the server came around to light candles at tables.

Where to after this? thought Merc.

She looked around at the patrons eating dinner. The joint was just the right blend of pop and casual. It definitely suited her more than the restaurants she visited in Georgetown, but still the people here looked kind of preppy.

Where are the creatives? she thought.

London could be the same if you didn't know where to go.

When it was sufficiently cooled, Mercury slurped her ramen. She was not disappointed. The flavours were bright and rich, and complemented the comfort and simplicity of noodles and broth.

When she came into the restaurant she'd seen some arcade machines in the bar next door. She decided that after dinner she would go down and try them out. She finished up her bowl, paid, and made her way downstairs.

The long, narrow room was lined with vintage game machines that ran on quarters. Mercury walked down to the back where the bar was situated, checking out the selection. The pinball machines looked so cool but the novelty wore off after one or two balls. She spied Donkey Kong.

Perfect, she thought. *I'll be back for you.*

She walked up to the bar.

"So how does this work?" asked Merc.

"Two dollars per credit. You buy them here and I give you tokens."

Petty cash mostly died out with the last generation. Mercury was the first generation of youth who had never used coin.

"I'll take five. Add a ginger ale to that as well," said Mercury, holding out her wrist where she had an implanted chip.

"You don't see a lot of those here," said the bartender as he scanned her—*ding*. "I heard it's caught on in New York City though."

"Everyone's got em in London."

"I guess that's where you're from then?"

"Yea. Mercury," she said, holding out her hand.

"Jason," said the bartender, shaking her hand.

He poured her ginger ale. "You sure you don't want something stronger?"

"Not tonight, thanks," said Merc.

She took her drink over to *Donkey Kong*. Someone was already playing. She leaned against the machine and looked around the arcade. There were some low-key punk vibes happening. She was getting closer.

"You want to play next?" asked the girl on *Donkey Kong*.

"Take your time," smiled Merc.

"Go for it." The girl stood up.

"Thanks," said Mercury.

She sat down and put in her quarter. When she turned around the girl was gone.

After three rounds of DK, Mercury took a break. It was completely dark outside. There were more people and the arcade was filling up. Just as she looked at the door, two guys came into the bar. They both had long hair and one was wearing a bomber jacket not unlike her own. The other had streaks of paint on his pants. He locked eyes with her as he came down toward the bar.

"You paint?" she asked with a smile.

"Sometimes," he laughed. He was wearing eyeliner.

"I'm Jezz," said the boy with the jacket.

"I'm Mitt," said the boy with the painted pants.

"Mercury." She held out her hand for a shake. Jezz fist bumped it.

"Cool accent," said Jezz softly.

"I'm sort of new in town," said Merc.

"I like your style. We're heading to a rave in Ivy City later, you down?"

"Sure!"

They grabbed a table and chatted for a bit. Jezz and Mitt were nineteen and twenty one, but Jezz had a fake ID. Jezz was a student at Washington Studio School and Mitt worked at a coffee shop called

Bukowski in Dupont Circle.

The boys had a few drinks and then it was time to go.

"How far is it?" asked Mercury.

"Pretty close. We can just walk," said Mitt. They headed out.

The summer night felt friendlier as she walked with the two guys.

"Let's connect on Virtual in case we get split up," said Mercury. She held out her wrist.

"Whoa, we don't have the chip here yet really," said Jezz.

"I don't have Virtual Reality Connect either," said Mitt. "Can't afford that shit. But I do have the Virtuous hack." He grinned.

"What's that?"

"The latest knockoff."

"That's highly illegal in the UK," said Mercury. "Those hacks are engineered in China and Russia, you realize."

"VRC is insanely expensive though."

"In England the price is regulated by the state. They don't want all that data going straight to other governments."

"Big business around here would never let the government regulate it."

Mercury shivered and said nothing. Her programmer mind thought of all the ways the lack of foresight could go awry.

Do you really want some half-assed nanotech broadcasting in and out of your brain? she thought.

"I can connect to your Virtual with Virtuous," said Mitt. "You won't get in trouble here, I promise."

She looked at him.

I can always disconnect later if I need to, she thought. Her VRC was highly secure.

They exchanged information.

They walked along a quiet industrial street. Mangy cats dug through bags of trash by the side of the road.

"Getting close," said Jezz.

It didn't feel like there was a club nearby.

They kept walking, and then Mercury heard the beat. It grew louder, and she heard young people's voices. A purple light glowed from an alley onto the street.

The party was a pop-up event called Purple Passion that never took place in the same location twice. Tonight it was hosted in a run-down auto shop.

"Side door," said Mitt. They ducked into the alley where the music boomed as people slipped in and out. Mitt pulled a slip of paper out of his pocket and showed it to the chick at the door with a mouthful of piercings. She let them in.

The place was packed from wall to wall. Portable floodlights were set up around the room casting purple and pink beams on the crowd. A disco ball glittered from the ceiling. The sound system was better than most clubs.

"Cool right?" said Mitt, catching the huge grin on Merc's face.

They wove in deeper and picked up the beat. Mercury was instantly transported to her happy place. She could dance for hours.

Jezz held a small purple pill up to her with a question in his eyes.

"What is it?" asked Mercury.

"An upper. Like ecstasy with a dash of LSD."

Merc grinned and shook her head. "Nah!" she said. She didn't need it. Plus, she was in a strange city with strange people. She needed to get herself home tonight.

They danced and danced. Jezz and Mitt introduced her to some of their friends. Mercury was really glad she ran into them tonight. This crowd was more her jam than the matching couples in boutiques in Georgetown.

Everything's gonna be okay, thought Mercury.

After a few hours they led her over to the old garage grease pit where the organizers had set up tanks of hooch to brew a few weeks before. People were taking turns drinking out of grimy hoses.

Someone passed Mercury the hose.

"Looks nasty," she laughed.

"No one's gone blind yet," he said.

"Well now I absolutely have to try it."

She grabbed the hose and took a swig.

"Oof!" Her lips puckered at the intensity.

"Not too bad right?"

"Tastes exactly like I thought it would. We'll call that a once in a lifetime experience."

Someone handed her a flyer. It felt rough in her hand like it was made of homemade paper. She looked at it.

M Street Underpass. Our most ambitious Passion yet.

It was her invite to the next one. Purple Passion was organized by an anarchist collective called Second Coming. Loosely inspired by Pussy Riot, they never met anywhere legally.

"Thanks," she said.

"Hey, where are you from?" asked the girl who had given her the flyer.

Mercury flinched slightly. She hated that question.

"Why do you care?" she said.

"Sorry. I just like your accent."

Mercury softened. She knew it was hard to strike a balance between genuine interest in someone's life story and making someone feel like they don't belong. Mercury decided to give this girl a chance.

"London. I'm just sick of that question."

You should wait until you know someone before you ask it, she wanted to add. But she didn't have the energy to get into that conversation right now.

"You've got great style," said the girl.

"Thanks. I'm Mercury by the way."

"Elaine."

"Pleasure."

"So what are you doing in DC?" asked Elaine.

"Computer programming at Georgetown this fall."

"Really." Elaine's interest was piqued. "The collective could use more digital if you ever want to get more involved."

"Honestly I'm just here to party, but that does sound like a good way to make new friends."

Elaine laughed and they exchanged information.

Mercury tucked her invite to the next Passion into her jacket and then went back to the dance floor to lose herself in the music. She was really proud of herself. Usually she was a bit shy and awkward but she was really outdoing herself with trying to meet new people.

Finally it was time to head back up to Georgetown. She looked around for Jezz and Mitt. She didn't see them anywhere.

Where are you? called Mercury in Virtual.

Sorry girl, said Mitt. *Jezz just finished her period so we left ;)*

Mercury heard laughter over Virtual Reality Connect in her head.

She was silent.

You okay? asked Jezz softly.

It sounded like things were getting hot and heavy on the other side.

Yea I'm fine. Have fun guys. Thanks for taking me out tonight. Night hun.

She disconnected. Her friends in London would never leave without telling her—not that Jezz and Mitt were her friends yet, but it still made her feel like they didn't care much. Maybe that was just how people were in this new place. She would have to get used to fending for herself.

Isn't that why you moved so far away in the first place? she thought.

It was time to figure out how to get home. She looked up the transit situation. It was pretty grim; there was nothing until the morning schedule. Walking would take over two hours. She felt her stomach growl.

Might as well get a bite to eat and catch the 4:30 am when it starts, she thought. There was a 24 hour diner twenty minutes away. She started walking.

Almost every overhang and stoop had a huddled form curled up beneath it. This neighbourhood had a lot more homeless people than Georgetown, she noticed. Mercury had read that a lot more people here in the United States did not have access to internet than she was used to. She could see firelight crackling in the windows of abandoned buildings here, and she started to get an understanding of why.

America's version of 'off-grid', she thought.

A man moaned in an alley. Mercury felt a chill down her spine and walked faster. She could see the lights up ahead of a built-up intersection. The diner was not far.

She reached the street. There were men standing outside of a pool hall smoking cigarettes. They looked like patrons of the bar, but they also looked like the homeless people she had seen on her way here.

She pulled out her device to see if she had to turn left or right to get to the diner. The blue glow of the screen illuminated her face.

Left.

She felt strong arms grab her from behind and something cold and hard press into her stomach.

"What the fuck?"

She looked down. It was a gun. She felt cold shock from head to toe. She had never seen a gun before.

"Are you barking mad? It that actually a fucking gun?"

"Give me your phone," he snarled. "And your money."

"Or what? You'll blow a hole in me? Seriously?" Mercury's voice was shrill. She was in shock.

"He will," said another man, walking in front of her.

He reached out and snatched her phone out of her hands.

"Now your money."

"I don't have a fucking red cent."

"Bullshit." He reached toward her.

She snapped her hands into her pockets and pulled them out.

"I have this piece of paper and an arcade token. You want it?"

The man holding her loosened his grip. The hand holding the gun relaxed.

The other man took the token.

Mercury sneered.

"You got something to say?"

He took a step toward her. His teeth were yellow and his breath reeked.

"You got your fucking quarter, let me go," she said, yanking an arm out of the man's grasp.

"Help!" she screamed.

The man with the yellow teeth hit her right in the mouth.

"Shut up, you mouthy Blaxican bitch. I can do whatever I want to you right now, no one gives a fuck."

From the apartment above the bar, a woman leaned out the window.

"I called the police," she shouted. "Now get the fuck outta here."

"The police don't bother coming to this neighbourhood at night," said the man with yellow teeth.

"They will for me," said Mercury. "I'm an ambassador's daughter. I hit the alarm on my phone before you took it. They'll be here any minute."

The man holding her shoved her from behind. She stumbled to her knees.

"She's lying," said the yellow-toothed man, but Mercury could hear the doubt in his voice. She scrambled to her feet and ran left, away from the bar. There was the marquee of the diner, blinking neon in the dark street. She went inside.

The server came over with a greasy menu.

"What happened to you?" he asked. Her knees were scraped and bloody, her pockets were turned out and her hair was a mess.

"Blokes are the same all over I see," she said, wiping blood off her mouth with the back of her hand. "I'm going to the restroom. When I get out I need to use a phone. After that I want a big breakfast, whatever you got really, and lots of coffee."

She walked to the back of the restaurant and into the washroom.

Mercury turned on the taps in the grimy sink. She let the water get warm and then she washed up as best she could.

When she came out, there was a steaming mug of coffee waiting for her at a table. She sank into the bench seat and cupped it in her hands. She would have her coffee and then call the police.

She felt terribly alone.

"Here's a phone," said the waiter. He had a kind face and he didn't ask her about her night. She called the police. There was no answer, just an inbox service, so she left a message as detailed as possible about what happened. She included her Virtual information on the off chance that they could trace her phone before it got wiped.

The waiter brought out a plate of bacon and eggs with toast. She didn't eat pork, but today she just scarfed it down. Neena and Giddy Elmahdy would understand.

The man in the kitchen was humming along with the song on the radio. The tune was familiar, but she couldn't remember where she heard it before.

"Excuse me," she said to the waiter. "What is this song?"

"I don't know. I can find out though," he said.

He brought over his phone. "It's called *Answer*, by the Waves."

The Waves. It was the band Raif was listening to at Marley's Café.

The waiter showed her the screen. They were a small-time Canadian band currently touring. In a few weeks they would be performing in Halifax, an east-coast Canadian city just a few hours north of DC.

"Can you send me that? My phone got stolen tonight," she said.

"Sure."

She sent it to herself from his phone for when she got home. A concert would make her feel better.

The sun was rising.

"What do I owe you?" she asked, holding out her wrist.

"It's cash only," said the server.

Mercury's face fell.

"You know what? This one's on the house. Come back again, okay?"

"Thanks."

The morning bus rolled up to the stop outside the diner and she hopped on.

CHAPTER TWO

Jordan Barker, the lead singer of the band the Waves, was getting ready for his first show on the East Coast. He had never visited the Maritimes before.

After the small publicity explosion following their spot on CBC, Jordan, Jerome and Bubba found a new drummer. Emmet Hale was incredibly talented and bringing him on board levelled up the Waves to professional band. Hale found Cynthia Hing, a bass player he met when they studied together at the Victoria Conservatory of Music. They hired a publicist and manager, Mack Miller. The band was complete.

Jordan couldn't believe how easy it was to book gigs and publicity spots now. He almost felt bitter about it.

Every band needs a Mack, he thought. *We couldn't do it without him.*

The responsibility of managing the band overwhelmed Jordan to the point of mental breakdown. Hale and Cyn thought that hiring a proper band manager would level him out. It helped, but he was still fucked up.

Bubba and Jerome knew about Jordan's troubles. Hale and Cyn were only starting to realize now that Jordan's creative genius cast a long and intense shadow.

It was Canada Day. The Waves were playing a free show at the Halifax Commons to round out their first cross-Canada tour. As long as it didn't rain, it would be the biggest crowd they ever played for.

"Remember last year?" said Jerome. "That show in Montréal... that's where it all started."

"Look at us now," grinned Bubba. "We're a national treasure."

Bubba had been officially dubbed the Production Technician. He was the head roadie and he was happier than he had ever been in his life.

Jordan smiled but he was distracted.

We have more than I ever hoped was possible, and everything I ever dreamed of is in our reach, he thought. *So why don't I feel it?* He felt like any minute it could all slip away.

"You ready?" said Mack, poking his head into the offstage green room that was set up for the talent.

"Yep," said Cyn.

"Come check out the light setup this band's got, it's awesome."

They all followed Mack out to stage left. Jordan lingered behind. He pulled his necklace out of his shirt, opened up the small vial, and took a bump of coke. He capped the vial and slid the necklace back into his shirt. He inhaled sharply as the rush hit his senses.

"Right before the show man? You sure that's a good idea?" said Bubba, coming back and catching Jordan in the act.

"Are you worried about my singing?" said Jordan with a laugh. "You know I can sing anywhere, anytime."

"Okay, but seriously that shit will fuck you up."

"Trust me, I'm worse without it."

Bubba frowned, something he rarely did.

"Well then you gotta see a doctor bro," he said.

Jordan was suffering hard from depression, but he refused to seek treatment.

"I won't take antidepressants," growled Jordan. He thought antidepressants would diminish his soul somehow.

"How are these drugs better?" said Bubba softly.

Jordan glowered and pushed past him to join the others.

*

Valkyrie Snow was at her condo in Ottawa, the capital of Canada. She checked her bags one last time before calling her ride to the airport. She was following a lead and heading out to the east coast. Dr. Thaila recommended that she take it easy and not stress herself out too much, because it could cause long-term damage to her brain, but she was dying to remember why the music of the Waves was so important.

I need to be back with the sisters at Gray House anyway, she thought.

She was so grateful to have the sisters for support while her health was so bad. The sisterhood was located on Cape Breton Island on the east coast.

Valkyrie was going to the Waves concert in Halifax, and then she would continue on to the sisterhood. She wore a small backpack with her overnight essentials and she was taking two large crates of things to Gray House. Supplies were more limited on their remote estate and the ladies requested tools, speciality foods and other items from the mainland.

"Your car is here," said the Oracle, her AIA (Artificially Intelligent Assistant). "Would you like help with the cargo?"

The robot in the car was already on its way up. It was also Oracle-enabled.

"Yes, thank you," said Val.

When the robot came into the condo, it tried to lift a crate.

"It exceeds its permitted weight bearing," said the Oracle. "Lifting this weight could damage it. I will call for more assistance."

"Sorry, it's the cast iron pans for Margarethe. Don't worry, I'll help."

Valkyrie lifted one end of the crate. The robot lifted the other. Together they brought the crate out and loaded it into the car. They came back for the second one.

"Did I forget anything?" asked Valkyrie.

"I don't think so," said the Oracle.

"Okay. Lock up for me please."

"Affirmative."

They headed to the airport.

Valkyrie Snow was nervous and excited. She hated that her memories of the last year of her life were hazy and sporadic. She was desperately hoping for this lead to help her understand what was happening to her. She slid her passport to the agent at the desk.

"I'm sorry but it seems that you cancelled this ticket."

"What? That can't be," she hissed. "Check again."

The agent tapped away at the keyboard.

"It says here you booked the flight six days ago, and you canceled it yesterday."

"I did not. That's a mistake."

"It's not, ma'am."

Valkyrie looked at the clock. The flight would be boarding soon. She always came to the airport at the last minute because she had a Nexus pass for expedited boarding.

"Well put me on the flight then."

The agent tapped the keyboard.

"I'm sorry but we have a policy that we don't book any seats less than an hour before boarding. The flight boards in twenty minutes."

"Get your manager over here and put me on the plane," she snarled.

The agent signalled a manager to come over.

"Hi there, what can I do for you?" asked the manager.

"I'm supposed to be boarding the plane to Halifax in fifteen minutes."

"She doesn't have a ticket," said the agent.

"You left this a bit last minute, didn't you?" joked the manager.

"No! Somehow your system screwed up and now I'm not on the flight manifest. I bought a ticket and I have a confirmation message from your company!"

"Let's see..." said the manager, reviewing the information on the agent's screen.

"It says here you cancelled the flight. That's a scam I've seen before, you know."

"I'm not a scammer! I'm a Nexus pass holder!"

"Our records say that you cancelled the flight."

"Fine. Just get me back on it," said Val, sick of arguing.

"It is against company policy to—"

"—to book a flight with less than an hour before boarding. I heard. That's why I called you over. To fix this problem."

"I really can't—"

Valkyrie cut him off again. "If your foolish mistake makes me miss my flight, I'll put this whole airport on blast."

The manager looked at her for a moment.

"See what's available," he said to the agent.

"There won't be anything in first class..." he said to Val.

"That's fine."

The agent tapped away at the computer.

"It's fully booked," he said.

Valkyrie slammed her fist on the desk in frustration. Several people looked over at her, alarmed.

This was uncharacteristic behaviour for Valkyrie Snow, but spikes in aggression and intense emotion were a side-effect of the brain condition she was suffering from.

"I can't believe this," she said. "When is the next flight?"

"In four hours," said the agent.

She turned away in frustration.

"Oracle," she said.

"Yes?" At home she heard the voice over her sound system but here at the airport it floated into her mind.

"Make sure my cargo is on the next flight. Book me a hyperloop please."

"Affirmative."

She walked out of the airport.

*

"Showtime," said Mack with a grin. The band burst onto the stage. The crowd cheered.

Hale crashed in on the drums. The Waves were off. They opened with one of the old reliable songs from their first album with a great beat to build the crowd up.

As Jordan sang, his heart lifted up into the sky. Being on stage and singing for a crowd was the same feeling as being in love for him. In these moments the world faded away, and all of his thoughts were silent; his voice was a channel for all that was good and pure and radiant in him, and the audience could feel it. On stage, Jordan's anxiety was gone.

"What a beautiful place," he murmured into the microphone as the song ended. He closed his eyes and faced the direction of the setting sun basking him in gold.

The crowd cheered. Jordan's smile was angelic as they snapped pictures and livestreamed from below.

"Shout out to my pal Bubba's parents who are here watching the show with us today," said Jordan. "I couldn't imagine my life without him."

Bubba laughed offstage. Although he went to high school in Ottawa, he was a Haligonian in his heart. His ancestors had lived in the city since the 1800s; they survived the forced relocations of Black Canadians in the 1960s. Bubba's parents moved to Ottawa for work when he was fifteen years old, but they loved the east coast and visited his grandmother there often. She still lived in the house he spent his childhood in. Mr. and Mrs. Rose waved from the sea of faces in the crowd.

The Waves took the crowd on a journey as the sun went down, from up-tempo to slow and melancholy and then back up again. Finally, they played the anthem that gave them so much mileage through CBC.

From offstage, Mack smiled as the crowd joined in.
It's so damn catchy, he thought. *A money-maker.*

Where will I be when the revolution begins?
When you call I will answer
When you call I will answer
Reach out and touch me, I'll take your hand
You have to start it
You have to start it

Logging my hours, spending my life
To make someone else's dreams come true
There has to be
More
Than
This

Where will I be when the revolution begins?
When you call I will answer

When you call I will answer
Reach out and touch me, I'll take your hand
You have to start it
You have to start it

House I hate, car I can't afford
Kids I don't want, marriage I don't need
Becoming what I'm pretending to be

Where will I be when the revolution begins?
When you call I will answer
When you call I will answer
Reach out and touch me, I'll take your hand
You have to start it
You have to start it

The crowd was pulled into the energy of the performance. Mercury Elmahdy stood in the centre of it all, staring up at the band on stage. Coming to this concert was a nice break from the stress of starting school in Washington. As the band began to play, she realized that the concert was more than a nice distraction; the music called to her deep inside. This was it. She felt it. A turning point in her life. As strangers pressed up around her she had a brilliant idea. It crashed over her like a wave, and as she listened to the words of the song her creative and analytical mind whirred into action, neurons firing as she thought up all the ways she could make it happen and bring her idea to life.

She pulled out her device to jot down some notes. Thought-to-text technology was not perfect yet but she would be able to make sure she got most of it right by checking the screen. After her phone got stolen Mercury upgraded to the latest Augmented Reality device. She was meaning to get one for a while. Thankfully she didn't even need to tell Neena and Giddy Elmahdy that her other phone was stolen. They didn't need to worry about that. Mercury learned her lesson and she would be more careful at night.

Hunt in a pack, she thought.

She was still working on making new friends. People in Washington D.C. were more reluctant to let people into their friend groups than anywhere Mercury had ever been.

She finished her notes, pausing before closing the app. The *Title* bar was empty.

Mercury's Small Great Act, she typed.

She felt a shiver of excitement from head to toe.

As the Waves finished up and the headliner band came on Mercury let herself relax into the next set. She loved live music.

*

Valkyrie Snow arrived in Halifax just as the sun was starting to set. She jumped in a car. If she hurried she would catch the rest of the show.

The streets were packed with people dressed in red and white. There was cheering and singing, and a lot of drinking. The car crawled through traffic as crowds of partiers moved through the streets without paying attention to signs or lights. Valkyrie debated getting out and going on foot but she decided to try and be patient. She didn't know the city and the car would surely get her there faster than walking.

This struggle now is all part of the journey, she thought, trying to calm her mind.

Minutes ticked by on the clock. She knew that she would only catch the tail end of the concert if she was lucky.

Finally the car pulled up to the edge of the park. Valkyrie could see thousands of people between her and the performance onstage across the field. She jumped out and ran to the security table, validating her ticket and weaving through the crowd. The music itself was not familiar, but when the singer's voice rose in heart-wrenching cadences, she felt her body react and her head throbbed. She forced herself forward.

The band ended the song with a bang.

"Thanks everybody, Happy Canada Day and goodnight!" said the man onstage. "I love you."

Valkyrie's head jolted with a pain so intense that she almost fainted. She growled and pushed on, forcing her way closer to the front of the stage. The people around her were annoyed but she didn't care. She was almost there.

Valkyrie looked up at the man onstage. The light shone bright on his beautiful face and a soft lock of hair fell gently into his eyes. He pushed it back and then held his hand up as the crowd cheered.

Then he and the band exited the stage.

Jordan Barker, she thought.

The stroke of pain in her head was so intense that this time, she did pass out.

*

After the show, the Waves went to an after party hosted at a mansion off Belmont on the Arm. Most of the day's performers were there. It was a great opportunity to mingle with other musicians.

"Make sure everyone in the room takes a selfie with you for social," said Mack with a smile. He had his camera out and he was taking pictures too. Mack had taken over management of their Instagram account and with a few well-selected endorsements by Influencers they had over twenty thousand followers.

There were studio lights set up everywhere, and the lights of many cameras flashed. The food and drinks were great and the house itself was incredible.

Jordan grabbed a cocktail and went out to the balcony overlooking the ocean. On the beach far below, a group of people hooted and hollered around a bonfire, drinking and jamming on banjos and guitars. It looked like fun.

"The stars are so clear out here," said a voice behind him.

He turned. The woman walked over and leaned up against the balcony. He looked up into the sky.

"They sure are," he said.

"I'm Skyla."

No shit, he thought. Of course he knew who she was. Skyla Bright was one of the biggest female artists on the scene right now.

"Jordan."

They enjoyed the stars for a moment.

"I caught your set today. You've got a great voice."

"Thanks," said Jordan.

He felt a flutter of excitement. This was one of those moments he dreamed about over and over as he washed dishes at the Cherry. He wanted her to snap a picture of them together for social, but something in him painfully wanted her to think he was cooler than that.

They were silent again. Jordan wanted to say something but he was terrified to say the wrong thing.

"So what are you drinking?" he asked. It was all he could think of to say.

"I don't even know," she said. "Someone handed it to me." She laughed awkwardly.

She's nervous, he thought. He felt a thrill. He turned to her and locked her with his green-eyed gaze through the soft hair falling on his face. Skyla smiled.

She's into this. He could feel it.

Flash. Mack took a picture from across the balcony.

The moment was over.

"Well it was nice to meet you," she said, walking back into the house.

Jordan looked at Mack, who winked.

CHAPTER THREE

Mercury woke up early in her flat-share on Morris Street in Halifax. She was renting it for a few days so she had some time to explore the city before heading back to D.C. This was just the adventure she needed before she started gearing up for school in the fall. She headed down to the Halifax Waterfront Boardwalk; she had signed up for a sailing tour of Halifax. The tour guide tapped directly into her Virtual Reality Connect and as she looked out over the rollicking waves at the Nova Scotia shore, she listened to stories of bygone days. She held up her Augmented Reality phone, and it displayed on the screen in real time pictures of what the landscape looked like in the past. There was no mention of the slaves who had laid the oldest stones of the harbour when Canada was just a European colony.

It was a glorious day; the sun was bright and the sky was perfectly blue. She even got to chat with British tourists and it was comforting to hear the familiar accent. She found the land and the ocean incredibly inspiring and that night when she crawled into bed, she slept better than she had since she left London.

Jordan Barker slept in late the day after the concert. He was emotionally exhausted and the comedown after a show was intense. That evening, he picked himself up and he and the band went out for dinner downtown. They had the local specialty—heaps of delicious seafood.

Jordan was getting bigger. He ate a lot more food these days than he ever did before in his life. He didn't realize that food could taste so good. He was used to eating junk. He was still exercising every chance he got, and instead of getting fat, he was building muscle. He was also hitting second puberty—the one that men go through in their late twenties—and he swore he was getting taller.

After dinner, they went from bar to bar, and then as students started coming out to hit the clubs, they went back to the hotel. Jordan stayed out. His legs were jittery from a day in bed and he loved walking the streets of a new city at night. He walked through the bright lights of downtown and then through residential neighbourhoods, imagining all the people in their homes living their lives. He wondered if any of them were happy. He hoped they were.

The next evening Jordan walked along the waterfront. He found a quiet spot where he could sit on some rocks and listen to the sound of the waves lapping the shore. It was mesmerizing. He got out his phone and recorded the sound. Maybe he could sample it in a song later.

*

Mercury Elmahdy was out for a walk along the Halifax Harbour front too. She noticed that the whole city of Halifax that she could see looked like the neighbourhood of Georgetown in Washington.

The colourful wood houses between old limestone buildings lining the streets contained shops and apartments for mostly childless couples. Buskers played music on the boardwalk as the sun went down.

Merc enjoyed the salty breeze blowing gently as she walked down to the water. She sat on a bench and popped in her earphones to listen to her favourite tunes as she relaxed.

I can't imagine writing a song, she thought. *What is it like to have music in your head?*

She thought about the Canada Day concert. *Jordan Barker is so young to have it all figured out.*

Mercury was still figuring things out. She knew she was great at computer programming, but she wasn't sure where it would take her. So far, it had taken her to Washington D.C. and Halifax. She remembered the brilliant idea that dawned on her at the concert. When she got home to Washington she would take her notes and really start planning it out.

Home. The word sat heavily on her mind. Washington didn't feel like home yet. She hoped that when she moved into residence that things would come together.

The sky darkened slowly, and by night time, it was just Mercury, the last seagulls, and a young man sitting on the rocks by the shore.

Finally, Mercury stood up for a stretch, and headed back to her flat-share for the night.

*

The next morning there were pictures of Jordan all over the news. The front page shot was he and starlet Skyla Bright. She was leaning in and looking at him with a coy smile and he looked like a soulful poet about to spout sonnets. He almost laughed.

Reporters mined his data on social and there was a catalogue of his old content posted for the world to see. There were no pictures of his family. He didn't have any.

Who is Jordan Barker? they wanted to know.

"We're cooking now," said Mack, slapping his hands with glee as they packed up to leave the hotel.

"Great promo," said Hale, rubbing Jordan's back.

"Did you actually bang Skyla Bright?" asked Bubba.

"Nah dude, she talked to me for like, one minute."

"The perfect minute," said Mack.

The headlines ran wild with speculation.

Mack's phone rang.

"Hello?"

He stepped away to chat with someone on the other end. Then he hung up.

"It was Skyla Bright's manager. He wants to talk about how we're going to play this."

"Are we going to meet up in the real?"

"Probably not."

It was all a game to the managers. The spin game.

"He was surprised at how intense the reaction was, since the Waves are still pretty unknown. That must have added to the appeal. Anyway, it's been good for sales."

"Shit, how about our sales?"

"Grand slam," said Mack. "This will seed our next tour."

"Really? Awesome! This calls for some serious celebration," said Cyn.

They had a team hug.

The Waves left Halifax on the highest note they could and caught the Loop back to Ottawa.

*

When Valkyrie Snow collapsed at the concert in Halifax, someone called an ambulance and she was taken to the hospital. The doctors weren't sure what happened to her. They determined that she didn't have a stroke, but when they were able to bring her conscious, she could hardly speak. She was in acute pain. They checked her medical records and contacted Dr. Thaila.

"The baby..." she croaked.

"The baby is fine," said the doctor, holding her hand. "Is there someone we should contact?"

"Chanda Rani," said Val. "Oracle, send the doctor her contact information."

She closed her eyes. The light was unbearable.

The next day, Chanda and Farrah arrived at the hospital in Halifax to get Valkyrie.

"She's suffered some brain damage," said one of the doctors quietly. "She is highly sensitive to light. You will need to keep her in a dark, quiet place to properly rest."

"Valkyrie, what have you been doing?" scolded Farrah. "You should never have left Gray House!"

Valkyrie squeezed her hand weakly and said nothing.

"No need for that now," said Chanda quietly. "It will be enough to get her back now."

Each woman dealt with adversity her own way.

"The baby?" Chanda asked the doctor quietly.

"She's still pregnant, yes."

Farrah exhaled with relief, kissing Val's hand. "Everything will be okay."

Valkyrie tried to smile but she could barely think.

They bundled her up in a shawl and put her in the car.

When they got to Gray House, the communal house on Cape Breton Island, Margarethe burst out the door. Her white hair was wrapped in a turban and she wore ropes of red beads around her neck.

"Valki!"

The ladies helped Val into the house and up to Margarethe's bed.

There were children playing on the floor by the bed and the old woman shooed them out.

"No noise in here! She is sick darlings!"

Margarethe insisted that Valkyrie spend the next few days in bed with the blinds closed. No one was allowed in to disturb her. Margarethe slept with Chanda.

Finally, Val was feeling well enough to make her way downstairs. Her brow was creased in a frown. She could barely open her eyes. Even the smallest amount of light burned.

The ladies fashioned her a wimple out of cloth with a veil she could bring down over her face to block out the light.

"I'm going to call the contractors," she said quietly, her voice muted by the cloth, "and get someone over here to work on my cottage. I'm moving there immediately. I won't put you out of your bed."

"Nonsense!" said Margarethe. "I like sleeping with Chanda."

"I'll move as soon as possible," continued Val. "I will need to get ready for the baby, anyway."

"Of course dear."

As soon as dusk came, Valkyrie went to the little stone house. It was a mess inside. She set to work hauling old junk out. An iron bed frame rusted into the floor, and piles of wood trash were in various stages of decomposition. The floor beneath a major hole in the roof was ruined. Still, there were large parts of the wide oak floorboards that were salvageable beneath the detritus. There was only one small window in the building. The first time she looked at the cottage she envisioned blasting out a wall to make a window to look out over the ocean, but now she saw the darkness as a blessing. Her head throbbed permanently.

Valkyrie hummed as she worked, dragging the ruins of a past life out of the cottage—feebly, at first, and then stronger as she picked up momentum. Finally, after many hours of work, the main space was clear. Covered in sweat and filth, she lay down in the centre of the room and fell asleep just as the sun started to rise.

For the next several days, no one bothered her. She came up to the farmhouse to get a bite to eat and a drink when she needed it, and otherwise she was busy stripping down and scrubbing the stone house on her hands and knees. She bathed in the ocean salt when she got too dirty to stand it and then continued to work.

Valkyrie was a resilient woman. When she divorced Baron she was forty-one years old. Their friends treated her like she might as well just go die. Instead she went back to school, built a company, and rebuilt herself. She didn't even start to understand who she truly was until her fifties. Now she was fifty seven years old and getting ready to have a baby for the first time. Life was full of surprises.

Valkyrie had almost done as much as she could do. She surveyed her work. The cottage was tiny, but it would do nicely for one person.

...and a baby... she thought.

The wooden front door opened into the undivided main room. A woodstove against one wall would need to be replaced and a stovepipe installed. Solid wide stairs led up to a triangular loft where the floor was rotted completely through in one corner. The walls were a mess of plaster that would need a total overhaul, but the bones beneath were solid.

Stone bones, she thought. *Like mine.*

The contractor arrived the next day and Valkyrie threw herself into planning the stone house. It sat away from Gray House where the sisters lived, and away from the peninsula where the arcology was in the process of being built. Valkyrie Snow was an architect and the massive carbon-neutral arcology was her legacy project coming to life.

Work on the arcology was progressing quickly. The metal and wood scaffolding rose from the plateau on the peninsula like dragons' bones. The base of the citadel was massive. Valkyrie was impatient and watching it grow was both exciting and torturous. She focused on getting the cottage in working order. It stimulated her enough to keep her from thinking about her memory troubles but it also didn't stress her out.

Every day Valkyrie did an hour of meditation in the morning and an hour at night. She focused all of her energy singularly on healing her brain. She willed the nanites to heal instead of block. After she finished her meditation she always felt more calm and relaxed.

*

Jordan Barker was back home in Ottawa. He lived in a run-down student ghetto place called Animal House. He and Bubba had rooms in the basement and a few other people lived upstairs. The rent was covered by hiring out the main floor space for events. It was surreal to be back here after staying in hotels and rubbing elbows with celebrities on tour. Even though they made a name for themselves, the hustle wasn't over. The money was re-invested back into the band and they were still humble. They had new phones and Virtual Reality Connect, and they could afford groceries, which was nice, but it wasn't like in the movies.

Jordan was glad to be back in the city that he loved. He experienced a lot of firsts here, the good and the bad. Ottawa had made him a man.

Barry heard he was back and came by to see him. Barry was a drug dealer. He seemed pretty friendly, but Jordan had seen him threaten to cut someone with a broken bottle so he knew different.

"Nothing tonight, I got plans," said Jordan, throwing on his hoodie and heading out the door. He didn't want to get stuck in any difficult conversations.

Barry didn't say a word, he just watched Jordan walk out the door with a frown.

Jordan walked west to the transitway and then down to the canal. It was a beautiful walk and he missed it. He realized he was walking fast. He slowed down to enjoy the night air. He loved the feeling of his Blundstones on the pavement. They cost three hundred bucks. It was the most he ever spent on anything in his life except rent. He always wanted a pair and it was the first thing he bought when Mack put money into his bank account.

If everything goes to shit at least I'll have these rad shoes, he thought. He smiled ruefully. It wasn't a bitter thought like it could have been on another day. Tonight, Jordan felt great.

*

Baron Toussaint's world was on fire. The family's Ottawa-based company, Toussaint International, was unravelling. They were in the import-export business, and like most companies, they bended the rules any time it suited their bottom line. The loose end that finally started the unweaving was actually unrelated to lumber at all.

Larry Nix, an upper-level manager at Toussaint, was photographed in a brothel in Arkansas with underage sex workers. Toussaint's competitors bought the images and dug in deep, distributing them in press worldwide.

In the old days, it was easy to cut guys like Larry off like a gangrenous limb and keep the company uncontaminated by the bad press, but there were hundreds of images on social media of Larry having drinks after hours with other high-level employees, not to mention promotional content of Larry with people in the international business community who fell over running backwards trying to get away from Toussaint. Pictures of other unsavoury activities surfaced. A young prostitute in Belarus alleged that Baron Toussaint himself had drugged and beaten her on a business trip.

"She's confused," said Baron to reporters calmly and sympathetically. Inside, he was seething.

That lying bitch, he thought. The truth was that he did drug and beat her, but he rewarded her with a sizable payoff—it was the kind of money that was a game-changer in her circumstances.

She should be grateful, he thought.

The press was laying Toussaint International's dirty laundry bare.

I'm too busy for this, thought Baron.

Not only was he under an incredible amount of pressure in the changing economy squeezing him from down south, but he had other responsibilities—personal ones, the kind that could not be delegated to other people.

His unexceptional car rolled up to a run-down looking warehouse in St. Laurent. Baron got out and the vehicle drove off. He didn't want any surveillance clocking too much activity. The reporters were hounding him enough as it was.

Baron updated his security on the warehouse to a two-step punch code authorization.

Can't be too careful these days, he thought.

He had to be especially careful with the recent setbacks in his treatment plan for Valkyrie. It was harder than he expected to get her back on track. Usually he liked a challenge but in this case he was having a lot of trouble figuring out what was wrong with her. He thought that Jordan Barker was the problem, but taking him out of the equation produced zero results.

Baron let himself in the back of the building. The lights were motion sensored and they flicked on as he walked down a long hallway. He paused between two doors.

Who to visit first? he thought.

He entered the door on the left.

"Hi baby," he said, shutting the door behind him.

Click. The bolt lock auto-engaged.

The woman in the corner looked up at him, her expression vacant. She was pushing herself back and forth in a rocking chair with her bare feet.

"Hello," she said.

He leaned down and kissed her softly on the forehead.

"How are you?" he asked.

"Fine."

"Good."

He sat down in his chair beside her.

The room was decorated like a nursery. Teresa's little bed covered in quilts stood in the corner, surrounded by soft toys and a large shelf of books. There was a fake window on one wall fringed with fluffy pastel curtains.

"What have you been doing?" he asked.

She pointed listlessly to the bookshelf.

Baron smiled. "I have something for you."

Teresa's eyes registered emotion for the first time since Baron arrived. She held out her hands.

He pulled a book out of his jacket pocket.

Fables of Ancient China.

Teresa made a happy noise and held the book to her chest. She loved fairy tales. She rocked faster in the chair.

Baron put out his hand to slow the chair.

"You know I don't like that," he said softly.

She stopped rocking and put her head down. She knew. Baron was easily annoyed.

"Are you happy?" he asked.

"Yes." There was no other answer he would accept.

She held the book tight, waiting for him to leave so she could read it.

Baron looked at her downturned face. She was looking old.

You never know how a woman will age when you meet her, he thought.

He reached out and stroked her cheek.

"Good."

Teresa married Baron a year after his divorce with Valkyrie. She was ten years his junior. Teresa was once a soft and expressive woman, but she was deteriorating rapidly. In the eight years she had lived in this facility, she aged thirty. Her once lively gentle face was lined with worry and pale as a corpse.

Baron waited a few minutes longer and then stood to leave.

"I love you," he said.

"I love you. Thank you for coming, I missed you," she said, her eyes completely dead. It was also the right answer.

Baron unlocked the door and left. The bolt engaged behind him.

*

Rachel's graduation from law school was coming up and Jerome wanted to plan a party for her.

"The ceremony is in September," he said over Zype at their teleconference meeting, "so we can't be touring then. This is really important. I'm inviting her parents and everything."

"Aww, that's sweet," said Hale.

"Are we playing?" asked Cyn.

"Well yea, I was thinking that would be cool," said Jerome.

"We can get a film crew there, it'll be a great opportunity for some intimate shots at a controlled venue," said Mack.

They all laughed.

"What?" said Mack with his usual grin.

"Okay so let's get some shows set up in Ontario for September," said Hale. He and Cyn were back home in British

Columbia.

"Sounds good."

After the teleconference was over, Jerome, Bubba and Jordan headed out to Elgin Street Diner for a bite to eat.

"So... has anyone heard from Matt?" asked Jerome.

Matthew Doyle was the Waves' first drummer. He quit the band before their CBC spot.

"Nope," said Bubba.

"No." Jordan shifted awkwardly.

"I was making an invite list for the graduation party, and I wasn't sure if we should invite him or not."

They all had mixed feelings about Matt.

"I don't think so," said Jordan.

"Yea it might be weird bro," said Bubba.

"But he's still our friend, even if he isn't in the band anymore..." said Jerome.

Jordan looked uncomfortable.

"What it is?"

Bubba and Jerome both looked at him.

Jordan looked back at them. This was a conversation he had been avoiding for a long time.

"Nothing..." he said. He couldn't do it.

"Jord, we know you. Something's up. Just tell us."

Jordan sighed.

"Matt... forced Jesse's roommate to have sex with him."

"What the fuck?"

"Yea, after the first concert at Animal House."

"You mean, he raped her?"

Jordan coughed and looked around the restaurant uncomfortably.

"Yea."

"Holy shit," whistled Bubba. "Okay well point taken, let's not invite him."

"Hold on," said Jerome. "What happened? Like how is she doing? Did she tell the police?"

"I don't know," said Jordan. "I didn't know what to do."

"Jordan this is serious man. Like, shit."

"Well what would you do?"

They were all silent for a moment.

"Can I talk to Rachel about this?" asked Jerome.

"Umm, I don't know..." said Jordan.

"Rachel's a lawyer man, she'll know what to do."

Jordan didn't want to get dragged into this. He didn't want to talk about it at all. He didn't want to testify in a court or in a police statement.

You fucking low-life coward, hissed Snake, Jordan's inner critic. He shifted uncomfortably.

"Yea, maybe that's a good idea," he said quietly.

After they finished their smoked-meat-poutines at Elgin Street Diner, the boys headed home.

"Everything's gonna be okay, don't worry," said Jerome, giving Jordan a hug. "Rachel is a badass, she knows all about this stuff."

"Thanks," mumbled Jordan.

Jerome hopped on the bus and headed back to his apartment in Westboro where he and Rachel lived.

Jordan and Bubba walked home to Animal House.

As they approached the front door, Jordan noticed a big black spot on the house.

"What's that?"

They got closer to inspect. A chunk of plastic siding was missing. It looked like some drunk student had thrown a bottle at the house last night.

"Student ghetto man," said Bubba.

"We should call the landlord..."

"Nah, she'll notice it eventually."

"But it looks like shit."

"Don't worry so much Jord. It's not like we'll be living in this dump forever," said Bubba.

Jordan snorted. "We can't afford to move."

The Waves were gaining major momentum, but they were investing all of it into advertising, Mack's salary, the tour... there wasn't much left.

"Eventually."

"Yea."

They walked up the steps and into the house.

I like it here, Jordan realized. He was attached to this place.

Animal House was the first standalone honest-to-goodness house he ever lived in. From childhood to now he had only ever lived in shithole apartment buildings.

An image of Glasshouse floated into his mind. He choked it down, willing it to go away. Valkyrie Snow's Glasshouse felt more like a dream than reality to him now.

I never lived there, he thought.

"I'm calling the landlord about the siding," he decided.

CHAPTER FOUR

Mercury was nervous and excited for her first day of college. August twenty-fourth was coming up quickly. She moved out of the rooming house and into residence. She was excited to get her things set up more permanently so she could start to feel at home. The Georgetown neighbourhood was getting comfortable for her. She was getting to know its rhythm.

Her room was tiny, but she didn't have anything to put in it anyway. It came with all the basics. She would pick up some art for the walls and a plant or two in the next few days.

On her first day of school, Mercury took a seat in the middle of the auditorium. The course was Cryptography. Within the first ten minutes, she was hooked.

This is where I'm meant to be, she thought with a shiver.

Her other courses this semester were Introduction to Computer Science, Calculus, Data Structures, and Cyber Threats.

Mercury didn't talk to anyone at all during her first week at school. It seemed as though her cohort was a bit anti-social. She was lonely. She tried to meet up with Raif a few times, but it never worked out.

"I like your lipstick," said the girl beside her one day in Calculus.

"Thanks," said Mercury with surprise. "I like your..." she looked the girl over. "Your necklace." The girl wore a long chain with a piece of yellow citrine in the pendant.

"Thanks."

The girl smiled and touched the citrine.

"I'm Mercury."

"I'm Anastasia. Ana."

They both smiled.

"So are you in Programming too?"

"Statistics," said Anastasia.

The class was about to start.

"Oh," said Merc, disappointed. "Figures. I can't seem to meet anybody in my program."

The professor started to speak and they turned their attention to the front.

"So want to go for a coffee?" asked Mercury after class was over.

"Umm, ya sure," said Ana.

They went to a café on campus. Anastasia also lived in residence. She was a nice girl. Mercury went back to her dorm with a smile. She finally made a friend.

*

Matthew Doyle was scrolling on social looking for job posts. The company he was working for, Toussaint International, was going through a major publicity crisis and the top brass fired him. He was hoping that after things cooled down he could go beg for his job back. In the meantime, he was broke. He had student loan payments and he was living in an apartment he could no longer afford. He hated the thought of working some poverty wage job after being Junior Export Compliance Specialist at Toussaint International, so he was holding out for something better. As he scrolled through job search forums and found pages of posts for occasional work, sprint contracts, and part-time paid hours where they expected you to do a lot of extra work from home, he realized that things looked pretty lean.

Matt came across a post from the Waves congratulating Rachel on graduating from law school. He gritted his teeth. He hated Rachel. He scrolled through the comments. They were having a party to celebrate her success. It looked like all their friends were going. Rage boiled up inside him. He opened his contacts and found Jerome.

The phone rang.

"Hello?"

"Hey Jerome."

"Uh hey Matt, what's up?"

"Just wanted to see how you're doing."

"Oh. I'm great. Super busy, but yea things are good."

"Good, good."

There was an awkward silence. The last time they spoke was when they moved out of the Centretown apartment they were all living in together. Since then Matt left the Waves hanging for a gig and then quit the band.

"And how are you?" asked Jerome.

"Oh same-old same-old."

"Great."

"So I saw that Rachel is graduating. Good for her man."

"Yea! I'm super proud of her."

"For sure."

The tension grew.

"Okay well, good to hear from you bro—" started Jerome.

"Wait, wait a minute. Aren't you having a graduation party for her?"

"Oh. Um ya that's the plan."

"Okay... so... am I invited?" Matt laughed a little, trying to hide that he felt a bit pathetic.

Jerome coughed.

"Well it's like a family thing, sort of..."

"Oh so no friends are invited?"

"Well ya, but... you never really liked Rachel anyway man."

"What? But she's your girl. That's your choice, I don't have to like her for us to be friends right?"

"I dunno, it's her graduation party..."

"Okay but I haven't seen you guys in a while..."

"Ya I just don't think it's gonna work Matt. Sorry but like it's just not gonna work."

Matt was stunned.

"Maybe some other time man, okay? I gotta go."

Jerome hung up the phone.

Matt was humiliated. He felt the distance between he and boys growing but this phone call sealed it. They were cutting him out of their lives.

Fuck, he thought. He was jobless and now friendless.
He opened up Tinder.
Time to find someone to bang it out, he thought.

*

Mercury was thriving in school. She loved the lectures, the readings, and even the work. There was a lot of it, but she got a kick out of pushing herself. She was quietly competitive. She would look over other people's work and say nothing, but secretly she was working to be the best. Her teachers noticed it too. When they called on the class she never raised her hand, but then when no one would answer a question she would put up her hand to get the conversation rolling. She delivered answers with a quiet and absolute certainty that professors remembered.

Mercury did not forget about her brilliant idea. When she got back to Georgetown from the concert, she looked over her notes. The idea was simple, perhaps a bit silly, but the fire in her was lit and she knew that she would make it happen someday. Every morning when she woke up, she would work on "Mercury's Small Great Act" for one hour.

Mercury headed out to the restaurant where she was meeting Anastasia for dinner. The air was crisp tonight. It was October and still warm but the smell of death was creeping into the air. Mercury was excited to experience the changing seasons in this foreign land that was her new home.

She showed up to the restaurant ten minutes early.

"Hi, two please, I'm waiting for someone," she told the hostess.

She nestled into a seat by the window. The sun was setting. Mercury liked being early; she liked to settle into a space all by herself.

"Eating alone?" said the guy at the table beside her.

"Hmm?" Mercury turned to him. "Actually I'm waiting for a friend."

"That's quite an accent. Are you from out of town?"

"Yea."

"Welcome to D.C.!" He grinned. "Have you checked out the National Mall yet?"

"Not so much into malls really," said Merc.

The man chuckled.

"It's not a mall, it's a display of the world's greatest monuments and museums!"

Mercury laughed. "No, I'm from London," she said.

He smiled blankly. He didn't understand what she meant.

Anastasia walked into the restaurant.

"Well there's my friend," said Mercury. "Have a lovely dinner."

She stood up to hug Anastasia.

"Hey girl!" She pecked her on the cheek. Anastasia blushed crimson and sat down.

"Hey," said Ana.

"I'm Greg," said the man at the table beside them, holding his hand out to Anastasia.

"Oh hello, I'm Ana," she said.

"I was just telling your friend about the joys of D.C. So where are you from?"

"Cleveland Ohio, sir."

She told people she was from Cleveland, Ohio. Technically she was from Warren, a suburb town that people from Cleveland proper didn't consider part of Cleveland.

Greg told them about his life and the different Ohio football teams as the waitress took their orders.

The girls smiled and nodded politely.

"What do you think of this?" asked Mercury, showing Anastasia an article she read that morning about consonance and dissonance and calculus in chord geometry.

Ana looked it over and then looked at Merc's face.

"It's interesting," she said. "You love math more than anyone I've ever met," she laughed.

"Let's see," said Greg.

Mercury obliged.

Greg read the title and turned back to his meal without comment.

The conversation turned to calculus as their meals arrived. Greg paid the server for his meal and left.

"Nice to meet you girls. Have a good night," he said.

After dinner, Anastasia and Mercury headed out to the movies.

"Greg was kind of good-looking, for an older guy," said Ana as they walked to the theatre.

"Was he?" Mercury could barely remember his face, even though they saw him only twenty minutes ago. She didn't think about things like that a lot.

"Maybe not," said Ana. "What kind of guys are you into?"

"Umm, I don't know," said Merc. She had never been in a relationship before. "How about you?"

"Well I have a crush on Jeremy Witt, but that doesn't count."

"Who's that?" asked Mercury.

"You know, the film star."

"Oh like someone from American movies?"

"Yea." Anastasia had never seen a movie that wasn't American.

Mercury thought about it. Did she have a crush on any celebrities?

"I'm definitely not into older guys," said Mercury.

"Oh, me neither."

Anastasia was a bit of an amoeba. She agreed with everything because her family taught her that disagreeing was bad manners.

"I think I'm just focusing more on school right now," said Mercury. "My grandma and grandpa keep telling me not to get distracted and I think it's working," she laughed.

"Yea, my parents too."

"What are your parents like?" asked Merc.

"They're good Americans. They watch football and go to church. How about yours?"

"They're... well they died, actually."

"Excuse me, I'm so sorry," said Ana, red with embarrassment.

Mercury squeezed her arm. "It's okay," she said. "I was raised by my grandparents. They grew up in Egypt, and when things went super conservative in the 80's they moved to London. My parents were born and raised in London, and then they went back in the 2010's when there was a lot of hope and revolution in Egypt. I was born there. Then they died in the secularism riots of 2021. I was seven, and I went to live with Neena and Giddy in London."

"Wow." It was all Ana could say. "That's crazy."

They walked on. It was nice to talk to someone about something real.

"What are they like?" asked Ana.

You must miss them, she thought, but she didn't say it.

"They're obsessed with Queen," laughed Merc. "Hence my name. Freddie Mercury."

"Who's that?"

"You know... *Bohemian Rhapsody... We Are the Champions...*"

"Oh okay."

"They're just like stereotypical grandparents. They love me to pieces. They're like oldschool realness."

"I love my grandparents too, even though they're crazy."

They both laughed.

"So do you remember Egypt at all?"

"Not really. I know a lot about it through my grandparents and the community in London but I'm not connected to it the way they are. And even then, the Muslim community in London is more Pakistani than Egyptian anyway so it's hard for me to even know what's really Egyptian, and what's part of the London Muslim scene."

"So... you're Muslim?" Ana's face turned red. She didn't know why. What did it mean to be Muslim? The news said it meant you were stupid and old-fashioned and backwards, and at the same time you were a super-cunning terrorist. It was very confusing. Mercury seemed... pretty normal.

"Umm yea. Well no, not really... I don't know. My ancestors were Muslims a few generations before me and goddess worshippers before that, and cat worshippers before that. I think I'm still figuring out what I am."

"That's okay, I don't mind," said Ana, her face still red. She tripped over the words awkwardly. "I mean, not that I would mind. I mean... I'm sorry..."

"It's okay," said Mercury. "You think I'm okay." She laughed.

"Yea. More than okay," said Ana earnestly.

"I like you too," said Mercury.

They reached the theatre.

The girls got their tickets and went to see the movie.

*

After Rachel's graduation everyone headed to her parents' house. It was a beautiful property east of the city, past Orléans. A photographer floated around taking pictures of the guests in their graduation robes. The Waves were set up to play some songs in the corner of the yard. There were tables with food and little tents in case it rained. Twinkling lights were strung from the trees. Rachel's parents took a lot of pride in their home and it was the kind of place where the trees, the lawns, and even the patio stones were meticulous. Rachel's mother and her sister were wearing white summer dresses and her father wore a summer suit. They were beaming with pride.

"Thank you for organizing this," said Rachel's mother Shirley to Jerome. "It was such a great idea."

"I just got the ball rolling," he said. "You did most of the work!"

"Rachel's dad and I... we really love you. You're part of the family now."

They hugged.

Everyone chatted and took photos as servers came around with appetizers. After a few hours the Waves played their best tunes and everyone danced as the sun went down.

Jerome gestured to Jordan. He wanted the mic.

"I need everybody's attention," he said. Suddenly his throat was dry. He looked out over the faces of all their loved ones. The moment was surreal. Time stopped for him and suddenly Jerome realized that this was the moment that he was no longer a boy and he became a man. He cleared his throat. Everyone looked at him, waiting, wondering what he was going to say.

"Rachel. I am so proud of you. Not only because you graduated from law school—and I'm so proud of you for that—but also because you are the most incredible woman I've ever met. You're kind and caring, and so damn smart. You're beautiful. You're my best friend."

Rachel smiled at him with love shining in her eyes.

Jerome reached into his pocket. The mic scraped along his shirt and his hands were shaking.

"Uhhm..." he was awkward for a moment. He cleared his throat again. "I need to ask you something."

As he got down on one knee, everyone gasped. Phones whipped out, recording the moment.

"Rachel, will you marry me?"

She ran up into his arms.

"I love you," she said.

They kissed and everyone clapped.

"I want to marry you before our careers blow up," he whispered in her ear. "So we stay strong and grow together."

Rachel's eyes held a tiny shadow of uncertainty. What if her job took her far away? What if his did? She stepped back, looking him up and down, holding his hands. She appraised her man. Was this who she would promise to spend the rest of her life with?

She decided.

"Yes," she said. "Yes I want to grow together with you."

She put on the ring, and just like that, they were engaged.

"So you'll be my groomsmen, right?" said Jerome to Jordan and Bubba.

"Honoured man, of course," said Bubba.

"Yea. This is unbelievable," said Jordan.

"It is, but like, I just know. She's the one."

"Good for you man."

They had a group hug.

Suddenly reporters were flashing photos over the fence into the yard. Mack called in an anonymous tip that Jordan Barker and Skyla Bright were getting engaged just for the confusion and the attention.

Rachel and her family just waved awkwardly. They started to realize what they were getting themselves into.

*

During his next visit to the Barn—that was his name for the St. Laurent warehouse facility where Teresa lived—Baron decided to visit the room at the end of the hall on the right.

He opened the door and slid inside. It auto-locked behind him. There was a woman in a hospital gown tied with leather straps to an electronic medical bed. She was hooked up to a variety of machines, including a colostomy system so she wouldn't have to get up to go to the bathroom.

It was his wife.

Courtney was Baron's third and current wife. He married her in 2032, five years after he locked up Teresa. It was a tumultuous relationship from the start. She was pure arm candy, from her blond hair and matching cantaloupe tits to her daddy issues and drinking problems. Their relationship progressed very quickly from hot and heavy to high stakes fights where police were called. Baron literally chased her around the house with a baseball bat once, roaring like a lion. She screamed like a steam engine, her throat raw and bloody, rivers of mascara flowing down her cheeks. He stopped because she ripped the clothes right off of her on the front lawn and he didn't want the neighbours to get curious.

"I would never have hit you," he whispered into her hair afterwards.

They both secretly loved the drama, but then it got old. The love turned quickly into hate. Everything became a power struggle. Courtney joined Teresa in the Barn.

He looked at Courtney, strapped to the chair, her mouth covered with a gag. Her once lustrous hair was greasy and dull. Lying in the bed for months wasted away her muscles and her skin was ashen grey. It was called deconditioning—the effects of prolonged bedrest on the body.

I won in the end, he thought.

Her eyes opened slowly, and when she realized he was there she snapped to attention. She hated him with every fibre of her being. Her forearms were scarred from gnashing against her restraints. She had to be gagged and tied because she tried to escape so relentlessly.

Baron was surprised at her tenacity. He expected less from her, to be honest. Teresa accepted her fate far quicker, although Baron had used the experimental memory treatment on her, and that quickened her deterioration.

Courtney looked at him with cold determination.

My chance will come, she thought. *I'll fucking kill him.*

"What conniving little eyes you have," laughed Baron.

He was getting bored with this. When would the Stockholm Syndrome kick in? He expected her to be begging him for sex by now.

"Are you going to be nice?" he asked. He unbuckled her gag.

Courtney said nothing.

"I brought you real food," he said.

She was on a nutrient drip.

She looked at the plate. She dreamed of real food sometimes. Not from Baron though. The thought of eating the food he brought made her want to scream. She set her mouth in a tight line.

"Courtney..." he said gently, lovingly.

"No," she said quietly.

He set the warm plate on her lap in the bed and sat down in the chair beside her.

Twenty minutes passed and neither said a word.

I would decorate the room however you like, he thought. *If you would only just break.*

When he first trapped her here, he tried the same cancer trick on her that worked on Valkyrie, but Courtney didn't buy it.

Valkyrie is so naïve, so trusting, he thought.

Courtney saw through it immediately. She surprised him. She even guessed that Teresa was here too.

She's not as dumb as she looks, Baron thought.

Baron made one major mistake with Courtney. He locked her up before they got divorced. Technically they were still married.

It's not fair to Valkyrie, he thought. He wanted to re-marry Valkyrie, but in the back of his mind he would always know that it wasn't right. Courtney was his Bertha Mason.

He knew that he would probably just have to kill her and be done with it, but he didn't want that weighing on his conscience either.

Teresa's mind was mostly gone, but even still; Baron made the mistake of telling her that he was infertile, so she could never go free. No one could know.

"Will you eat your dinner, darling?" said Baron.

"No."

He stood up and walked over. He grabbed her chin in his hand and squeezed.

"I have somewhere to be, but we'll talk about this later," he said.

He left the food on her lap, just out of reach in her restraints, and left the room.

Baron was heading to the Friday Club. It was a monthly ritual for him and his friends to get together and share their indulgences.

"Just got back from the Barn," he said.

The Friday Club knew about the Barn.

"How's that going?"

"Courtney was being really difficult today."

"It's all this fucking feminism," said Harold, lighting up a cigar. "These cunts think they're men. If you want a real dirt-eating *woman* you have to go to a third world country. Those women know how to treat me right."

They all laughed.

The Friday Club was part of a wider network of communities called the Fraternity. There were many chapters and groups. The Friday Club was for millionaires only. There were groups for lower class men—they had other names: the Rebels, Proud Boys, the Kings.

Baron was so grateful for the Friday Club. These men were incredibly loyal. They would never tell another brother's secret to the outside world.

"How is the witch hunt against you going?" asked Harold.

"It's terrible. There are reporters outside my house. I have to watch my every move. Filthy liberal scum looking for lies to spew about me."

"Sorry to hear that old chap. Maybe a vacation is in order?"

"I was thinking of going down to the Caribbean for a few weeks, but you know how I hate leaving the wife for too long."

"They don't call it the ball and chain for nothing."

The salt and pepper of Baron's hair was looking decidedly white around the temples. He was stressed.

*

The Waves rode the high of Jerome and Rachel's engagement into the kickoff of the next tour. This time, they were touring the west, starting in Vancouver and working their way back to Ontario.

"Hey, aren't you the singer from the Waves?" asked a man in line at a coffee shop in Mount Pleasant. Jordan was surprised.

"Yea man."

The guy shook his hand and took a photo. It was surreal.

This was the kind of thing Jordan longed for when the band was playing shitty bars in Ottawa because it was a sign that they had 'made' it. Now that it was happening, it felt more bewildering than anything else. It was also a bit terrifying. Somewhere in his mind he expected that he would play bigger shows, make more money, and have a bigger online presence, but he never considered how it would change the fabric of his everyday life, like his morning coffee.

After their show in Vancouver, the band made their way to an exclusive party on the rooftop of an office building in Yaletown transformed into a nightclub. The city glittered in crystal around them as searchlights reflected from skyscrapers in the downtown core.

"This is next level," said Hale, grabbing a beer and surveying the small but important crowd. There were real celebrities here.

"Make some serious connections," said Mack before they went in. Mack wasn't invited.

Vancouver was an international hub for music and film, and at any given time in the city you could find some very interesting creatives if you went to the right places.

"I heard you were coming," said a woman softly.

Jordan turned around. It was Skyla Bright.

"Hey," he said.

"Hey."

"Who told you that?"

"Your publicist told my publicist. He's really trying to get this Skyla Bright-Jordan Barker—Skydan—thing going in the media."

"Oh yea? That's weird."

"My publicist isn't sure about it yet."

"I don't blame her."

They both laughed. It was the first time Jordan laughed in a really long time.

Skyla was mesmerizing in real life. Her eyes were massive and amplified by makeup like a 1920s Hollywood starlet. Every hair was perfect. Her body was like a work of art. Skyla was technically in the music industry, but she was winning in the branding industry. Her personal brand was flawless. She had taken Sarah Weinberg, her childhood self, and molded her with sheer will, work, and sometimes surgery, into the goddess that was Skyla Bright. Her presence here in the real was every bit as staggering as the Skyla Bright image.

"So how did your show go?" she asked.

"It was great. This city has great energy."

"It does. I spend a lot of time here," said Skyla.

They had a few more drinks and danced. Skyla even danced perfectly.

They took a break to stand by the building's edge and look out over the city.

"We're looking at the stars again," laughed Skyla.

"Yea." Jordan's eyes connected with hers. It was the perfect romantic moment, crafted by the universe itself from his ego's desires, but Jordan felt nothing. His expression was tortured. He wanted to reach out and touch her, brush her skin with his and feel the kindle of connection, but he could not.

Skyla felt the intensity in his gaze and then felt his energy retreat from her. It was tantalizing.

"What do you want to do now?" she asked.

Jordan thought about it.

"Want to get out of here, hit up a regular nightclub?"

Skyla was surprised. Her eyes danced. It was like the plot of an old 90's film. Her followers would love it.

"You know what, sure. Let's do it."

Jordan had Oracle on his new Augmented Reality phone.

"Oracle, show me the best clubs right now in Vancouver."

"Affirmative."

'She' cast holographic images of the scene in ten clubs. The Oracle Big Data Network sampled the voices of every Oracle AIA user in the world to create a composite voice for communication. The resulting voice sounded slightly more feminine than masculine so Oracle was sometimes called 'she'.

"How about that one," said Jordan, pointing to a place with blue lights and glints of silver. It matched Skyla's dress.

"Good choice," she said. "Let's go."

They grabbed a car and took off.

The bouncer let them straight in.

There was no great announcement of Skyla Bright's arrival but the crowd buzzed as the story passed between lips. Phones whipped out.

I guess this is happening, thought Skyla.

"I need to feed the beast," she said.

"Pardon?"

"I haven't updated my believers in a few hours. They need content or they'll go nuts," she laughed.

And if they see this from someone else before me, they'll feel betrayed, she thought.

She turned the phone into selfie mode and snapped a video of the two of them together.

It populated onto her social streams and instantly the comments rolled in.

Jordan was stunned.

"What?" she asked.

"I can't believe you're sharing that with millions of people," he said.

"These are my fans," she said. "They are everything to me. They make me who I am. I live for them."

She turned the phone back on herself and recorded live video.

"Believers, you are my everything. I live for you." She blew them a kiss and disconnected.

Jordan thought about his fans, and then felt that same sensation of bewilderment he felt at the café this morning when the man snapped his photo.

"...but it's so personal."

"Is it?" She looked him square in the eyes.

Is this personal? thought Jordan. *Or is this just business?* It seemed like a kaleidoscope of overlap for Skyla.

"I guess not," he said.

'Personal' was a matter of perspective. Who was the real Skyla Bright? Sarah Weinberg was dead. Skyla was everything.

"If you want to become everything, you have to give them everything," she said.

If you want to be their godd, she thought.

She was dead serious. She had a cult of loyal followers who would kill someone if she asked them to. Skyla Bright was shooting for legendary.

CHAPTER FIVE

Valkyrie Snow moved into her stone cottage. The floors were sanded down and shellacked, and anywhere that new wood had to be put in was covered with a thick woven rug. The walls were repaired by a mason and the stonework restored to its former glory. The exposed beam along the ceiling was cleaned of cobwebs. The big cast iron woodstove was fitted with a gleaming new stovepipe ready to heat the place in the winter. The carpenter put a beautiful carved banister on the stairs and the pitched-roof loft was filled wall-to-wall with a big comfortable bed piled with blankets.

The land around the building site for the arcology was changing quickly. Refugees continued trickling in from down south, and the acreage was a small village. Farrah, Margarethe and Chanda were joyfully organizing.

Val's stomach was starting to bulge and her breasts were sore. She felt terrible all the time. She needed more sleep than usual, but when she was awake she felt more alert than usual, like her thoughts were clearer than they had been in months. She forced herself to eat healthy for the bump, and she relaxed as much as possible. It was still surreal to her that the cluster of cells inside her womb was growing and developing and would one day become a human, if everything went right. She didn't quite believe it yet.

Sometimes in the darkness of her house Valkyrie saw scenes play out like a movie. She tried to disassociate herself from them. If she watched them from a detached standpoint instead of like memories then she could hold off the excruciating headaches. Her eyes were still sensitive to light and she wore her veil over her face any time she left the house in the light of day.

Valkyrie knew that the singer onstage at the concert had something to do with her forgotten year. She saw his green eyes in her mind and in her dreams and she knew.

As her stomach grew and her cramps worsened, she started to remember.

Kale accompanied Valkyrie to Toronto to visit Dr. Thaila, the brain specialist working on her case. Last year Valkyrie's cancer treatments were infected with bioengineered nanites that attacked her long-term memory system, causing the headaches and brain damage she had been suffering from.

Dr. Thaila performed a full checkup.

"We're working on a treatment," he said. "We can't administer it while you are pregnant, though."

"Why not?"

"Not only would it possibly harm the fetus, but it appears that the hormone changes from your pregnancy are disrupting the effects of the nanites attacking your memory," said Dr. Thaila. "There would be no way to monitor the effects of our treatment with your hormones changing already, and the treatment is experimental. We would be relying completely on observation. It would be dangerous for your brain."

"So you're saying that these visions I'm having are probably repressed memories?"

"Yes, but please don't push yourself to remember. It will only cause further damage. That fainting spell in Halifax did a significant amount of damage to your brain. Take it easy Valkyrie, please."

Kale rubbed her back beneath the veil, frowning.

"I will." Val looked from the doctor to Kale and back again.

"I really will."

"It's for your own good."

"So you're saying that the pregnancy hormones are fighting off the nanites?"

"To put it colloquially, yes."

"Could I be cured naturally then?"

"It's possible, yes, that the nanites could be overpowered by your body's defense systems and either expelled or absorbed into the body in other ways. But the damage to your brain will require a lot of rehabilitation either way."

"What will happen after I give birth?"

"We can't know."

*

Matthew Doyle saw the pictures in the news of Jerome and Rachel's engagement alongside the video clip loop of Jordan and Skyla Bright partying together in Vancouver. He seethed with bitterness. That should have been his night. Instead he met up with a girl with a stinky vagina from Tinder who looked a lot different in her pictures than she did in the real. To top it off, after they hooked up she told him not to call her again when she found out he was unemployed.

They owe me, he thought. *I put in the time, I applied for gigs for us, I came up with ideas,* he thought. *The Waves owe me.*

He tried to get on with his day, but he couldn't stop obsessing. *I own that success as much as they do,* he thought.

He looked up lawyers. He was going to sue them and get his rightful piece.

Mercury Elmahdy loved school. She never missed a class and

she gobbled up all the extra reading material. When a professor mentioned a book, she took note and went to the library to get it. She hardly did anything but read. She was fascinated by computer systems and she was learning by leaps and bounds.

Mercury's personal style of eclectic Cairo punk was radically different from her classmates. Most of the boys wore khaki pants like it was the Georgetown uniform. The girls showed up to class dolled up to perfection with a mask of makeup and their hair blown out. They wore pearls and fake eyelashes and tank tops with cute bralettes peeking out the sides. They wore sweatpants on the bottom though.

Once a month Mercury danced at Purple Passion. It was her break from the books. She also did some computer work for them. It included minor hacking that bordered on illegal, but it was anarchist art culture stuff. Nothing serious.

Neena and Giddy Elmahdy could tell that she was happy and they were relieved for her. The news reported that Muslims were being targeted and attacked in the United States, but she was happy spending her time reading in Georgetown cafés and things were going well.

Mercury found it easiest to hide her Egyptian ancestry. Many people she encountered did not have a very strong grasp on geography outside of their small region and they would stare at her blankly if she mentioned what her background was. Sometimes they would have some vague sense of what Egypt was.

"Egyptian?" they would repeat, and she could see in their eyes the vision of an emaciated child with eyes covered in flies, and ancient dead kings entombed in gold.

Others would treat her with suspicion; Egypt was recently added to the growing list of banned countries in the United States, started in 2017. She tried her best to avoid the "what are you?" question.

Mercury was happy to spend her time reading and she resigned herself to having few friends. She and Anastasia went to the movies sometimes, and they helped each other often with calculus. Ana was anxious to find a boyfriend, but Mercury didn't really care about dating at all. She just listened while Ana talked. She enjoyed spending time with another person.

Anastasia could tell that Mercury was bored with their

conversations and she longed to make a friend she could commiserate with. She joined a sorority, a particularly American cultural institution dedicated to inscribing young women with ultra-hetero femme ideals. Her parents would be pleased. She hadn't told them yet that she was friends with a Muslim and she didn't think she ever would.

The sorority quickly dominated her time; the women expected Anastasia to participate in their events several times a week. They promised to find her a boyfriend though, and they spent a lot of time talking about boys. For Anastasia it was a worthwhile trade-off.

Mercury noticed that Ana started blowing out her hair and wearing pearls.

"Hey Merc? The Zeta Psy Psy Thetas are having a Fall Fling vacation and we're all supposed to bring a PMN."

"What's a PMN?"

"Oh. Potential New Member."

"I don't really think I have time to join a sorority though Ana, sorry."

"You could come out for the event and maybe you'll change your mind. Or just come out for a fun weekend. The Alpha Alpha Deltas invited us to their beach house on the Potomac River."

It actually didn't sound bad.

"Tell me more," she said.

"Well the boys are going to cook for us and wait on us, *topless,* it's going to be a lot of fun."

Mercury imagined the khaki jocks in her classes serving dinner on silver trays wearing only bowties and tight underwear.

"What else?" she asked.

"There's going to be drunk Olympics, with relays and teams."

"I don't drink," said Mercury.

"Really?" Ana found it hard to imagine being young and not drinking alcohol considering the constant pressure at Zeta Psy Psy Theta events to drink. They were always saying it was normal.

"Is it, like... a Muslim thing?"

"It sort of started out that way, but now I just don't. I don't really get the whole drinking thing."

"Okay, well, you could come out and swim in the river," said Ana.

Mercury imagined going along to Alpha Alpha Delta House and swimming while everyone else got wasted.

"I just don't think it's my jam, Ana. You'll have to tell me all about it when you get back."

*

Matt found a lawyer willing to take his case. He assembled any material he could to demonstrate that he was an integral part of the band and that he was entitled to a share of the music profits. At the very least, he owned part of the rights to the first album.

The lawyer served Jordan and the rest of the band members with the suit.

"This is the old drummer?" asked Mack, surveying the paperwork with a critical eye.

"That fucking dickhead," said Jordan. He whipped out his phone.

"Wait, what are you doing?" asked Mack.

"Calling him."

"Please don't. Let's think about this."

"I'm calling." Jordan punched in Matt's contact.

Mack scrambled to get out his phone to record the conversation.

"Put it on speakerphone at least," he said.

Jordan did.

"Hello?"

"I just got your letter," growled Jordan. "What the fuck is this Matty?"

"You know exactly what it is. You guys owe me my fair share."

"Was it fair when you bailed on us at our house show?" asked Jordan.

"Don't be so fucking childish. This is serious."

"I'm dead serious. You quit the band, and that's something you'll just have to live with."

"I never quit! You guys pushed me out!"

"You bailed! You cared more about your stupid fucking fancy job than the band. But us, we care about the band more than anything. That's why we made it and you didn't. You still don't care. You're just mad you lost your stupid job. Well go find another one and leave us alone."

"Jordan you owe me and you know it."

"I know I don't owe you shit. And I also know what you did."

"What do you mean?"

Now that he started, Jordan couldn't stop.

"What you did you Jesse's roommate."

"What the fuck are you talking about... you mean that I banged her? What, were you into her or something?"

"You fucking raped her, you piece of shit."

"That's bullshit. Yea I fucked her, but she was into me."

"She was sleeping and you forced yourself on her. You're an asshole and you always have been. The band outgrew you and now we're successful. Fuck off with this lawsuit shit or we'll let everyone know what a monster you are."

Jordan ended the call.

Mack whistled and ended his recording.

"I better let Skyla Bright's publicist know about all this," he said.

Matt went forward with the lawsuit anyway. Who would the media believe, a serious young educated man or some slut he banged? He would bet his word against hers any day. Hell, in most countries, it took two of her testimonies to even equal one of his.

News of the lawsuit hit the media and the connection between the Waves and Skyla Bright skyrocketed it worldwide. Matt was front and centre in interviews just like he wanted. He told reporters that he wrote the music, that he planned the gigs and set up the lights and came up with the name.

Jordan was furious.

"He doesn't have a fucking ounce of creativity in his body. He's not even a good drummer," he said in a clip on Instagram.

Mack deleted it, but it was too late; it was viral. It only fanned the flames.

"Sending out good vibes to my friend Jordan," said Skyla, blowing a kiss to her fans on her livestream.

There was that word—*friend.* Jordan felt her blowing him away with that kiss.

Mack decided to play hard. He chopped up an editorialized version of the recorded phone conversation—removing anything that made Jordan sound bad—and released it.

"It's a real conversation," he avowed. "The Waves parted ways with a rapist. We had to censor parts of the conversation to protect the young lady's identity."

Matt denied the conversation.

Then Jesse released a video.

"She didn't want anyone to know, but I convinced her to let me come forward to protect our friend Jordan," said Jesse. "Matthew Doyle is a rapist. Jordan kicked him out of the band to do the right thing."

Suddenly Jordan was re-cast as a hero, the dark and brooding protector of rape victims.

"Jordan Barker is my hero of the day," said Skyla to the believers. They scurried over to his social and he gained a few hundred thousand followers.

CHAPTER SIX

Anastasia Simon boarded the coach to the Fall Fling. The vacation property they were heading to was called Camp Alpha Alpha Delta as a nod to Camp David. Everyone in Washington D.C. was obsessed with politics and most of the boys in Alpha Alpha Delta secretly thought that he would be President one day.

"Ladies!" trilled a young woman standing at the front of the bus. "Take your seats!"

Anastasia nestled in with the other rusher newbies. They all looked up expectantly at Buttercup Eberhart.

"Are you ready to have some fun?"

They all cheered.

Buttercup smiled. Her face was a bit frozen because she had gotten injections in preparation for this weekend yesterday, but her cheekbones looked fabulous.

"I am so proud that Zeta Psy Psy Theta was invited to be the guest sorority at the inaugural event for Camp Alpha Alpha Delta. You should all be so proud sisters!"

The girls whistled and cheered.

"This is going to be the best weekend of our lives. Until our wedding days of course!"

They laughed.

"Let's raise a glass to us! Let the games begin!"

The girls beside her popped the corks on bottles of champagne and as the bus rolled off they clinked glasses and started drinking.

I'm so lucky to be on the bus with Buttercup, thought Anastasia. She felt sorry for the girls stuck on the other two coaches.

Buttercup was the best Chapter President in the history of Zeta Psy Psy Theta. This was her second year as President and she wrangled this opportunity to be the first sorority to visit Camp Alpha Alpha Delta through her incredible charm and grace. This would be the pinnacle of her tenure as President.

The girls sang cheers and chants all the way to the Potomac. The Zeta Psy Psy Theta song itself had thirteen verses that the rushers had to commit to memory by the end of the bus trip.

Buttercup told them stories about the Alpha Alpha Deltas.

"There's Nick, VP Finance, he's a very serious money guy, and Geoffrey Waters, the VP Social. Watch him, he's allll hands..."

The other girls laughed knowingly. Anastasia smiled along with them, even though she didn't really know what that meant.

"And then there's Jensen..." started Violet, the VP Membership for the Zeta Psy Psy Thetas, looking at Buttercup.

Buttercup smiled coyly.

"Yes, Jensen."

"Your future husband?" said Brittany.

"Oh shh..." blushed Buttercup. "Maybe!"

They all squealed with delight.

Everyone knew that Jensen Decker had a soft spot for Buttercup Eberhart. They were like the king and queen of the Greek Life world.

This weekend would change her life forever, she knew it. Whatever it took, she was going to prove to Jensen that she had what it takes to be his first lady.

The bus rolled up a winding laneway lined with trees. It crunched to a stop in front of a big timber-frame lodge. The boys lined the front porch, flexing their pecs and waving to the arriving busses.

They chatted excitedly. This was going to be an epic weekend.

Buttercup stepped out of the bus first, and the other women followed. Jensen came down to greet them.

"Miss Eberhart," he said with a grin.

"Mr. Decker," she said, arching her back.

"Welcome to Camp Alpha Alpha Delta."

"We're delighted to be here, aren't we ladies?"

The Zeta Psy Psy Thetas tittered their assent.

"Where should we bring our bags?"

Jensen laughed.

"Get down here boys!" he gestured.

"We don't expect beautiful ladies like yourselves to carry your own things at Camp Alpha Alpha Delta!"

The men tumbled across the lawn and onto the busses spastic with energy like a pack of wolves, nipping at each other jostling to grab the most bags. They were excited too.

Anastasia preferred to carry her own bag, but it was swept away in the heat of the moment and she didn't say anything.

A young rusher came around with a box.

"No phones allowed," said Jensen. "Put it in the box."

There were murmurs of reluctance.

"Sacred Law number one: what happens at Camp Alpha Alpha Delta stays at Camp Alpha Alpha Delta! Sacred Law number two: no phones!"

Buttercup dropped her phone into the box.

"No problem," she said.

The other women followed.

"Are you ready to go swimming?" said Jensen.

"Are we ever!"

Buttercup pulled off her dress, revealing her freshly shaven and tanned body in her new swimsuit. Jensen looked her up and down with eyes that told her his dinner was prepared just the way he liked.

"We're going to have fun this weekend," he said.

The girls headed toward the beach. There was a large rocky outcropping on one side, high above the water line, and a long sandy shore.

Mercury would have liked this, thought Anastasia, looking out at the water.

She wished Mercury came. Ana felt a bit out of place with her sensible bathing suit and her pale lumpy body.

There were volleyball nets set up on the beach and some of the girls headed that way, taking off their tops and throwing them courtside. Others headed down to the water.

"Wait, not that way," said Jensen. "You can't swim in the river. There's a pool over there if you want to swim." He gestured to a garden behind the lodge.

Sewage discharge overflowed directly into the Potomac River and there were signs on both sides of the beach that warned swimmers of the danger.

So that's what the smell is, thought Anastasia.

This entire area was once a lush kingdom teeming with life and governed by the great Algonquin Piscataway, the Mattapanient, Nangemeick, Tauxehent, Anacostank, Pamunkey, and others for thousands of years, who built green cities and respected the river. Now dead fish floated alongside plastic bottles and human excrement.

Anastasia headed to the pool.

The large park behind the lodge had several hot tubs and saunas alongside the pool. The Alpha Alpha Deltas had built themselves a really nice retreat here.

They must have some kind of endowment, thought Ana.

Before long it was time for dinner. The ladies took their seats at a long table laden with plates of luscious foods. As promised, the boys served them cocktails dressed in hotpants, bowties and black gloves. The ladies ate very little and then went to their dorms to change for the after dinner party in the garden.

The garden was decorated with lights and tiki torches. Grass hut mini-bars were erected and rushers were bartending. There were tables set up for beer pong and other drinking games. As the ladies came out back the men were already hooting and chugging beers. Long rows of shots were set out and challenges were issued. The alcohol was flowing and anyone without a drink in their hand was forced to take a shot.

"Buttercup!" shouted Jensen. "Where are you?"

All the girls looked around expectantly. The boys looked at Jensen hungrily. The carnal energy crackled.

"Right here," she trilled, coming over to him, stumbling a little with intoxication.

"Want to come in the hot tub with me?"

"Mmm, that sounds fun," she said.

"Just one thing," he said slipping into the hot bubbling water. "Chicks have to be naked in the hot tub."

The men howled.

Buttercup gasped with false shock.

"So naughty Jensen."

She dipped her toe in the water.

He pushed her foot back out.

"I'm serious. It's a Sacred Law at Camp Alpha Alpha Delta."

Buttercup looked around the garden. If she said no it would ruin the vibe. She wanted to keep things light and fun. She wasn't ashamed of her body; quite the contrary. She would love for everyone to get a look at her naked majesty. She worked hard on it. But she didn't want to be known as the slut who got naked first. It was a difficult situation.

"Are you sure?" she asked quietly.

"Sacred Law number one: what happens at Camp Alpha Alpha Delta stays at Camp Alpha Alpha Delta," said Jensen loudly. "Right boys?"

"Yea! What happens at Camp Alpha Alpha Delta stays at Camp Alpha Alpha Delta," they chanted, over and over, louder and louder.

"Come on, Miss Eberhart," said Jenson softly.

At least there are no phones, thought Buttercup.

"Fine!" she laughed.

Every eye watched her close as she slowly peeled off her top and two tanned grapefruit breasts were exposed.

Jensen laughed.

"Isn't she beautiful? Keep going gorgeous..."

Buttercup pulled down her bottoms slowly like a striptease. The men hooted.

She slipped into the hot tub.

"There. Satisfied?"

"Not totally, but we'll get there..." said Jensen.

"Let's get this party started!" he hollered. "Crank up the music!"

He gestured and the music blared.

The girls relaxed as the night went on. Within a few hours the hot tubs were full of naked ladies. Anastasia was a bit overwhelmed and she kept her glass full of soda, pretending to drink alcohol. This party was out of her league and she could feel it slipping into an energy she wasn't comfortable with. As the hours passed people coupled off and went to dorms and beach houses and hammocks to get closer. Drunken men scrapped on the beach and women puked in the bushes.

Anastasia thought about Mercury and how she didn't drink.

What's the point? she had said. Ana found herself thinking the same thing.

After Jensen was done with Buttercup, he went to find boys to bring out more kegs of beer.

So many things on one's mind when one is President, he thought.

"I'll take a turn here," he said to a rusher stuck behind a grass hut bar.

The rusher looked at Jensen with admiration in his eyes.

"You're the best," he said.

Jensen leaned on the bar, looking out over the lodge garden. Everyone was laughing and having a great time. The event was already a huge success. It would go down in Alpha Alpha Delta history. Security cameras all over the garden were catching great shots they would put in the fraternity spank archives. Jensen hoped there was a good shot of Buttercup's tits. That would be legendary.

"Well howdy Captain," said a tall muscular man coming toward him and handing him a cigar. "Congratulations, this is epic."

"I'd say," said Jensen.

They lit up, smoking their cigars.

"These girls are all sluts," said Geoffrey Waters, the VP Social. "Do you think all girls are actually sluts?"

"Probably. Your mom is for sure."

Geoff made a fist and fake-punched Jensen in the gut, stopping just before making contact.

"Uhhn," he said.

Then they laughed.

"We're living the dream," said a shorter guy, coming up beside them.

"Hey Scabbers," said Geoff.

Andrew hated his frat nickname at first, but after a while it grew on him. Most of the other guys never read Harry Potter anyway and they didn't know the reference. He nicknamed one of this year's rushers Kentucky Cunt Chickenshit and it made him feel a lot better.

"Got one of those for me?" he asked.

"Yea sure," said Geoff, pulling another cigar out of his pocket.

"This is what growing up is all about," said Scabbers. He took a deep suck on his cigar and choked, coughing.

Jensen and Geoff laughed.

"Attaboy Scabbers!"

Jensen slapped him on the back.

"How's your night going boy?"

"I just finished working in the lab like an hour ago so I'm just getting started," said Scabbers.

"Don't worry we saved you lots of good leftovers," laughed Geoff.

Scabbers went off to find a woman to pester.

The next morning, everyone woke up late. Afternoon Caesars were passed around to cure hangovers.

"Good morning ladies," said Jensen as the women starting coming out of their dorms.

"Sacred Law number seven: After the first night, women have to be naked 24/7 at Camp Alpha Alpha Delta."

"Seriously?" said Buttercup.

"Seriously babe."

She only paused a moment and then shrugged her shoulders. "Fine."

She took off her clothes and went down to enjoy a quiet day sunbathing on the beach.

Anastasia went to bed early the night before and she felt okay today. She was the first one up and she went down to the rocks at the far end of the beach to sit and read.

She was proud of herself for staying out of trouble last night but she also felt a bit like she missed out on a potentially important coming of age ritual. She decided that tonight she would try to talk to a boy instead of just hanging out with the other shy girls.

"Hey, what are you doing out here?" said a voice.

Anastasia looked around.

Scabbers came over the rocks toward her.

"Hey. Just reading," she said shyly.

"Oh. Well this area is off-limits," he said.

Ana stood up.

"Oh okay."

"Wait," said Scabbers. He held out his hand.

"I'm... Andrew."

"I'm Ana," she said, shaking his hand.

"But you still have to go," he said.

Ana walked back across the beach to the lodge. She was surprised to see all the women lying on their towels naked. She felt a tremble of excitement.

Cool, she thought. *Very liberated.*

"Hey you. You're not supposed to be wearing clothes," said a guy as she walked by.

"But... you're wearing clothes..." she said, confused.

He kept walking.

She went to the dorm to put away her book. There were a few girls still in bed.

"A guy just told me we're not supposed to be wearing clothes," she said.

"Yea, it's one of the rules."

"Oh."

Ana crawled into her bunk and decided to stay there until dinner time. She wished she had her phone.

That night Jensen stepped things up. There was twice as much alcohol and twice as much pressure to drink. Things got out of hand quickly. There was a circle of young people playing Truth or Dare, and most of the dares involved women making out with one another. There was a fighting pit set up and men were brawling as women stood around cheering, their bare breasts bouncing in the light of the tiki torches.

Ana felt uncomfortable so she made a lei out of flowers to wear around her neck. It made her feel less naked.

"You're not supposed to be wearing that," said a drunk guy, grabbing at her.

"Hey, it's fine," said Scabbers, grabbing her by the elbow and steering her away from him.

"Oh, hi Andrew," she said.

"Hey. I don't remember your name."

He knew her name was Ana, but the Seduction Artist Handbook said to pretend that you don't remember.

"It's Ana."

"Oh okay," he said nonchalantly.

"So... what are you studying?" she asked.

Yes, it's working, he thought. *She wants to know more about me.*

"Pre-med bioengineering," he said.

"Cool," she said, surprised.

"How about you?"

"Statistics."

"Oh yea? You like math?"

Dammit, thought Scabbers. He wasn't supposed to show interest.

"I do."

"You seem pretty sober," he said.

"So do you."

They looked around at the shenanigans going on.

Jensen rolled out a cauldron.

"Gather round folks," he said.

Ana and Andrew turned their attention to Jensen.

"This is a special drink for the ladies."

Men dipped cups into the cauldron and brought them around to all the women.

"Cheers to you, Zeta Psy Psy Thetas, our first guests of honor here at Camp Alpha Alpha Delta. With this drink, we officially inaugurate the Camp, and award you the title of First Tribute!"

A brother came by with a cup and held it out to Anastasia. She looked down at it in his hand. She didn't want to drink it but she thought it would be rude not to. She took it. One drink wouldn't hurt. This was her moment to participate in the coming of age ritual so she could go home feeling like she really took in the full experience.

"Cheers to the First Tribute!" boomed the men as the women downed their drinks.

"To the beach!" shouted Jensen.

The men herded the naked women down to the dark waters of the Potomac River.

Anastasia woke up with white sunlight burning her eyes. She blinked in the morning light. Her body ached all over. She turned, feeling sharp rocks beneath her. She heard a moaning sound and then realized it came from her. She lifted her hand in front of her face. It was covered in small stones.

I fell asleep outside, she realized.

The last thing she remembered was everyone running down to the river in the dark.

Her body shuddered with cold. Her legs felt completely numb. She lifted herself onto her elbows and cried out in agony. Her whole abdomen was on fire. She looked down at herself, moaning uncontrollably. She was covered in blood from her stomach to her vagina and down her thighs.

Was I raped? she thought. She couldn't remember.

Suddenly she heard moaning beside her. She looked out over the rocks and saw that they were all there, all the women. They were waking up one by one on the cliffs, as bloody as she was. A murmur of pain rippled out across the bodies as they started to move, uncomprehending, crying out in agony, a sea of bloody mermaids weeping with pain.

From the caves below the cliffs, Jensen and several other men came out topside.

Jensen went straight to Buttercup with a towel, picking her up in his arms and wrapping her up.

"Hey, hey, shh..." he said gently, wiping away her tears.

"Last night got a little bit out of control, there, didn't it?"

The other boys smiled sheepishly.

Buttercup nodded tearfully. She didn't remember what happened. Why couldn't she remember? She couldn't stop crying. Her whole abdomen burned with pain, like all the other women.

The screams turned to quiet crying and they looked at each other in disbelief and shame.

"What happened?" asked Buttercup.

"Don't worry," said Jensen. "Sacred Law number one: what happens at Camp Alpha Alpha Delta stays at Camp Alpha Alpha Delta."

The boys took up the chant, murmuring softly over and over. "What happens at Camp Alpha Alpha Delta stays at Camp Alpha Alpha Delta."

"No one will find out about this, don't worry," said Jensen.

They can't, thought Buttercup. *No one can ever find out about this. If it gets out, we'll be the slutty sorority and that reputation will never go away.*

The boys continued chanting: "What happens at Camp Alpha Alpha Delta stays at Camp Alpha Alpha Delta."

"No one can ever know," cried Buttercup.

"Let's get you ladies to the showers, okay?" said Jensen.

The women started to get up, their tears soaking the cliffs. One woman kept screaming. As the boys came over with towels, she screamed louder. The sound was raw and blood-curdling. The other women recoiled with discomfort from the approaching men.

"Go take care of that," said Jensen to Buttercup.

More men started coming out of the garrison in the cliffs, rubbing their eyes, still sleepy from a long wild night.

Buttercup stumbled over with a towel.

"Shh, shh," she said.

Anastasia kept hollering like a lunatic, over and over, unable to stop.

"Shut up," shouted one of the men, rubbing his temples.

"Calm down, please, relax," said Buttercup, stroking Ana's hair out of her face. "Shh, shh..."

The other girls joined in silencing Ana's screams.

"Shh, shh," they said, eying the men nervously.

"Is this going to be a problem Buttercup?" asked Jensen through gritted teeth.

"No of course not," she said.

"Shh, honey, shh..."

"What happens at Camp Alpha Alpha Delta stays at Camp Alpha Alpha Delta. What happens at Camp Alpha Alpha Delta stays at Camp Alpha Alpha Delta..." the men continued to chant.

Anastasia Simon ran her hands over her bloody abdomen and held them up; her screams went on and on.

"Get up to the lodge and clean up," said Jensen.

Buttercup Eberhart stepped back from Ana and she and the others girls scrambled up the beach, clutching their bodies in agony.

Jensen and three other men on the Alpha Alpha Delta executive stepped forward with grim determination. The other men escorted the women back up to the lodge.

Jensen grabbed Anastasia roughly by the hair. His eyes were dark as he looked into each of the faces of his brothers. They all grabbed parts of her kicking and screaming and dragged her down to the waterside, her legs flailing and lacerated on the rocks. They kicked her until she was unconscious and then drowned her in the river.

From the mouth of the cave garrison, Scabbers watched them beat Ana to death. When it was done and she stopped moving, he went back to work, cataloguing the Tribute. In the frosty glass case there were a hundred bags dripping with blood.

The girls thought that they were raped, but Alpha Alpha Delta had harvested their uteruses.

"How did we do?" asked Jensen, coming up into the garrison, out of breath. His boots were caked with blood and sand.

"A great cull," said Scabbers. "One hundred successful extractions."

"The Fraternity will be pleased."

CHAPTER SEVEN

Fall was in the air. Jordan smelled it in every town he visited across western Canada; the sharp flavour of ripe fruit and the crunch of leaves underfoot reminded him of Glasshouse with Valkyrie. Jordan was sure that he would never feel anything like that again. Last year with Valkyrie was the most intense any human could ever love, he thought. And it all slipped away so fast, like sand in an hourglass.

He could only hold onto those memories and make music.

His phone rang.

No identification, just 1-111-111-1111.

He answered.

"Hello?"

Hi Jordan."

It was Skyla Bright.

"Hey."

"What are you up to?"

"Oh just wandering the streets of Saskatoon."

She laughed.

"Really?"

"Really."

"Where is your next show?"

"It's here, tonight."

"I see."

"How about you? What are you up to?"

"I'm in Portland. I knew you were doing a west coast tour so I thought maybe you were close by and we could meet up."

By Canadian standards it wasn't necessarily that 'far'.

"You want to come to my show tonight?"

"I could be convinced..."

Jordan laughed.

"Would you please come to my show? I'd like to see you."

He actually meant it. Skyla seemed like a lot of fun to spend time with.

"Count me in. I'll grab a hyperloop over there."

"Cool. See you soon."

Just like that, Skyla Bright was on her way to see his show.

*

Valkyrie Snow woke up in her cozy loft sticky with sweat beneath blankets but she didn't want to push them off because the weight felt comforting around her. She stuck her feet out the bottom of the bed and shifted onto her side. As her stomach grew she had to change positions more often.

Something about today felt different in her body. Her back still hurt, but she didn't feel sick. In fact, she was heavily craving a juicy steak. It was the first time she had a taste for meat in months. She ran her hand along her stomach. It was the biggest she had ever been, but it wasn't a big soft jelly like she imagined it would be; her stomach felt firm. She rubbed underneath, feeling the round curve of her belly. Suddenly she felt a spike of warmth between her legs. She reached down and touched herself with surprise. It was the first time she was horny in a long time. She kept touching, bringing herself to orgasm. She sank back into the pillows, relaxed.

Valkyrie got out of bed. She went downstairs to the small bathroom the contractor had built onto the cottage and splashed cold water on her face. She felt lonely. The feeling came suddenly with such intensity that she wanted to cry. She looked in the mirror. Even squinting in the darkness she could see that her skin was perfectly smooth and her hair was thick and lustrous.

She put on her veil and went out to find something to eat at the farm house.

"I'd like meat, if we have any," said Valkyrie.

"Meat?" said Margarethe. "You must be turning."

She came close, pressing her hands against Valkyrie's stomach over the veil.

"Let me see you, please," said Margarethe.

Valkyrie sighed. They went upstairs to the old woman's bedroom. Margarethe pulled the curtains firmly closed.

Valkyrie pulled off her veil and took off her dress. Margarethe inspected her.

"It's really happening love."

"I still don't believe it."

"I know. But you're far enough along that we can say it's really happening."

They smiled and hugged each other.

Valkyrie put her clothes back on and they went downstairs. Margarethe made her hamburger soup.

"I feel different," said Val.

"Everything is changing," said Margarethe.

Valkyrie ate her soup as the women came in to rub her belly and share the meal. Suddenly, her spoon clattered in the bowl. She put both hands on her stomach.

"What is it?"

"Butterflies..." she said. "Butterflies fluttering inside me..."

The baby was kicking for the first time.

After dinner Valkyrie called Mika Nakamura, the once-junior-now-senior designer at Snow Arcologies, a subsidiary of Valkyrie's architecture company, Hammer & Bone.

"How are you?" asked Mika.

Valkyrie had been off the map for months.

"I'm recovering. I'm ready to talk about the launch," said Val.

"I'm glad to hear that."

Mika was relieved. The financial situation was dangerously strained at the company and they needed more investors for the arcologies.

They sketched out a plan. They would host an event at the Mother House pilot site in Cape Breton to get investors excited. It would be mostly digital but those who wanted to come see it in person would be invited.

Valkyrie decided to sell Glasshouse in Ottawa. Although it was once her dream house, now it only reminded her of the trauma of the last year. The sale would generate a great deal of interest in Futurustic, her high-low-tech hybrid architecture venture. She expected the sale would garner many new design contracts. It made sense as part of her business strategy, even though her emotions were a jumbled torrent.

"Have the team spin up a massive campaign on social," she told Sukhwant, her assistant. "Selling Glasshouse must sell Futurustic as a lifestyle."

"I understand. Do you want me to have your personal things removed from the house first?"

Valkyrie thought about it.

"No. Stage the house and give away anything you can't use."

"Even your books?" asked Sukhwant, surprised.

"Yes."

Valkyrie saved those books to read in her retirement. With her fragile eyes she could hardly read anymore.

I'll make pottery in my retirement, she thought ruefully. *With Oracle dictating any book I want to me.*

She rubbed her belly, feeling a surge of emotion. *Or maybe this little person I'm engineering can read to me,* she thought.

Once she decided to sell Glasshouse, Valkyrie was relieved that she made a good decision. Futurustic would generate a good piece of income to fund the Mother House project, but not only that, Futurustic was a much easier sell than arcology technology. In twenty years arcologies would move into a more mainstream space, but for now, they didn't quite fit the late capitalism financial paradigm. Valkyrie's head was always in the future.

Valkyrie Snow wore thick sunglasses beneath her veil and walked along the beach barefoot, the wheels in her head grinding forward as she planned the launch. Children ran around chasing the birds, laughing in the sunlight. They were curious about the strange figure veiled in white, her stomach large and protruding.
"Is that a baby in there?" asked a little boy.
"Yes," said Val softly.
"My mommy grew one too," said a little girl, joining him.
"Where is the daddy?"
"Or the other mommy," said the little boy. His moms were Kale and Susanna.
"There is none," said Val.
Who was the father-pollen? she thought, not for the first time. James Ahote? Baron the Devil? Or the holy ghost with green eyes?
The children ran off again to play with the others.
Valkyrie continued walking and thinking, a strange Virgin Mary on the shores of Cape Breton.

Film crews came to Mother House to create a series of three-minute videos intended to go viral on social media. The millions of hits would be more successful at enticing investment than even the dream itself.
Many of the sisters worried about the publicity. Would it bring people of all kinds to their small paradise? How could they be so greedy, when they themselves crawled to these shores in desperation and found shelter and community? The village itself was in violation of building and farming codes, not to mention all of the illegal refugees living there.
"Dr. Snow would like you to focus on the construction of Mother House out on the peninsula," warned Farrah when the crews tried to film the bustling commune area. "Please respect our privacy and stay out of the village."

"And where is Valkyrie Snow, the creator of all this?" they asked.

"She is busy creating," laughed Margarethe.

"She's the ghost that haunts the land," added Chanda with a grin. "She is all around us."

Despite their best efforts to protect privacy, the commune fascinated the outside world. The videos went viral, but it was the commune that people clamoured to know better and even be a part of rather than the partially constructed citadel on the peninsula.

"The artists, the dreamers, they knew this future a generation ago in their hearts and dreams," said Val quietly over dinner. "These normal people are waking up to it because now they can see it before their eyes."

The campaign was a success and the investment they needed was secured. The filmmakers worked on developing a computer-generated simulation of what the arcologies would be like on distant planets. Valkyrie's plan to build Snow Arcologies on the moon and on Mars began to materialize on social and she knew it would happen in the real.

Mika Nakamura came to visit the pilot site.

"You've turned your company into a legacy," she said, walking alongside Val on the beach.

"*Our* company," said Valkyrie. "Your leadership at Snow Arcologies, especially during my health difficulties, has been invaluable. You are as much a part of this now as I am."

"I'm honoured to hear you say that," said Mika.

Valkyrie was her greatest mentor and Mika believed in her leadership with undying loyalty.

"I'm honoured to have you here. Your skills as an architect and project manager are extraordinary, but more than that, I know you believe in this the way I do. I trust you with my vision."

Mika understood exactly what she meant.

"My great-grandparents were tortured in an internment camp for Japanese-Canadians. I don't know if I ever told you that," said Mika.

"I didn't know," said Val softly. "Thank you for telling me."

"I won't let anything happen to the refugees," she said.

Valkyrie knew she could count on that.

Skyla Bright came out onstage at the end of Jordan's concert and waved at the crowd. Her fans went wild on social. Every once in a while she liked to surprise them.

Mack was grinning from ear to ear offstage.

After the show, Jordan and Skyla had a very publicized walk around downtown Saskatoon. They got ice cream and shopped in local stores.

"Just hanging with my new best friend ;)," wrote Skyla on social.

That evening they disappeared into Jordan's hotel.

"Thanks for coming onstage at the show," said Jordan. "You didn't have to do that."

"I'm having fun," said Skyla, jumping up on the bed. Her phone was in her hand, like it was a part of her body.

"I see that," said Jordan, climbing up beside her.

"You really are a great singer," she said. Her voice sounded different. It wasn't coy or cute. She sounded real.

"Thanks."

"So where to next?" she said. Her voice was back to falsetto.

"Hmm?"

"On the tour."

"Oh. We're heading down to Regina."

"I see."

"Are you an artist?" Jordan asked, out of the blue.

"An artist?"

"Yea. Do you consider yourself an artist?"

Skyla looked at her phone. Should she record this? It was an interesting question. *No,* she thought. *Not this time.*

"Yes," she said. "Yes I'm an artist. You don't think so?" She looked amused.

"Sorry. Yea. It just seems like your image is more than the music. If you don't mind me saying it... I don't mean it in a bad way. Just something I noticed."

"You're right, my image is everything. But my life is the art. Music is just the channel for me."

"So you're more of a magician than an artist," said Jordan.

Skyla turned on her livestream, turning the camera onto her face.

"My life is an artistic experiment," she said. "My life is my process. My life is my self-directed installation."

She gazed intensely into the lens for a moment and then she turned off the livestream.

"Carl Jung said 'the God-image is the God.' It's the same for us. Neo-godds. Image is what they see. Image is what is remembered."

Skyla was mesmerizing. Jordan believed in her and he had the benefit of looking right into her real eyes and hearing the words from her own lips. Her perfect lips...

He turned to her and leaned in to kiss her, and he realized she was waiting for him. His lips brushed hers softly and then harder. His body awakened from a long sleep, suddenly aching for this to happen. Their clothes came off and in a hotel room in Saskatoon, Jordan Barker made love to Skyla Bright.

CHAPTER EIGHT

As much as Mercury Elmahdy loved school, she was lonely. Her friend Illaria came to visit Washington for the first week of November, and they had a lot of fun catching up and visiting all of Mercury's new local haunts. It was really great for Mercury to be able to bring a friend to Purple Passion.

"Your new friends are a lot of fun," Illaria said.

They are, thought Mercury. *But I still feel like I'm on the outside looking in.*

"I do get lonely sometimes," she told her friend.

"Poor sweetie," said Illaria, hugging her. "Moving to a new place is hard."

"It is."

"Maybe you should check out the school clubs."

Illaria was back home in London now and Mercury was back to her solitary life of study. She noticed that Anastasia wasn't in Calculus class. She tried calling her but there was no answer.

Mercury took Illaria's advice and she looked up the school activities. The African Students' Association was meeting that day so she decided to check it out.

It might be fun to explore my roots more, she thought.

"Hi," she said shyly, coming into the room at the student centre where the meeting was being held. It seemed quite informal.

Everyone obviously knew each other already.

"Hey, can I help you?" said a woman coming over.

Mercury glanced around and noticed that she herself was very visibly the lightest person in the room.

"Hi! I'm looking for the African Students' Association."

"This is us," said the woman.

Mercury was introduced to everyone in the room and she stayed for the meeting.

As she walked home, Mercury felt relieved. Meeting many new people at once exhausted her. Even though everyone was very kind, she didn't really connect with anyone specifically. She felt a bit out of place. She had spent so much of her life insisting that she was from London that connecting to her Egyptian identity as an African was hard for her.

Anastasia didn't show up for class the following week either. Mercury tried calling her a few times and couldn't get through.

I hope she's okay, she thought.

Mercury decided to try out the Muslim Students' Club. Even though she was not a believer, per se, she was very socially connected to the Muslim community growing up and the thought of connecting here in Washington D.C. felt comforting.

The Muslim Students' Club had a house off-campus. Mercury dropped in and one of the club executives gave her a tour. It was a lovely warm space with lots of activities and events. Mercury took a copy of the club calendar and resolved to attend something soon.

There was still no word from Anastasia. Mercury was concerned. She stopped by her residence room and knocked on the door. There was no answer.

I don't think she's avoiding me, thought Mercury. *She hasn't been in Calc either.* The last she heard from Ana she was going to the Fall Fling.

Should I contact the sorority?

The thought of talking to the Zeta Psy Psy Thetas stressed Mercury out.

I could just hack her phone, see where she is... thought Merc. She wouldn't even need to mess with a telecom provider; the knock-off Virtuous would give her all the information she needed without much fuss.

No, that's immoral. But if it were for a friend? She was genuinely worried about Anastasia. If the trace indicated that she was back home in Ohio then Merc would know it was probably a family emergency. The trace could show that Ana was in the hospital.

Once the idea was in her mind Mercury couldn't let it go. She decided that her intentions were good so she should just go ahead and do it.

Mercury was amazed at how easy it was to hack Virtuous.

This is a serious security risk, thought Mercury. She was surprised that the United States funneled so much money into border control and defense but they left this massive gaping hole in their digital security.

The last place Anastasia was connected to the internet was Camp Alpha Alpha Delta two weeks ago.

That can't be right, thought Mercury. *She hasn't used her phone since then?*

Hacking Virtuous only raised more questions and Mercury was more curious than ever.

Mercury told Neena and Giddy Elmahdy that Anastasia seemed to be missing.

"I haven't heard from her for weeks, she hasn't been to class, and she's not in her room," said Mercury on Virtual.

"Tell her mother," said Neena.

"I don't know her mother," said Mercury. "I've never met her family."

"Does she have a boyfriend?"

"I don't think so."

It wasn't like Anastasia to run off with a boy anyway, even if she did have a boyfriend. If Mercury were in London, she would call the police. When her phone was stolen here in Washington D.C., the police did nothing. She had a feeling this would be the same. The police here showed up with guns to scare off criminals in the midst of crime, but there was no funding for investigative policing.

"Tell your teacher."

"Okay Neena. That's a good idea."

The calculus professor listened patiently after class as Mercury explained the situation with Anastasia.

"Does she have a boyfriend?" she asked.

"Umm, no," said Mercury.

Why does everyone think she ran off with a man? thought Mercury, confused. *Do they know something I don't?*

"Try contacting her family," said the professor.

"I don't know her family. Would you be able to get in touch with her parents?"

"I don't have access to any of that kind of information. Ana is a grown woman."

"Could you let the university know something's wrong? I don't want her to fail all her classes if she's in the hospital or something."

"That's not my responsibility. If she is in the hospital, I'm sure they let her family know and it will be her responsibility to make sure she gets medical leave from the university."

Mercury could see that the professor just didn't really care that much, one way or the other.

"Okay. Thanks for your time."

Mercury turned quickly and left, unable to hide the disapproval in her face. She would have to find out for herself.

That evening, Mercury decided to do some digital probing to see if there were any records of Anastasia Simon in hospitals here or closer to the Potomac. She spent the night investigating and found nothing.

After a week of searching Mercury was getting very worried about Ana. Should she try calling the police? She decided that might be the best course of action. She dialled and the phone rang. As usual there was no answer. She left a message, knowing that they would never call her back.

*

Jordan Barker and Skyla Bright were dating. It was official.

"I'm so happy for you man," said Bubba. "Now you can finally be happy again."

Was he happy?

Happiness. Such a strange concept.

Yes, thought Jordan. *Yes I'm happy. I have everything I ever dreamed of.*

He didn't feel overjoyed, but he felt safe, and that was a good start. He wasn't overflowing with ecstasy like he was with Valkyrie, but she was his first love. He would never feel that way again.

I just have to accept it and move forward, he thought.

Easier said than done, hissed Snake.

She broke me a little, he thought. *She broke me open. Now I'm healing and I'll be stronger than I was before. That has to count for something.*

He took solace where he could. In Skyla, for instance. He was ferocious in his desire, having sex any time he possibly could. Her body under him or floating above him was perfect in every way, like an angel on earth, taut and sculpted and radiant. When they were having sex he thought he loved her. As soon as he orgasmed though the feeling evaporated. He held her numbly, feeling absolutely nothing.

He couldn't even look at her because he was afraid that she knew. He didn't love her and he never could.

Skyla threw herself into her new relationship. She posted cutesy photos of them cuddling and holding hands in the park. Jordan became the night to her day, the brooding counterpart to her sunny online persona. It was perfect.

Jordan went to Skyla's shows when he could. She was actually a pretty good singer. He definitely loved her most when she was up on stage singing.

It's the only time he smiles, scribbled her fans on pictures of Jordan on social media. *When he's watching her sing.*

When they were sitting alone on a hotel bed, or in a café, and he had to look her in the eyes, it was a lot harder to love her.

Skyla was playing with the idea of her and Jordan doing a surprise show together, or even having him come onstage to sing with her at one of her shows. That was a big move though and she would definitely build up the anticipation online first and then plan the event in conjunction with a song or album release. For Skyla Bright, getting serious in the relationship was inseparable from the performance.

She would wait to talk to him about it. She felt him holding back from her. It wasn't because he felt nothing for her, she could tell—Jordan was a deeply emotional man and he must be bonding with her in some way. He lived with a lot of fears and anxieties. His walls were up to avoid pain and disappointment.

Those are the most dangerous men to fall in love with, she thought. *There is only so much of their heart they will ever give you... you have to decide if it's enough to live on.*

Skyla had her own walls.

"So. Boyfriend of mine..." she said one night as they lay in each other's arms after making love.

"Yes?" He held her tighter.

Skyla Bright is my girlfriend, he thought. It was still surreal.

"How do you feel?" she breathed.

"Really good." His body was completely relaxed.

That's not what she meant.

"Mmm," she said. "Me too lover." She swirled her finger on his bare chest.

"How about there," she said, pointing to his heart. "How does that feel?"

Jordan hated this conversation, even though he'd had it so many times.

He thought about Valkyrie. She taught him that even though lies slipped out easier, in the long run it was less painful to tell the truth.

"You feel good," he said. "You feel amazing in my arms." He kissed the top of her head.

"I'm really starting to feel connected to you," she said. "I miss you when you're not around."

"I miss you too," he said.

Skyla was the best distraction from his chaotic thoughts.

"Do you think you're starting to feel connected to me too?" she asked. Her words were plain with truth. There was no video voice, no calculated phrasing, just an honest question as she clung to him beneath the sheets.

"Yea I am," he said, also honest. "You're an amazing girl, Skyla."

She squeezed him tight, and he allowed himself to relax a little, letting some of her love energy flow into him. It felt good.

"You're so special Jordan," she said, looking up at him.

He looked deep into her eyes for once. She saw the pain there. His eyes asked so many questions.

"What is it?"

"I'm not special," he said, feeling a little stupid as the words slipped out.

Skyla laughed softly.

"I wouldn't be here if you weren't special," she said.

"Yea, I mean special like... the only one in the world kind of special. Like you."

Skyla was surprised. She kissed his lips softly. He was terrified of getting his heart broken.

"Jordan..." she said. She wanted to tell him that he was the only one in the world kind of special, that she'd never met anyone like him and that she longed to explore his heart-places and she couldn't live without him. She didn't say it. She didn't want to lie to him.

"Would you ever really love someone like me?" he asked in an uncharacteristic moment of vulnerability.

"I might," she said softly. She wasn't sure if it was a lie or not.

They kissed and kissed in the darkness and then made love again and went to sleep.

After Jordan's Toronto show he and the band went to a party in Bridle Path. There were several celebrities there and the host had trays of cocaine at the mini-bars along with the drinks.

Bubba watched Jordan like a hawk. Since he started dating Skyla, the drug situation had cleared up quite a bit. She wasn't here tonight though and Bubba was worried.

"Relax," said Jordan, going to the bar. "I'm just getting a drink."

He asked for a rum and coke.

"Get the fuck off me," growled a woman nearby. Jordan turned.

The man she was with looked around, embarrassed. He leaned in and started whispering something angrily in her ear. She pushed his face away with her hand. He stormed off. She came over to the bar.

"Here you go," said the bartender, handing Jordan his drink.

"I'll have a double gin and tonic," said the woman. She looked familiar.

Jordan sipped his drink.

"What are you looking at," said the woman, looking him up and down and fixing him with an intense and chaotic gaze.

"Have we met before?" he asked her. "You look kind of

familiar."

She snorted. "No."

"There you go," said the bartender with the gin and tonic.

"Thanks," she said, grabbing her drink and hobbling away in her massive black high heeled shoes.

"Who is that?" asked Jordan.

"She's Prunella Stokes," said the bartender.

Jordan shook his head. He had no idea who that was.

"You know, the singer..."

"Nah man, no idea."

Jordan went back over to Bubba.

"See?" he said, sipping his drink. "Rum and coke."

Bubba rolled his eyes.

"I saw you talking to Prunella Stokes," he said.

"Yea who is that?"

"Dude. She was on the show 'Marry a Stranger' and then she made a sex tape where the camera was literally in her vagina. I've seen it."

"The bartender told me she's a singer."

"She's a bullshit celebrity. Auto-tuned to shit."

"Oh."

The night went on and in a few hours people stopped drinking and were doing harder drugs.

"I'm gunna head out," said Bubba. "You coming?"

"Nah, I'm gunna stay for a bit and then take a walk," said Jordan. He wanted to try out walking in Toronto at night.

"Okay brother. See you tomorrow."

Bubba left. The rest of the band left hours ago.

Jordan watched wistfully as people rubbed powder on their gums and popped pills.

"You look thirsty," said a voice behind him.

He turned around and there was Prunella. Her dyed black hair was a mess and she had big circles under her eyes from her mascara. Her big lips were painted dark red.

"Pardon?"

"You look like you want a hit."

She smiled wickedly.

"Nah, I'm good."

"You can't fool me, I know what thirsty looks like."

"I see. Well I better not," he said.

"Suit yourself," she said, snorting powder out of a little baggie.

"It does look good," said Jordan.

She laughed.

"I'm Pru," she said.

"Jordan."

"I've heard your music. You're the real deal."

"Oh yea?"

"Yea. Old school."

"You're a musician right?"

Prunella laughed. She lit up a cigarette.

"Right. A musician."

Jordan looked around. He had a feeling that the owners of this house would not want Prunella smoking in here. He could tell she didn't give a fuck. On one hand it made him uncomfortable but on the other hand he kind of liked it.

"I don't actually have anything to do with the music part," she said.

"What do you mean?"

"My publicist creates the music. On the computer or some shit. It's all part of the business."

Bubba was right. She was a bullshit celebrity.

"Seriously? What's the point?"

"Fame and fortune," she said, blowing smoke in his face.

At least Skyla actually sings, thought Jordan.

Prunella finished her cigarette and then pulled out the baggie. She took a big snort. Jordan watched her hungrily. She held out the bag.

He hesitated for a moment and then broke.

"You know what..." he said, "why not."

He took the bag. He choked a massive lump up his nose.

Might as well just go all in, he thought. Especially since he wouldn't be talking to Skyla tonight. She never explicitly said she didn't like him doing drugs so much but he knew she would see it as a weakness. She was intensely career-driven.

The high hit him in just a few minutes. He sighed with release. It felt great to be back in la-la land.

"In the Neverending Story," he said.

"What?"

They both laughed.

"So where are you from?" asked Pru.

"East of Ottawa," said Jordan.

"Ew, poor you," said Prunella.

"How about you?"

"Born and raised right here in Toronto," she said.

They chatted some more. Prunella's parents were real estate millionaires. She was raised with a trust fund and although they had disowned her multiple times for bad behaviour—DUIs, drug charges, the sex-tape event—they were never more than a phone call away. This music career was just Prunella's latest distraction in a life of distractions.

They kept snorting her white powder. She seemed to have an endless supply.

Prunella was a crude woman but Jordan liked that she didn't care about what anyone thought. She also had a great sense of humour. The hours flew by and they chatted all night.

"I know a good after-hours place we can hit up," she said.

"Lead the way," said Jordan.

She took him to a filthy bar where there was no alcohol at all, just a cover charge and nooks to do drugs. Trance music played and neon searchlights flashed erratically.

Prunella found a guy she knew and produced two needles for them. Jordan did not object.

By this time they were both well and truly fucked up.

Jordan looked into Prunella's eyes. There was chaos and darkness there, but he feared it less than looking into Skyla's eyes.

"What?" said Prunella softly.

"I'm having a good time," said Jordan.

"I am too," she said.

He looked at her face. She was young, but there was something old about her.

Probably from the drugs, he thought.

Her breasts spilled over the low top of her tight shirt, and her black nail polish was chipped. Her eyes were kohl-framed like Theda Bara. There was something sexy about her, but Jordan suspected she was a night creature. He imagined that in the day she would look a mess.

"It's been a long time since I met someone I could really talk to.

Not too many people understand me," he said.

"You're a dark soul, like me," she said.

Jordan felt a strange sensation shiver up his spine.

No, he thought emphatically. *I'm not a dark soul. I'm good...*

Prunella looked at his expression and laughed.

"I gotta piss," he said, getting up to go to the toilet.

Every door was busted. Jordan stood on the cracked tiles in the middle stall with his dick in his hands, trying to pee. The spasmic lights continued dancing in the bathroom.

Jordan felt hands slide around his waist. He looked down. Chipped black fingernails.

Prunella squeezed him tight. He turned around to face her. She slid her hands up his chest and into the back of his hair, pulling hard. It felt good.

"Hey, um, I really shouldn't..."

Prunella grabbed his bottom lip in her teeth and pulled softly, threatening with lightly harder bites as she released. It awakened something in him.

She laughed as she saw it in his eyes. She reached down and grabbed him hard, rubbing him to attention. He was surprised to feel himself getting hard.

"Fuck what you should or shouldn't do," she growled. "Do what you want."

She was right. What was the point of life if you didn't do what you wanted?

He pushed her hard against the wall of the stall with his hips, grinding into her and kissing her hard. She laughed with delight. She pulled down her tights and he fucked her right there in the bar bathroom stall, the busted door banging.

"Want to crash at my place?" she said afterward. She had a condo in the city.

"No, sorry I need to walk," he said.

"Are you sure?" She slid her hand down his arm and held his hand.

"Yea."

"Are you okay?"

Jordan looked awful.

"I just... probably shouldn't be doing this."

"You mean because of Betty?" said Prunella with a coy smile.

Jordan pulled his hand away.

"Yea."

Pru just laughed.

"Such an Ottawa boy," she said.

Jordan set off walking as the sun started to rise.

Prunella Stokes grabbed a lift and scuttled off to whatever gutter she crawled out of.

CHAPTER NINE

Baron hopped in the back of his car to grab a Loop to the Friday Club. Today's gathering was in Vermont. It was hosted by Hiram Switzer, an old colleague and dear friend of Baron's.

"I have a surprise for you all," said Hiram, puffing on a pipe that contained a blend of tobacco, marijuana and opium. "You're going to love this."

The men boarded a limousine that took them to an old church once abandoned that Hiram reclaimed and renovated for his project. They filed into the old building and took their seats in the refurbished pews. He was not the only one to use an old church building or community hall for their meetings. It caught on, particularly among their American brothers because there were so many empty buildings to choose from after the recessions.

There was a large wooden box on the stage at the front of the church with a red velvet curtain door. When all the men were seated comfortably Hiram stepped up to the stage.

"I have something to show you," he said, puffing excitedly.

"What is it?" shouted a man with a dark green suit and black moustache.

"It must be expensive, look how excited he is," said another. They all laughed.

"Is it a toy?"

"In a manner of speaking..." said Hiram.

"Well get on with it, tell us what it is."

"It's a robot," said Hiram with a grin.

One man rolled his eyes and several others looked instantly bored. They had all tried out sex robots at one point or another.

"A robot?" snorted Baron. "Isn't that a bit... pathetic?"

"Not for sex," said Hiram. "A robot of myself."

He had their attention back.

"A robot of yourself?"

"For what?"

"Immortality," said Hiram, his eyes glittering.

He whisked back the curtain with a dramatic flourish.

It was a life-sized doll that looked like a taller, better-looking version of him. They were even wearing matching outfits.

"Wake up, HiramBot," said Hiram. The robot's eyes opened and it turned its head from one end of the church to the other, scanning the crowd.

"Hello friends," it said. It even had Hiram's voice.

Baron shivered.

Interesting, he thought.

HiramBot stretched out his arms as if waking up; it was how he was programmed. HiramBot was slightly more feminine than bio-Hiram. The designer added touches of makeup to accentuate and beautify his features. Renaissance artists had difficulties painting female figures since they didn't have many opportunities to view real nude women, both because it was taboo and also because many of them were gay. Their women often had muscular masculine physiques. The current designers of robots were used to making exaggerated feminine sex dolls, so the task of creating the HiramBot prototype of a lower-than-average-looking white middle aged man was not yet perfected.

"HiramBot is equipped with Artificial Intelligence. He learns and adapts. He has critical thinking skills. When I die, my memories will be uploaded into him. My loved ones will never be without me."

HiramBot shifted his position in the box. His movements were fluid. It was uncanny.

"But it won't really... *be...* you," said the man in the green suit.

"Why not? What makes me *me*?" laughed Hiram.

"How much did this thing cost?"

"A few hundred thousand."

"That's not too bad, really."

"I've made a significant investment in the company ImmortaBot," said Hiram. "If anyone else is interested in shares, let me know."

"I'd get one of these," said one man quietly.

A few others nodded their assent.

Hiram grinned. He knew this crowd would like the ImmortaBot. The possibilities were exciting.

"Back to the house, dinner should be almost ready," said Hiram after showing off a few more of HiramBot's tricks.

'The house' was actually a mansion estate. Hiram had his own small golf course and a separate building housed his collection of antique sports memorabilia.

"I have a treat for us after dinner," he said.

After their meal, the men retired to the smoking room to play cards.

Hiram's servant Betts brought around a tray of tumblers containing a bluish-silver liquid. Betts was the only woman allowed at the Switzer estate during Friday Club meetings. Even his wife and children spent the weekend away.

"Thanks to John Decker, we have a fresh supply to restock our vitality drink," he said, holding up a glass.

"Excellent," said Baron, taking a tumbler.

John Decker was Jensen Decker's uncle. He stepped forward.

"A toast to the boys at Alpha Alpha Delta," he said, raising his glass and nodding to a video camera that was set up to create a special video for the Alpha Alpha Delta executive.

The drink was the newest craze among the world's elite. It was supposed to make you younger. It also gave you an endorphin kick, so at least you felt younger. The men toasted and then downed their drinks. They went back to their card games and brandy.

Betts cleared up the glasses. She brought them to the kitchen to be cleaned. She was curious about the drink, but she knew it was probably a hoax, just like all the other drugs out there promising the fountain of youth. Still, she poured a drop or two from every glass into her mouth, just in case.

Like the Switzer family, Betts knew about Hiram's obsessive quest for immortality. He felt age weighing on him as his body slowly deteriorated and he was convinced that he would find a solution.

Betts was amused by Hiram's obsession with the robot. She knew he fantasized about HiramBot one day ruling the world, carrying on the legacy of Hiram Switzer for all time. When he talked about it, all she could picture in her head was HiramBot sitting in the attic of the estate, switched off, heavy with dust in a corner behind the other useless family heirlooms of bygone times.

What a fantastic weekend, thought Baron. This was just what he needed to get his mind off of his troubles.

"Congratulations my friend, this weekend was epic," he said, slapping Hiram on the back.

"Why thank you Toussaint."

The men of the Friday Club congratulated each other late into the night and then took off back to their respective domains in the morning.

I wonder what my wife is up to? thought Baron. This time, he was thinking of Valkyrie Snow.

*

Valkyrie Snow received a message from the Ashemore crew inviting her to their annual Christmas gathering.

Is it really that time of year already? she thought.

Her memory problems completely threw off her natural seasonal rhythms and she could not believe that winter was already coming.

She told her friends Lisbeth and Evander that her baby was due in February and she didn't want to risk travel in December. She didn't bother to mention that she would never be going to the United States again.

In the past year Valkyrie had suffered losses. She felt them like deep cuts in her heart and mind. Now the wounds had cauterized and her strength was returning; she could feel it.

Some years ask questions, she thought. *Some years answer.*

She learned that lesson many years ago. This was a deeper spiral of the same lesson. She smiled grimly.

Valkyrie felt herself changing into something new. She felt her entire being shifting and transforming beneath her long white veil. Not only did her belly grow like a new limb but she felt her life's purpose crystallizing and coming into focus as her diminished eyesight forced her to turn within herself. Where others her age were thinking about retirement, Valkyrie Snow was beginning the Third Act with a new baby and a colossal project to lead: the creation of Mother House and the community that was its lifeblood. Valkyrie's vision was a preview for the world of a new order of things. Suddenly, after many years of living idly, of waiting, of learning and planning and building without knowing why, her purpose in this world became clear. Nothing could stop it now, she realized; not Baron, or illness, or the loss of her eyes. Not even losing her mind. Valkyrie hadn't lost her mind exactly, but she could feel it re-ordering.

As she walked between the houses made of stone and wood and colourful glass, the women embraced her as their mentor. They looked to her as the silent commander of the ship. They spoke of her with reverence as their High Priestess. The online community tuned into the Mother House project and following it on social media understood that she was the Admiral of their community.

Valkyrie felt the truth of it all and accepted it without questioning it or overthinking it. She pushed for the continued construction of Mother House at all costs and prepared a warm nest to welcome the baby she was creating.

*

Jordan tormented himself about what happened with Prunella. His thoughts were a hamster-wheel of self-loathing turning through his mind.

You're disgusting.
You need to tell Skyla.
You'll never tell Skyla.
What is wrong with you?!
You're broken.
You'll never be fixed.

The thoughts spun on, wracking him with guilt.

I am my own worst enemy, he thought. *I am the architect of my own ruin and destruction.*

Ssss, sssss... laughed Snake. *So melodramatic. Grow up.*

Jordan's eyes burned. He wanted to cry but the tears didn't come.

Why couldn't he just grow up?

His phone rang. It was Skyla.

"Hello?"

"Hey handsome."

"Hey beautiful." The sweet words slipped out like honey. "What you up to?"

"Just thinking about you," said Skyla warmly.

"Are you?" Jordan's voice cracked.

He sounded sweet and vulnerable.

"Yes... I miss your kisses and your warm hugs," she said.

"I miss you too."

"You should come see me," she said.

Suddenly there was nothing Jordan wanted more. He ached missing her. How did he not appreciate how incredible she was before?

"Okay sweetie."

They made plans to meet up in a few days.

When Jordan reached Skyla's hotel, he was sweating with anxiety. He knew he should tell her what happened, but he just couldn't bring himself to do it. He already decided that he wouldn't tell her, but he still felt the decision weighing heavily on him.

It's better for her this way, he thought. *No need to hurt her more by telling her. You needed to do it to realize that you love her. Time to man up and focus. You have something amazing going with Skyla. Stop fucking it up.*

Skyla opened the door of her room. Her whole face lit up when she saw him.

Jordan swept her up in his arms and squeezed her tight, carrying her to the bed. He snuggled her, wrapping her up in his tight embrace, kissing her neck softly.

"I missed you," she said.

"I missed you too."

She looked down at him. He looked up into her eyes, gazing at her fully. She saw so much emotion there in his eyes.

"I love you," he said. The words tumbled out automatically as if on cue at the perfect moment.

There was intensity in his voice and in his eyes. It almost felt like sadness.

Skyla kissed him. "I love you too," she whispered softly.

They kissed more and Jordan pulled off his clothes urgently, kissing her neck, her breasts, pulling down her pants and sinking into the softness of her thighs with his mouth, pleasuring her with a frenzy that she had never experienced from him. She pressed into his lips, giving in to his attention until she came to orgasm. Then she pulled off the rest of her clothes and he climbed on top of her. He willed his heart to join with hers as their bodies connected. He could see her love surrounding him but it didn't pierce his heart. He tried and tried but he could connect with her in body only. Finally, after giving her several orgasms he let himself go. He collapsed spent in the bed and held her close.

"I love you," said Skyla again, as lovers quickly do after the words are first spoken.

"I love you too," he choked.

He hated himself. The words were nothing and now they would hang over him when he was with Skyla like an albatross around his neck.

He closed his eyes and willed himself to fall asleep.

*

Mercury Elmahdy reported that Anastasia Simon was missing to the Dean of the Faculty of Mathematics. He didn't seem to care. It was difficult to impress the seriousness of the situation on him when she couldn't explain that she had hacked public and private records to learn that Ana was not in the hospital, had not booked public transportation anywhere, and had not connected her phone to the internet in weeks.

"Can you please get in touch with her family?" asked Mercury.

"I can't do that. Her family's personal information is not of concern to the school. If you're really this worried about her then maybe you should file a police report."

With the Egyptian tag on her passport and the illicit activities she was participating in with Purple Passion, the last thing Mercury wanted to do was get heavily involved in a police investigation.

Mercury decided to take the matter into her own hands. She found Ana's parents online and called them. They hadn't heard from Ana in weeks either and they were also worried. Anastasia's parents got in touch with the police themselves. Mercury was relieved.

Soon Ana's picture was all over the news. An unofficial spokesperson for the Zeta Psy Psy Thetas revealed that Ana was depressed and may have committed suicide.

Mercury knew that Ana didn't commit suicide. What happened at the Fall Fling? As the fall turned colder and winter approached, a feeling grew in the pit of her stomach that something terrible had happened to Ana.

Jordan Barker decided that Bubba was right and he might need to see a doctor.

I think I'm actually truly fucked up, he thought.

He spent several days hanging out with Skyla, sometimes thinking that he really loved her, and sometimes thinking that he didn't.

This can't be normal, he thought.

His emotions yo-yoed throughout the span of a day. It was exhausting.

He did a great job of hiding it from Skyla. She attributed most of his moodiness to being a creative and left it at that. She had never struggled with depression and she didn't know what it looked like.

It didn't help that there was Christmas music playing everywhere. Christmas was always hard for Jordan, who was estranged from his family.

Skyla loved Christmas. She didn't understand how anyone couldn't enjoy the holidays.

"Where does your family live?" she asked.

Jordan frowned.

"Why?"

"Just wondering. I was thinking about Christmas, and thinking about family," she said.

Jordan didn't say anything.

"What does your family usually do at Christmas?"

"Nothing."

Skyla laughed.

"You have to do something..."

"I don't want to talk about my family," he said, turning away from her.

She put her hand on his arm.

"Come on, you can talk to me..."

Jordan flinched. Skyla felt his energy retract deep inside him. She pulled back her hand.

"You're welcome to spend it with my family, if you want," she said.

"I'll think about it," he said. Spending Christmas with Skyla's family sounded awful, but spending it alone sounded even worse. It

sounded dangerous.

Over time Skyla and Jordan became more comfortable with one another. She let him see her without makeup, an honour her fans had never experienced. She was letting down her barriers.

"I want to show you something," she said one night in bed after making love.

"What is it?"

She pulled out a box and opened the lid. There were analog photos inside.

"These aren't anywhere on the internet," she said.

She flipped through them, passing them to Jordan.

"It's Sarah Weinberg," she said.

Jordan looked at the pictures of a young, normal-looking happy girl.

"Who is she?"

Skyla said nothing, she just smiled as he looked at the pictures.

Realization dawned on him.

"It's you," he said. He could tell by her expression that he was right.

Skyla Bright was born Sarah Weinberg, a plain girl with a different nose, smaller boobs and brown hair. Over the years Skyla had other work done; she had a few ribs removed, and her jawline was sculpted in an incredibly painful but effective procedure that involved shaving the bone.

Jordan looked at the pictures and then at Skyla, noticing the changes. He didn't need to tell her that Sarah Weinberg was beautiful too. There was no point; Sarah Weinberg was dead and gone. The image Skyla Bright had crafted with blood and tears was here to stay.

"Thanks for showing me," he said.

"I wanted to show you in case you visit my family at Christmas," she said. "No pressure," she added quickly. "It's just that my mom calls me Sarah sometimes."

"I see."

"So who were you when you were young?" she asked.

"Me?" Jordan was surprised by the question. He imagined Jordan the little boy, living in a dump apartment with his brother Michael, waiting for their mother or father to show up. He felt a stab of sadness and shook away the memory.

"I was the same," he said.

"Show me a picture of you when you were little," she said.

"I don't have one," said Jordan. It was true. There were none to show her.

"What did you guys do last Christmas?" she asked, assuming he spent the holidays with his family.

Jordan's mind flooded with confusing images of the party at Ashemore Estate with Valkyrie Snow... Valkyrie's face beneath a million sparkling lights, Valkyrie's warm embrace... he choked back a sob.

"Are you okay?" asked Skyla, concerned at his sudden change of mood.

"Just leave me alone for a bit, okay?" he said, turning away.

"Jordan, I'm sorry!"

She wrapped her arms around him.

"What did I do? I'm so sorry..."

Jordan pulled himself roughly out of her arms.

"I said leave me alone," he snarled.

Skyla lay back in the cushions, confused and hurt. After twenty minutes of tense silence she left the bed and went to the couch in the adjoining room of the suite.

The next morning Jordan woke up first. Skyla was back in bed. He wrapped his arms around her and she woke up with him holding her. They ordered breakfast in bed and didn't talk about what happened the night before.

They spent the day together with Jordan following Skyla around as she shopped downtown. Skyla posted twice as many cute snaps and videos of them together as usual, as most couples do after a fight. It felt horribly disingenuous to Jordan as she tagged him in her feed with sweet photos and descriptions and little hearts. She could post those pictures but she couldn't talk to him about what happened. Jordan thought bitterly that everything was fake, all of it—the lights, the photos, Skyla's nose and her name, their relationship, his happiness, Prunella's auto-tuned voice. Augmented Reality was happening long before it was literal. He felt an aching need to break up with Skyla but he couldn't do it because he didn't want to spend Christmas alone. He had never learned how to be friends with girls.

He took off back home to Ottawa. The Waves were playing a

hometown concert at a café. Jordan was relieved to be getting back to basics. The only thing that was real to him anymore was his music. Jordan sang out all his feelings, his heart bleeding on anyone who would listen.

"Hey man, you want to come to Halifax for Christmas with my family?" asked Bubba. He knew Jordan didn't have a good relationship with his folks.

"Yea actually I would," said Jordan. "Thanks man."

Jordan felt tremendous relief. He went to the toilet and broke up with Skyla in a text message. Then he went outside for a smoke.

"How's the little lady?" asked Mack, who also smoked.

"We broke up," said Jordan.

Mack was momentarily stunned. Then Jordan saw the wheels in his head turning.

"You know what? She was our ticket, but we're in now. There's no stopping us."

"What?"

Jordan sucked the life out of his cigarette.

"Dating her was the best thing that ever happened to you. Everything she touches is gold. Platinum. Even if you split, she touched you, man."

"Huh."

"We can spin this," continued Mack. "We can spin a whole album out of this breakup."

*

Baron Toussaint rolled up to Valkyrie Snow's apartment for a visit. After their tense reunion and her treatments, he spent some time away from her to give her time to come to her senses. By now things would be back to normal and he could apologize and take her out for dinner tonight. He had made the reservation at Metropolitain on the way over.

He knocked on the door.

No answer.

He knocked again and then slid his key into the lock. It wouldn't go in. He jammed it in the hole.

She changed the locks, he thought with cold anger. Did this mean she was mad at him? He kicked the door.

He took a deep breath and calmed down. She wasn't home. He pulled out his phone and checked their transportation account. They both traveled a lot and since their combined flights resulted in more discounts, they did not close the account when they got divorced. Why bother? They were on good terms.

She must be out east, he thought. *She must have taken a Loop.*

When he cancelled her flight to Halifax to see Jordan's concert, he expected her to come back home, but she must have stayed at that business project she was working on.

He knew that the Mother House pilot was a big project. Valkyrie was testing new technology. She probably expected to be out there often over the next few years. Half of him resented Snow Arcologies, and the other half begrudgingly respected the vision and drive. Sometimes he checked up on her progress and he knew the company had locked down the Mars project. That was a big deal.

Where was all that power hiding when we were together? he thought. He pictured young Valkyrie, timid and beautiful. She seemed to have evolved into a different creature.

But she's still my wife, he thought.

He took one hard look at the locked door and felt the flash of anger. He turned and left.

Baron rode over to the Barn. He had other women to attend to.

He went straight to Teresa's room.

"Hello," he said.

Teresa was sitting in her chair, reading. She slipped the book into the seat beside her and sat at attention.

"Hello Baron," she said. Her expression was blank.

"How are you doing Teresa?" he asked her. "Are you happy?"

"Oh, yes."

"On this special day, you get a treat," he said.

"Thank you."

"Here you go little dove, put it on." He handed her a Santa hat.

She pulled it on. It felt ridiculous, and she felt a pang of emotion thinking of Christmases in the past. She choked her emotions deep down inside. She would deal with them later.

"Follow me." He opened up the door and beckoned her out.

Teresa hesitated. Was this a test?

"Come, come little dove," he laughed at her expression.

So sweet, he thought.

She followed him tentatively, her arms folded tight to her chest. Her head was turned down but her eyes were glued to Baron, watching for any sudden change of mood.

He opened the door at the end of the hall and summoned her inside.

Teresa stood in the corner of the room shivering. There was a woman in this room strapped to her bed. Teresa had no idea who she was or what would happen next.

Courtney's eyes widened at the sight of Teresa. Baron put a Santa Claus hat on her greasy hair and pulled off her gag.

"Merry Christmas darlings!" he said.

He set down his duffle bag on the table. It was full of all sorts of goodies.

"I thought we could celebrate all together, like one happy family," he said. "Does that make you happy?" he asked Teresa, handing her a candy cane to suck on.

She nodded and took the candy.

"Yes thank you," she said softly.

"Does that make you happy?" he asked Courtney, his eyes flickering darkly.

She frowned and said nothing.

"She's jealous of you, my little dove," he said to Teresa. "She always had jealousy problems."

He stroked Courtney's cheek.

"No matter. It's Christmas. We can put aside our differences today, can't we?"

Courtney wasn't sure how to play this. She wanted to get Teresa on side but the woman looked totally messed up. She was frail and pale as a ghost. Her once lustrous hair was snow white and her cheeks were gaunt as though Baron had sucked the life out of her. Her eyes were haunted. Courtney felt sorry for her, and then she felt a pang of terror run through her body.

That's what I'm going to look like, she thought. She wanted to sob.

"How long have you been here?" she asked. The words

croaked out of her. Her throat was raw from screaming.

Teresa's eyes flitted around the room. Baron and Courtney were both looking at her and their combined gaze burned her like fire. She wanted to curl up in a ball.

"So you are who screams," said Teresa finally. Then she froze with panic and looked at Baron and back at Courtney.

Baron just laughed.

"We are putting aside our differences today, remember?"

Teresa nodded furiously.

"Merry Christmas!"

"Merry Christmas," whispered Teresa.

Baron pulled three holiday Swiss Chalet dinners out of the duffle bag. He handed one to Teresa, who sat down on the floor to eat it.

"I'd like to let you loose to share in our Christmas meal," said Baron to Courtney.

Courtney contemplated for a moment.

"Fine," she said finally.

Baron grinned and unbuckled one of her arms.

She sighed with relief and stretched it up as far as it would go, and then pulled herself up in the bed. Her entire back was raw with sores. Baron put the tray across her lap and opened up her chicken dinner. He cut apart the barbequed bird and then handed her the plastic fork.

"There darling," he said. "Enjoy."

She forked a soggy fry and put it in her mouth. The food scraped along her raw throat. She set down the fork.

"What, it's not to your liking?" said Baron.

Teresa turned to look at Courtney sharply out of the corner of her eye.

"It's... my throat is dry."

"I see."

Baron pulled a can of Canada Dry out of the bag. He cracked it open and popped in a paper straw. Single-use plastic straws were illegal now in Canada. He held the straw to her lips.

Courtney sipped the drink. The cold crackling ginger burned in a soothing way. She drank as much as she could handle.

"Thank you," she said. She meant it.

She ate a few pieces of chicken.

Baron turned on his phone and put on his Christmas hits playlist. He grinned as he ate his dinner.

"What a great party, right?" he said.

Teresa nodded.

They finished up their chicken. Baron unwrapped Courtney's chocolates for her since she only had one arm free.

"Yummm," he said.

He pulled out a present for each of them, wrapped in shiny red paper.

Teresa got another stuffed bear for her room. Baron wanted to get her a nice little lamp but he was afraid she might strangle herself with the cord. Solar power wouldn't work for obvious reasons. He thought of getting something battery operated, but she might swallow the batteries.

Can't be too careful, he thought.

Courtney got a fluffy pillow in a red silk case. She propped it behind her head.

"What do you say?" said Baron.

"Thank you." She adopted Teresa's blank tone.

"Merry Christmas," he said warmly.

"Merry Christmas," said Teresa.

"Merry Christmas," muttered Courtney.

"I'm going to leave your arm free," said Baron. "But if the doctor tells me it's caused any trouble you'll be strapped up again."

"Thank you," she said with relief.

Baron grinned. This was a great Christmas. Things were going well.

"Alright little dove, time to go to bed," he said. "Help me clear up these things."

Teresa collected the chicken containers and the wrapping paper and stuffed them into Baron's garbage bag.

On her way out the door, Teresa turned to look at Courtney.

"Eight years," she whispered.

"What?" boomed Baron.

"Eight years," she repeated softly. "I've been here eight years."

She scurried back to her room.

Baron walked down the long hall. A light above him flickered and buzzed. He made a mental note to get it fixed.

Having wives is like having children, he thought. *Almost.*

He opened the door to outside. Snowflakes fell softly from the sky, illuminated by distant streetlights on the roadway. Baron got in his car and hummed Christmas songs all the way home.

At home, Baron packed his bag. He was heading out the next morning for North Carolina. Every year he attended a Christmas party for the rich and powerful at Ashemore Estate, a fabulous neo-renaissance castle.

The Ashemores and their friends were an interesting group of people that had grown over the years from a dozen or so to over a hundred. Many attendees were business associates but there was no business at the party; it was strictly pleasure. Every taste and desire was acceptable at Ashemore Estate.

Baron met the Ashemores when he and Valkyrie were married. Val met Evander at a luxury yoga class in Westboro. They hit it off immediately. Evander was the only male friend that Baron was comfortable with Valkyrie having because he was so feminine.

Val loved Evander's goddess energy. His embrace of his feminine power inspired her to reach into her own masculine side. Evander and the powerful women that he introduced her to at the Ashemore Christmas party reawakened her dream of getting her PhD.

Baron showed up at the estate the night before the big celebration. The divorce did not stop Baron from coming to the parties. He made his own friends here at Ashemore over the years, and although it was tense for a time after the divorce, they made it work. By the time Baron married Teresa, things were fine. In fact, during the time between his marriage to Teresa and his marriage to Courtney, Baron and Valkyrie shared a room at the Ashemore Christmas party like old times.

This year Baron was alone.

Maybe Valkyrie and I can come together next year, he thought.

Again he found himself wondering what she was up to. After the holidays he would do a deeper investigation.

Baron mingled with friends wearing a costume he had made for the party; he was a French courtier in deep crimson velvet. He wore a handcrafted black mask with a sinister expression.

More than once, Baron found himself having something of an out-of-body experience. As he chatted with partygoers he felt like he was looking in from outside rather than living in the moment. He hated losing control so he avoided doing drugs, even though almost everyone else here was high on something. He considered taking something to relax. He signalled a servant. The young man came over with a tray of illicit substances.

"Have you tried this yet?" said Lisbeth Ashemore, floating over in an emerald green gown. She held out a crystal goblet with blueish silver liquid.

"Of course," he boomed, interpreting her friendly conversation starter as a challenge. "In fact, the Fraternity may have supplied you with this."

"Oh yes, the Fraternity," she said, sipping from her goblet. "It's possible. I have no idea where it comes from."

The Fraternity was the world's leading supplier of vitality drink.

"I'm in the Friday Club, of course," clarified Baron.

The Fraternity was for all men. The Friday Club was reserved for the *best* men.

"Of course. Well have a lovely evening," said Lisbeth, floating away. Baron's intensity was harshing her mellow.

Baron finished the evening with a pair of prostitutes. They were synthetic twins. He usually found paying for sex with robots disdainful, but it was Christmas.

Might as well go all in, he thought.

In the morning Baron woke to the sounds of chanting and sirens.

"Nothing to be alarmed about," trilled Lisbeth at the breakfast banquet. "Just some local student protesters who think they understand what's going on here." She laughed.

Ashemore Estate's private forces rode to the gates and fired rubber bullets at the students. They dispersed, one holding their eye flowing with blood.

A few guests looked shocked. Some just looked uncomfortable.

"They all have rich parents anyway," said Lisbeth Ashemore defensively. "What do they have to complain about? If they care so much about tent city they should share themselves."

"Or combine forces," said one patron quietly.

There was a collective shiver.

Tent city had doubled since last year. More and more people were living in America's 'off-grid'. In some ways it was like the community at Mother House, but here there were guns and all manner of night-time violence. Utopia twisted in knots.

"Everything's fine," said Evander calmly.

"Wasn't that us out there once?" said a guest quietly. "Sometimes I feel like we've become the monsters."

Baron let out a loud dismissive bark of a laugh.

The Ashemore crew only scratched the surface of monstrosity. They turned a blind eye to environmental destruction and exploitative labour for the sake of dollars, true, but the Friday Club members were flesh dealers and death dealers. They sniffed out and took advantage of war and suffering like pigs fattening themselves in a trough of human misery.

"Monsters? Hardly," he said so tenderly that she felt reassured.

"Let's have a round of vitality drink," said Lisbeth to lighten the mood.

Bluish-silver liquid was passed around in crystal goblets. Lisbeth raised her glass.

"Let's make a toast to dear Valkyrie, the oldest but probably prettiest pregnant woman there is."

Baron stiffened with shock as they all drank in her honour.

His hand shook as he sipped. He wanted to ask for more information but his pride wouldn't let him.

How could she do this to me? he thought. *How could I not know?*

*

Valkyrie grew large with child beneath her long white veil. By now her womb leapt and danced and Valkyrie knew it would not be long before a child would emerge earth-side. Her little house was prepared with wood stacked high along the wall to feed the stove. She stopped visiting the main house because it grew too difficult to strap on her snowshoes with her massive body, and her feet were swollen and sore. Mika went out every evening with a shovel to clear away the new snowfall so that Val could take a small walk around the cottage. They had a simple supper together and Mika updated her on construction of the citadel. It was too cold to build upward but work was being done inside the completed lower levels.

Valkyrie put a hand on her stomach.

Mika tensed.

"Just kicking," said Val.

Mika relaxed.

"Do you want me to bring your nightingale over, now that the cottage is finished?" she asked.

"Nightingale?" Valkyrie frowned as a sharp pain spiked in her mind and she envisioned the green eyes. "Where did it come from?" she asked softly.

Mika recognized a brain damage migraine coming on.

"Don't worry," she said quickly. "It can stay at Mother House. We'll worry about it after the baby is born."

They continued eating their dinner. Valkyrie did a meditation exercise to relax her mind.

"Mr. Ahote will be returning in March to complete the Heart installation," said Mika after a while. She paused. "Does he know about the baby?" she asked softly.

"No."

Mika wondered if perhaps James Ahote had provided the sperm but she didn't want to ask.

"You're wondering if he is the father," said Val, smiling under the veil.

"Not that I'm assuming anything, but I thought maybe... is he?"

"I don't know," said Valkyrie honestly. Last year was just a blur of partial confusing memories for her, and her body remembered people that her mind did not.

"Are you scared?" asked Mika. She felt silly as soon as the words came out.

Dr. Snow is afraid of nothing, she thought.

"No," said Valkyrie. "Not afraid of the birth. If anything happens to me, I know the sisters will raise the baby the way I would want."

Mika nodded.

"I'm afraid of other things," she continued softly. "Afraid of dying before I can understand the mystery of my brain injury. Maybe I'll never know how this happened to me. Maybe I'll never know why."

"Dr. Thaila will get to the bottom of it," said Mika.

"I'm changing. I'm transforming again. After my divorce I died and came back to life as someone utterly new. It's happening again..."

Mika didn't say anything. She let Valkyrie process her thoughts.

"Sometimes thinking too hard frustrates me and gives me a migraine. So I'm thinking with my emotions. My eyes are broken, and I'm seeing with my emotions. I can think and see further than my thoughts or my eyes ever took me. It's hard to explain."

They continued eating in silence.

Valkyrie changed the subject.

"Do you have a partner?" she asked, thinking that Mika would be a wonderful companion.

"No," said Mika. "I was engaged to be married once..." she trailed off. "It was a terrible idea."

"Was he no good?"

"He wasn't cruel," said Mika. "It wasn't that. He wasn't stupid either. He just... expected me to play a role for him that I wasn't willing to play."

"I see."

Valkyrie knew better than anyone that being in a relationship with someone needy and domineering was like getting dragged along behind a car that someone else was driving.

She looked at Mika and tried to imagine her in a relationship. She relaxed her mind and pictured a gentle man who was quietly disappointed that Mika didn't fulfill his expectations of a helpmate. Looking at Mika through the eyes of this man, Valkyrie could see that Mika was rather small and imperfect.

"Better to be alone than limited in such a way," she said, snapping back to reality.

Mika smiled with appreciation.

Val looked at the woman in front of her as she was.

Warrior of wisdom, she thought immediately.

Mika was calm with a sharp intellect. She was trained in martial arts and a plain woman, in a way, but to Valkyrie she was fiercely beautiful. Mika was soft-spoken but her words held depth and valence as if spoken loud. Her strengths were great but completely out of tune with traditional patriarchal evaluations of women.

"Mika. I need to talk to you about something important."

Mika felt the weight of the conversation shift.

"Yes?"

"I want to transfer ownership of this land from me to you. Just in case something happens to me."

"You're going to be fine," started Mika.

"Don't argue, please. Just give me this peace of mind."

Mika agreed and they made a plan as the snow fell and day turned to night.

PART TWO: ALLAT

CHAPTER TEN

Mercury sat alone in her residence room at Georgetown trying to will away the feeling that she needed to cry. She had one very difficult exam left and she was feeling an incredible amount of stress, but she was also lonely. Campus was quiet as students packed up and took off for the holidays. Mercury decided in the fall that she wouldn't go home over the holidays. There were several reasons. With the recent escalation of political turmoil in the United States about Muslims, she thought it might be best not to leave the country until she was leaving for good, just in case she couldn't get back in. She wouldn't want to miss any school next semester due to silliness or a misunderstanding. She also thought that maybe she and her new school friends would go on a road trip over the holidays so she could visit more of the country. Instead everyone was going home to their families and she was all alone.

Mercury took a break from studying to make a list of things to do over the holidays. She would finally go to these museums everyone in Washington was always raving about. She would take some time to check out the statues. It comforted her to have a plan.

Mercury relaxed and went back to studying.

After a few hours, her anxiety ramped up again and her back

ached from being hunched over her books all day. She decided to finish up for the night and take the bus downtown. She decided to check out the White House, the French-looking white-painted building where the head of the American state lived and worked.

It was already dark outside when she left. December days were short in D.C. She zipped up her purple coat as she got off the bus; it was cold out tonight. The streets appeared to be dead, but she heard a commotion. As she turned the corner and the white building came into view at the end of the street, she saw a large group of protesters with signs gathered.

It's late to be out protesting, she thought. *And cold.*

The protesters were barely dressed.

They must be freezing, she thought, eying a woman in a black leather mini-skirt that barely covered her butt-cheeks.

Mercury realized that these were mostly women, and they appeared to be sex workers. She got closer, passing a woman with a hot blue synthetic wig. The woman turned to look at her and Mercury realized that she was a robot.

Suddenly she realized that they all were.

So realistic, she thought.

While wait staff and service employees were often styled as cutesy androgynous robots, these units emulated a drag performance of ultra-femme aesthetic. Their exaggerated lips and eye makeup, and their archetypal clothing and wigs obscured whatever bio or mecca essentialism might be beneath well.

Sex robots—both male and female-presenting—were around for ages, but they were mostly private expensive toys owned by middle class men. With the advent of Oracle AI technology, mecca sex workers collectivized and now they wanted to unionize.

There were lots of female-presenting robots around, in private and public spaces. These didn't seem to bother people very much, since older generations dominating policy-making tended to objectify bio-women already. Male-presenting robots started to become popular a year ago with the creation of ImmortaBots, which were almost exclusively male. The first ones were carefully provided for in the last will and testaments of their wealthy owners. Now the knock-offs were flooding the market. They were more affordable, but still expensive and ultimately worth enough money that they were showing up in pawn shops. Inevitably they ended up in sex work.

There was a tension between old men who wanted special rights—not quite human rights, but almost—for their clone robots, and the potential awkward implications for the female-presenting robots manufactured specifically for sex work. It was a peculiar and tenuous ally-ship that the sex workers were now taking advantage of.

Mercury pushed through the crowd to the gates of the White House. She reached her phone through the fence, past the protesters, and snapped a photo of the building.

I'll send it to Neena and Giddy, she thought.

She lingered a few more minutes. She wasn't sure what else to do now that she was here. She walked further down the block, snapping a few more pictures of the building from different angles. Then she caught the bus and headed back up to Georgetown to get to bed so she could get an early start studying in the morning.

The next day Mercury studied hard. Her exam was the following day. She took a break at dinner time to call her grandparents.

"We're so proud of you," they said. "Keep studying. You will do well."

They told her to go to bed early tonight and eat a big breakfast in the morning. She sent them the photos of the White House and then they wished her goodnight.

"We love you," they said.

The next day Mercury made sure to eat a proper breakfast along with several cups of coffee. Her hands were shaking on the way to write her exam.

She walked into the auditorium. She handed her student card to the exam proctor at the front of the room.

"Mercury Elmahdy." He read her name out loud and paused. He looked up at her for a moment, scanning her face.

"Go out in the hall," he said. "There's someone here to talk to you."

Mercury did as he asked, puzzled.

As she walked out of the exam auditorium, a man standing by the door looked up at her.

"Mercury Elmahdy?" he asked.

"Yes... Is everything okay?"

Mercury was suddenly worried. Did they find out what happened to Anastasia?

"Come with me, we have an urgent matter to discuss."

"But I have to write my exam..."

"Don't worry about that right now, just follow me. We aren't going far, just a private room."

Mercury followed the man. She had a terrible feeling in her stomach, which was already in knots over her exam.

He led her into a nearby empty classroom and went inside. He closed the door behind her.

"It has come to the school's attention that you are Egyptian."

He said it matter-of-factly, looking over the rim of his glasses at her with an expression that suggested she had done something wrong.

"Actually I'm British," she said.

"You don't look British." He pronounced it the American way, with the 't' as a 'd', as though he had a cold.

"Have you ever been to Britain?" She enunciated the 't' softly and clearly, exaggerating the difference between her accent and his.

"No. Are you or are you not Egyptian?"

"I was born in Egypt but I don't remember it," said Mercury. She couldn't lie. She didn't want to lie, but she felt somehow like she should.

Harsh white light reflected from his glasses and she couldn't see his eyes as he stared at her.

"The United States government has declared everyone born in Egypt an enemy of the state. Georgetown University has not declared you an enemy of the state, Mercury Elmahdy, but you are no longer a student here. As of this morning you withdraw your registration."

"What? That's mad!" she burst out. "I have to go write my exam!"

She moved to leave the room.

The man held out his arm.

"You won't be writing that exam, or any other. You are no longer a student at this university."

"This is ridiculous! There are going to be serious repercussions for this."

"Trust me, this conversation is a courtesy. We have not alerted the authorities. My advice to you is to get out of the city today, and get out of the country as fast as possible."

Mercury was stunned. She didn't know what to say.

"Go pack your bag and get out of here."

"You can't be serious."

"This conversation never happened," he said, leaving the room.

Mercury stood alone in the room for a few minutes, absorbing the information more fully. She shook her head, walking out into the hall and pausing in front of the exam auditorium. She wanted desperately to go inside and write her exam like nothing had happened, but there was no way she could write an exam right now. Her mind was spinning. She kept walking and went straight home to get on the computer and see if the man was telling the truth.

In her dorm, Mercury logged onto her university account. All of her course selections for next semester were cancelled.

What is going on? she thought, completely shocked.

She did a deep trawl online. The man was right; mass arrests were taking place. People were disappearing left and right. She felt a cold shiver up her spine.

Enemy of the state, she thought.

Suddenly she felt a wave of anger overcome her.

I should never have come here, she thought. She watched the meltdown with the Rebels last year online and everyone told her not to go, but she never thought in a million years that this would happen to her.

Enemy of the state.

Her Calculus books were spread out over the desk where she was studying for the past two weeks. In a burst of rage she pushed them all onto the floor.

I'm not going to cry, she thought. *I'm not going to cry...*

She clenched her fists.

What should I do? she thought.

Then suddenly she knew. It was so simple, like the universe had created this moment with these circumstances for this to unfold just like this. Mercury opened the folder on her computer where she had been working on her Small Great Act. She snorted. This was an idle project she half expected she would never implement, and certainly not for many years if she did. It was the programming equivalent of doodling. Dangerous doodling. Her mouth was set in a grim line. It was happening now. Her fingers flew on the keyboard as she took the necessary steps to set things in motion.

I'll show them, those ignorant bastards, she thought.

Mercury was up all night, and she didn't stop working until the sun was up in the sky. She inserted the final piece of code and then went to the bathroom to shower. She packed up all her favourite clothes, her laptop and a few necessities, and left Georgetown University.

Mercury decided that booking a flight home was too dangerous. She would never make it.

How about Loop? she thought. *I could get to Canada by land. I could return to Halifax.* Halifax was the only place in Canada she had ever visited.

She decided to stick to the old rickety bus. Fossil vehicles were almost obsolete, but they were low-tech enough to be untraceable. She made her way to the bus depot.

Taking the bus up to Maine and into New Brunswick by fossil bus would take days, but the Loop system might document her and that would get her caught fast.

Mercury Elmahdy went to the filthy washrooms at the bus station. She looked in the mirror. She pulled up the hood on her sweater under her coat. She didn't wear her blue lipstick today, or any makeup at all, because she wanted to keep as low a profile as possible. She headed to the main depot to check a bus schedule. As she scanned the chart, she felt tingles of warning in her fingertips.

Dammit.

Mercury realized that she couldn't pay for a bus ticket with chip; that could be tracked. She shook her head, laughing at herself. She took off to a nearby grocery store.

"Do you do cash back?" she asked.

The teller looked at her with a blank expression. "Yes..."

"Great."

Mercury got soup and a sandwich from the hot counter for today, and a box of nutribars and some apples for the road. She could eat light for a few days. She didn't want to carry a bunch of grocery bags.

"I'd like five hundred dollars cash," she said.

"Our maximum is two hundred."

"Fine."

Mercury got her cash and sat on a bench to log onto the local wifi. She quickly confirmed that there were no geo-tracking measures enabled on her phone or computer. She fired off a quick text to Anastasia.

Mercury:

I miss you. I'm hitchhiking out to Ohio to spend Christmas with your family! See you soon.

She knew that as soon as the police figured out the connection between Mercury Elmahdy and Allat, they would be checking all her phone records. This would hopefully give her an extra day to escape.

She left the grocery store.

When she returned to the bus depot she bought a ticket to Bangor, Maine. They would want to check her passport if she drove through the border on the bus and she didn't want to risk any wrinkles so close to Canada. If she hitchhiked up the 95 from Bangor and got off to walk through the border she could book a flight home to England from Canada.

Mercury bought her bus ticket. She imitated the local accent and made herself look as bored and tired as possible, like all these other normies in the bus station.

She remembered the men in the dark street who stole her phone back in the summer.

Blaxican.

In this moment she was grateful that Americans read her as Afro-Latino rather than Egyptian.

She yawned as she handed her ticket to the bus driver. She wasn't faking it. She was exhausted.

As they took off, Mercury couldn't sleep. Every sound put her on edge. She knew she might as well get some rest. She would need it. Trapped on this bus, there was no way she could run away if police figured out she was on it. If she ran they would just shoot her down. She shivered.

Why the fuck did I come to this place? she thought.

Finally, after Baltimore, she slipped into a deep sleep.

The bus drove on, sometimes stopping for hours at different cities. She stayed awake at those times, sleeping while they drove.

She was tempted to get out at New York City just to see it, but she didn't dare.

I was stupid enough to think I would be safe here, she thought. *No more risky mistakes.*

The bus stations were filthy, crumbling holes. They represented the dying fossil industry, but also America itself. The floors were littered with takeout containers and used condoms. Homeless people slept in nests of crumpled advertisements. There were stands selling what looked to Mercury like inedible non-food, but slobby people in stained sweatpants with their guts spilling all over the place mashed it into their mouths. Where was the country Mercury saw in Hollywood films? Augmented Reality had sold her a mirage of the desert she encountered in real life.

As she rode on that bus, the gentle, carefree and rambunctious youth that was Mercury Elmahdy felt a bit of iron enter her heart. Once she trusted and embraced everyone, but as she looked around at these people and saw them for what they were, she realized what they saw when they looked at her. She was their enemy.

Enemy of the state.

The world had betrayed her. This was Mercury's second great betrayal, after the death of her parents. It tasted bitter in her mouth.

On the second day of her journey to Bangor, Mercury was deeply tempted to check her phone and see what became of her Small Great Act, but didn't want to risk it.

The bus station at Hartford, Connecticut was surprisingly clean and well-lit. Mercury had a few hours to kill so she allowed herself a quick walk outside to stretch her legs. She went into a Mexican restaurant near the station to grab a snack and fill her water bottle. She ended up ordering a plate of tacos. They were delicious. Just as she was eating the last one, a story came on the news on the television screen at the bar.

"New development on the Gendergate story. Police suspect that the attack was carried out by a network of Muslim terrorists. Who are Allat? What do they want?"

Mercury felt her blood get cold.

Muslim terrorists?

She quickly paid cash for her tacos and headed back to the bus station.

She crawled up tight on the bus. She needed to get to Canada fast.

Mercury was relieved when the bus continued north. She slept when she could and stayed awake to watch the scenery flick by as they drove along the ocean for part of the journey. The landscape reminded her of Halifax and she felt more at ease. As they drove she noticed the snow getting deeper. She was glad she had a nice warm coat. The walk through the border would be cold.

When the bus arrived in Bangor Mercury resisted the urge to use GPS on her phone and asked for directions to the highway. She trudged twenty minutes up to the turnoff and stood beneath the sign pointing north on 95 with her thumb out. Within ten minutes of standing there her feet were numb. She looked down at her little boots. They were definitely made for the city. She pulled her coat tighter. When she had to get off the 95 highway and onto the 6 she would get a pair of warm woolen socks. She didn't have enough cash left for new boots.

Finally someone picked her up.

"Where you headed?" asked a large man who looked to be in his early fifties.

"Up to Lincoln," she said. She tried to mimic his accent but it felt strange in her mouth.

"Hop on in then," he said.

He seemed friendly enough.

"Thanks," she said, getting in the car.

"Normally I don't like strays but I couldn't leave you out there at Christmastime," said the man. "I'm Orville."

"Anna," said Mercury. She cursed under her breath. That was stupid.

At least I didn't say my own name, she thought.

They drove in relative silence for most of an hour. Mercury was thankful that Orville wasn't a chatty type.

"Now I'm headed up to Medway," he said, turning off the 95, "but I don't mind taking you into Lincoln."

"Really? That is so nice."

"It's just a few minutes out of the way. No problem."

"Thank you so much."

"Where can I drop you?"

"Any store is fine, I need to get... a gift," she said, remembering the importance of holiday gifts.

He let her out at Nat's Department Store on Main Street.

"I really appreciate your help." She smiled at him with genuine thanks, wishing him good karma.

"Merry Christmas," he said.

She shut the door and he circled back up the way he came.

Mercury went into Nat's. She bought a pair of sturdy gloves, a pair of woolly socks, and a flashlight.

"Hi there," said the cashier. "Last minute shopping?"

"Yea," Mercury laughed. She paid with the last of her cash. She used the toilet and put on her socks, tucking everything in securely. She refilled her water bottle in the restroom sink.

Mercury walked a few blocks up to highway 6. She trudged along the side of the road with her thumb out.

Dear Universe, she thought. *Please send me an angel. Thank you.*

Mercury walked for over two hours. She was glad it was still daytime. There were no towns in sight, just long stretches of forest with occasional turnoffs onto rugged roads.

At least walking is keeping me warm, she thought.

Finally someone stopped to pick her up.

"Where you headed darlin?" asked the woman.

"Up to Vanceboro," said Mercury.

The woman made a disapproving tutting noise.

"Get in, I'm going as far as Topsfield," she said.

"What are you doing out here?" asked the woman as they got underway.

Mercury could tell she was chattier than Orville. She swallowed hard and focussed on keeping her British lilt masked and sticking with the story she came up with while she was walking.

"I'm sort of in a fight with my mom so I'm visiting my friend for Christmas," she said.

"Your friend? Or your boyfriend?" said the woman, alarmed. She didn't want to be helping this girl run off with a man.

"No just my friend don't worry," she said.

"How old are you?"

Mercury was quiet a moment. If she said she was too young the woman might turn around the car or call the cops. But if she said she was too old it would seem suspicious.

"Eighteen."

The woman's mouth was set in a grim line.

"I saw you pause. You're not telling me you're eighteen so I won't call your mother, are you?"

Mercury would have smiled if she wasn't terrified.

"No ma'am, I'm eighteen."

"Hmph."

They drove half an hour into Topsfield and Mercury avoided talking as much as possible.

The woman stopped the car.

Mercury put her hand on the door handle.

"Well thanks so much for driving me, it was so kind of you to pick me up," she said.

"Now hold on a minute. Don't you get out."

Mercury froze.

"I can't just leave you here to get to Vanceboro on your own like this."

"I'll be okay," started Merc.

"You're a child, of course you think you'll be okay," snapped the woman. "Look at those boots!"

She's observant, thought Mercury.

"I'll take you up," she said.

"Oh no, don't worry about it, someone will pick me up, really."

"And how long were you walking when I picked you up?"

Mercury didn't answer.

"That's what I thought. I won't be able to sleep tonight if I don't take you myself. Just buckle back up and I'll drive you."

Mercury buckled her seatbelt back up.

"Thank you so much. I can't thank you enough."

"I'm Irma."

"Anna," said Mercury. It felt like less of a lie to use the same name again.

Irma drove her the rest of the way up the 6 to Vanceboro.

"Where Church Street meets the 6 please," said Mercury.

"Alright."

They arrived at her destination.

"Merry Christmas Irma," said Mercury, opening the door.

"Call your mother," she said.

"Sure."

Irma grabbed her sleeve hard. Mercury turned to look at her.

"Promise me you'll call your mother."

"I promise."

"Happy Holidays Anna."

Mercury got out and watched Irma drive back up the highway. Even though she hadn't cried about her parents in a really long time, she felt a tear sting her eye.

She turned to face the snowy road in front of her. The sun sank low in the sky. She felt a shiver of fear and then an injection of resolve.

I can do this, she thought.

CHAPTER ELEVEN

The breakup between Skyla Bright and Jordan Barker was splashed across the news. Skyla was playing the heartbroken songstress on social.

Did I break her heart? thought Jordan. *Could she have really loved me?*

He didn't trust himself to make that judgement.

The press hounded him. The only blessing in all this was the explosive publicity for their record sales. That Jordan was the one to end it didn't reflect poorly on him at all. It only made Skyla look bad. It was amazing. The other blessing syphoning attention from the Skydan breakup and giving Jordan some relief was Gendergate. Someone had changed all the pronouns on the internet. Every web page in the English language had their 'he', 'she' and 'they' switched. Canadians mostly thought it was a hilarious and clever joke.

Americans believed it was a Muslim terrorist group. Scandinavians hailed it as a stroke of genius and the Feminist Party of Sweden proposed implementing such a program on the Swedish-language internet. The Russians were immediately accused of participating in the plot, but they were themselves concerned about the security implications of such a far-reaching breach of global digital networks. Overzealous teenage bloggers criticized the lack of 'ze', 'zir', 'ey' and 'xie' pronouns. Testamenters (Christians and Muslims) were in full-blown panic mode. There were Christian groups calling for the apocalypse, and Muslim groups decrying the blasphemy of calling Mohammed 'she'. There was also the matter of the curious avatar of the hacker who supposedly carried out the attack. S/he was called 'Allat'. 'Allat' was the ancient goddess from whom the more modern male god 'Allah' derived his name. What did it mean? No one could figure it out.

Jordan headed to Toronto for a music gala before spending Christmas with Bubba's family out East. He was winning a songwriter's award for Heartsong. It was a small-time award but still an accomplishment. Dating Skyla Bright had inflated his ego.

Jordan accepted the award, awkwardly bumbling offstage and saying few words. He didn't really want to be here. Skyla was here and he didn't want to see her.

"Congratulations," said Prunella Stokes, walking over at the after-party.

"Thanks," he mumbled. He eyed the award in her hand. "You too."

"This thing?" She grinned. "Thanks, I worked hard for it."

She set it on the bar table beside them.

Prunella wasn't even slightly embarrassed that she was a pop star who didn't make music.

Jordan felt all the eyes watching him talking to her. What were they thinking? He shrank smaller into the floor.

"What's wrong with you?" she said loudly.

Jordan flinched.

"Everyone's watching me," he said.

Prunella threw back her head and laughed a full throaty laugh like he said something hilarious.

"Nobody gives a fuck," she said. "Really and truly. Nobody cares."

Jordan looked around. Was anyone watching? Did anyone actually care? He relaxed his shoulders.

"You control *them,*" she said. "*They* don't control you."

"What?"

"Didn't you learn anything from Betty?" Prunella lit up a cigarette. "She's the master."

"She sure is."

"So who did you write Heartsong for?"

Jordan was taken aback by the question.

"My first love," he said.

"I see."

She blew smoke in his face. A few people around them scowled and moved away.

"And where is she now? Where's the breakup song?"

"I'm just figuring it out now," he said. "I can barely think about it... let alone sing about it."

The entire next album was heartbreak. Jordan was working on it slowly. Each song was a different stage of grief.

"I don't believe in true love anymore," he said quietly. He had never spoken those words out loud before.

"That bad huh?" murmured Prunella.

"Love fucking sucks."

"But it hurts so good." She smiled wickedly. "There's nothing more fun than falling in love over and over."

"I'll never fall in love like that again," said Jordan.

"Probably not," said Prunella.

All the relationships I have after Valkyrie will be pale imitations of the real thing, thought Jordan, but some part of him desperately wished he could fall in love again. *I wasted it on someone who didn't love me back.* Intense bitterness rose up inside him and he chugged his drink to wash it down.

"Hey, I'm just kidding," said Prunella, seeing his pained expression. "I'm sure you'll meet some lovely bird to fly away to paradise with."

Jordan frowned at her. The reference to a bird hit close to home—Valkyrie Snow called him her nightingale.

Prunella just smiled at him with her coy expression. She was mildly telepathic. She took the bird cue from the lyrics of Heartsong and inferred the rest, her clever mind and her intuitive powers purring along as she chatted. It helped that people almost always underestimated her.

Jordan grabbed another drink from a passing servant.

"What's the point of getting into some scripted relationship with someone where we follow some bullshit pattern set out for us by movies? There's no space for my individuality in that."

"So don't."

"But that seems to be what everyone else wants..."

Prunella snorted.

"Is that what Betty wanted? Really? Did you ask her?"

Jordan didn't say anything. He didn't know what Skyla Bright wanted from him.

"It's one thing not to care about what anyone thinks. It's another thing to assume what they're thinking. I make fun of little Betty, but she's more complicated than you think."

"I guess."

"Look, I'm heading out. Want to come over?"

Jordan frowned. He looked at her for a moment. He liked that Prunella Stokes didn't care what anyone else thought of her. He wanted to bring more of that energy into his life. He downed his drink.

"Lead the way," he said.

Prunella put her lighter in her purse and started walking to the door.

"What about your award?" called Jordan.

"My publicist took a picture of it. We're good."

They left the party.

The next morning Jordan woke up in Prunella's bed. She was nowhere to be seen.

Jordan stretched out. The bed sank low in the middle like all the springs were dead in the centre. The sheets smelled sour and faintly of mildew. He groaned and sat up, putting his feet on the floor. The room was small and dark. There were water stains on the ceiling, and piles of discarded clothes on chairs and tables and the floor. Jordan found his jeans beside the bed and pulled them on. He saw needles and powder on a large piece of glass balanced on dirty clothes on top of the dresser. He walked into the next room. It was a massive space with a vaulted ceiling. Large dirty windows let in a flood of light. There was a kitchen area along the back wall where every surface was covered with soiled dishes. He smelled the faint odor of rot as he passed them. The main area had couches scattered around the room and old lamps. The space had incredible potential but it was underperforming. There was no care or sense to how the furniture was organized. The place was obviously well-used by many people—Jordan could imagine a large party in here—but it felt somehow unloved by a personal touch. He glanced at the kitchen area, wanting a cup of coffee, but he decided against searching for some. He didn't want to see what was in the fridge either. He sat down on a couch and clicked on his phone.

Jordan lost himself in social media for almost an hour when the front door opened. It was Pru.

"Hey," she said. She was wearing the clothes from last night. Her night makeup looked strangely out of place in the morning light shining in the windows of the condo.

"Hey."

"How you feeling?" she said, going over to the fridge. "You need a hangover beer?" She pulled out a cold one.

"No thanks." Jordan felt okay. He didn't remember what they got up to last night.

Sex, drugs and rock and roll, he thought.

"You couldn't keep up with me," she laughed. "I had to put you to bed."

Jordan realized that Pru partied all night and was just coming home now.

She came over and sat down beside him. She smelled like sex.

"I need coffee…" he said.

"I need sleep. Here's a key," she said, pressing one into his hand. "Let yourself in and out whenever you want."

Jordan wondered how many people had keys to this place.

"Cool. See ya." He leaned over and kissed her on the cheek. It was a robotic gesture that felt strange as he did it, as though he was just now realizing that it was programming and no more. He stood up to get his shirt from the bedroom. Prunella followed him and crawled into bed in her party clothes, curling up to fall asleep. Jordan finished getting dressed and left to get a coffee.

Jordan had a week to kill before heading out east for Christmas with Bubba's family, so he spent it with Prunella. She demanded nothing from him, simply his company while they got messed up on drugs. They had sex once or twice but it was a purely physical gesture, like ŽIŽEK's Dating Machines. She was a night creature. She slept all day and came alive after dark, slithering around to her favourite city haunts. Jordan felt himself pulled into the night rhythms.

One evening she took him to a bar her friend owned. As usual, they were starting the night with alcohol, and he was serving up shots at the bar.

"Who's this loser?" he laughed. He knew exactly who Jordan Barker was.

"My siren," she purred, rubbing Jordan's leg.

The other man laughed.

"Jordan, this is Panam," she said. "Panam, Jordan."

They raised their glasses together and took a shot.

As the night went on Panam talked about his wife. They were having some problems; she wanted children and he did not.

After they were sufficiently smashed, Pru took Jordan to their next stop.

"I got the feeling he didn't like me very much," said Jordan after they left.

"He's jealous of you," she laughed. "He's one of my usual lovers..."

"Oh. But isn't he married?"

"That's not my problem," said Prunella.

The night progressed to dancing and cocaine, and then to more illicit activities.

When the after-hours bar closed, Prunella invited several friends back to her place. They followed her home, where they continued doing drugs. Panam showed up after he closed his bar for the night.

"I miss you," he murmured, running his hand up into Prunella's hair. She laughed, kissing him sweetly on the lips.

"I have a guest tonight," she said, looking at Jordan and pulling out of Panam's arms.

"Forget about him." Panam pulled her gently back in.

She leaned up and whispered into his ear.

"Go convince him to let you join us." She grinned.

Panam pulled back to look at her face. He loved that grin.

"You little snake," he growled in her ear.

She laughed and wriggled in his arms, kissing him.

She pulled away.

"Go," she said.

Panam poured two drinks and walked over to Jordan.

"Hey loser," he said, handing Jordan a drink and sitting beside him.

His tone was kind.

"Hey homewrecker," said Jordan with a smile, taking the drink.

"Sorry for being a prick earlier."

The apology caught Jordan off guard.

"You actually seem like a decent guy," said Panam.

"No worries man."

They sipped their drinks.

Panam leaned in close.

"Look at her, such a pixie."

They both looked at Prunella. She was cackling at some joke, smoking like Cruella De Vil.

"So do you love her, or what?" asked Jordan.

Panam relaxed. He could suddenly see this guy wasn't in love with her. He was just passing through.

"I'm not sure," he said. "Honestly sometimes I feel like she's cast a spell on me and it's out of my control. Is that love or magic?"

He grinned at Jordan. His pupils were massive. He was stoned.

"I'm glad she's got you," said Jordan. Then he remembered Panam's wife.

This can never end well, he thought. *Tainted love.*

Panam sensed what Jordan was thinking, or perhaps the guilt of his wife lingered always at the edge of his thoughts anyway.

"We can't help who we love," he said.

He moved closer to Jordan.

"We live one life. There's no sense in holding ourselves back from pleasure."

Jordan himself was heavily stoned, but through the fog he felt this man's energy reaching out to him, trying to connect with him. He breathed in his smell. It wasn't unattractive. He looked at Panam's face. He was handsome. His face was smooth like a woman's, and his brown eyes danced. Jordan could see why Prunella was attracted to him. Jordan wondered what his wife was like. He suspected Panam didn't see her much if he spent his evenings at the bar and his nights partying hard.

"I want to ask you something Jordan."

Jordan looked at him and felt suddenly afraid.

"What."

"May I spend the night with you and Pru?"

It sounded like a perfectly reasonable question.

"Sure," said Jordan. "It's up to Prunella." After all, it was her house.

Panam cast a quick smile to Prunella, who started ushering people out of the house. She locked the door behind them.

"Are we ready for bed?" she asked.

Part of Jordan thought they were going right to sleep and part of Jordan knew something more was going on.

He and Panam stood up and headed back to the bedroom. Prunella followed. Panam took off his shirt and slipped into bed.

Prunella took Jordan's hands and pulled him in for a kiss. He mellowed out into the kiss, his brain foggy but his body responding warmly. She pulled off his shirt, giving him some attention with her mouth as she pulled off his jeans. He was ready. She pulled him into bed. She kissed him and pressed up against him with her thighs in bed. Panam pressed up against him from behind. Jordan gasped softly with pleasure. The feeling of Panam's warm body and wide chest behind him was a new sensation. It felt good to be held from both sides. Prunella turned him around to face Panam.

Suddenly Jordan was face-to-face with another man in bed. It was unfamiliar but stimulating. He felt safe to explore. Panam closed his eyes and kissed him. Jordan felt strange about the kiss and pulled away. He put a hand on Panam's chest. He felt a spike of pleasure. He ran his hand down Panam's chest but stopped short of reaching further. He was not ready to go there yet. He closed his eyes and pressed up against Panam, enjoying the new sensation of their chests touching without the softness of breasts and a woman's belly. Panam's erection grew and their penises touched. Jordan didn't know what to do. It didn't really fit or make sense the way he had practiced sex all his life. He reached out for Prunella.

She climbed on top of them, sinking in between. She moaned with pleasure. Jordan put an arm over her and pressed up against her back as she and Panam kissed. Eventually Pru climbed on top of Panam and they kept going while Jordan passed out.

When Jordan woke up the next afternoon, Panam was gone. The whole thing was like a strange dream. Jordan hopped in the shower. He hadn't washed in days. He noticed the Kurt Cobain poster behind the bathroom door. Cobain was a musician who blew his brains out when he was twenty-seven years old. As he washed away a few days of hard living, Jordan thought about the dark day last year when he ended up in front of traffic.

It's a good thing guns aren't easy to come by around here, he thought. He might have blown his brains out that night too. Jordan looked at the needle tracks on his arm. He sighed heavily.

I need to take it easy, he thought.

Jordan would be twenty-seven this year himself.

He and Prunella went out to eat at a diner where they could get breakfast at five pm.

"This is just normal life for you," said Jordan, digging into his eggs.

"Life at its best," she said.

Prunella was a huge celebrity but it didn't seem to change her. Jordan suspected she lived just like this before she was famous. He respected that about her.

"I couldn't keep up with you if I was here all the time," he said. "It would kill me."

They both laughed, but it was true.

There were pictures of Jordan and Prunella dancing at after-hours bars all over the news.

Skydan Ripped Apart by Party Girl Prunella Stokes! screamed the headlines. *Are They Dating?*

Jordan read the text with a frown. He felt as though his life was not his own anymore.

That night Jordan was done partying around midnight.

"I just can't go anymore," he said. "I'm heading home okay?"

"It's your last night with me," said Prunella. "Suck it up."

"I seriously can't. I need to sleep."

"We slept all day," she hissed.

Jordan had never seen her angry like this before.

"Yea but day sleep isn't restful for me."

"Don't be a pussy," she said.

"I have to fly tomorrow. I want to feel half decent."

Jordan was leaving the next day to spend Christmas with Bubba and his folks.

"Fine. I'll take you back to the condo."

"You don't have to, seriously, I can get back on my own."

"It's our last night!"

"Really Pru, I don't mind. Go on and party."

"Fuck off. I'm coming."

They got a lift back to Prunella's condo.

Prunella kissed him. This time Jordan didn't feel into it. He just wanted to go to sleep.

He pulled away and went to the bathroom. When he came out she was waiting for him in bed naked. Jordan had been drinking but he wasn't stoned at all and the sour smell of her bedsheets and dirty clothes repulsed him. He crawled into bed.

"What's wrong?" she asked.

"Nothing."

She pulled out a needle and spoon from the bedside drawer. She started shooting up. She got the needle ready and handed it to him.

"No thanks," he said, but his eyes lingered on the sharp tip, hating and loving the sight of it.

"Are you sure?" her voice was gentle with the tiniest edge.

He was silent.

One more time, he thought.

He took the needle and shot up.

They had sex but it was strange. Jordan was rough and angry, hating it and enjoying it at the same time. After he finished he set his alarm so he could get up in the morning to catch his flight.

Jordan woke to the sound of his alarm in the dank bedroom. He turned it off quickly so as not to wake Prunella. He slipped out of bed and pulled on his clothes quietly. He gathered up his things and went to the other room. The light from the windows was bright and he felt it enter his squinting eyes and send radiating pain into his head. He made a mental note to pick up some painkillers at the pharmacy on his way to the airport.

As Jordan walked out into the sunlight of the new day he squinted harder. The bright winter light was intense. As the sun soaked into his skin, he felt incredible relief to be leaving Prunella's house. He was grateful for the week of escape but it was time to move on.

He grabbed painkillers and a massive coffee and took off for the airport.

As the plane took off Jordan's headache grew worse. His heart was racing. He tried to look out the window to calm himself down but it made him more anxious. He was never afraid of flying before. Suddenly he took ill and hurried to the airplane bathroom to vomit.

Definitely the worst flight of my life, he thought.

When he sat back down in his seat, his hands were shaking. He felt sweaty and lightheaded. The stewardess brought him pretzels and Canada Dry.

He popped a bunch of painkillers and leaned back in his seat with his eyes closed, willing himself to relax. He fell asleep for about five minutes and the plane landed soon after.

Bubba was waiting for him at the airport. As Jordan came out the Arrivals doors, he saw Bubba's big grin.

The Music Man, said the sign he was holding.

Jordan was so happy to see him. He ran up for a big hug.

Bubba sniffed him and frowned. As they drew apart, he smiled again.

"Missed you buddy," he said. "Let's get you home."

They headed out to a lift.

Bubba looked Jordan over as they sat in the back seat of the car. He looked a mess. His hair was stringy and greasy, his skin was pale and greenish and there were massive dark smudges under his eyes. He looked like he hadn't slept in days.

"You look a little sick bro."

"I threw up on the plane. I'm glad to be back on earth."

"You're never on earth," laughed Bubba. "Where have you been?"

"I spent a week hanging out with Prunella Stokes," he said.

"What? Really?"

"Yea. She parties hard."

"I can imagine." He paused. "Did you guys... hook up?"

"No. Well, yes..." said Jordan. "We hooked up but it was no big deal."

"She's not really your type..."

"You're right. But it's just what I needed right now."

"What do you see in her man?"

Jordan searched for words. "Pru... just gets me. She lets me be myself. Everything about Skyla was fake. Prunella's not, like, perfect or anything but I don't have to pretend with her. It is what it is."

"Okay, I could see that," said Bubba. He was worried about Jordan.

"We're not dating or anything."

"But sometimes *you* think you're not dating but *they* think you are," said Bubba gently.

"Not Prunella."

"Okay, cool."

The car drove up to a simple little vinyl-sided house in a Halifax suburb. The icy wind tunnels off Lake Ontario swept the streets of Toronto clear of snow. Here on the coast, the snow was heavy. A blanket of crystal shone from every surface, and the snow-covered yards tucked in the houses in a wintry sleep.

Bubba's house was lined with blinking lights in every colour. *Bleep. Bleep. Merry Christmas,* it seemed to say.

"Thanks for inviting me," said Jordan.

"You're family bro."

As Bubba's parents swept the boys up in their arms and peppered them with kisses, Jordan felt safe for the first time in a long time.

CHAPTER TWELVE

"Alex, Jordan is sleeping with you, take him down to your room," said Bubba's mother. His parents called him 'Alex'.

A little boy barreled by, followed by another chasing each other around the house.

"Jenny, send them outside!" she called. Bubba's sister Jenny had four kids and they were at grandma's house for the holidays. The house was full of noise and good smells.

Bubba took Jordan down to the basement.

"This is my old bedroom," he said. Everything was exactly as he left it when he moved to Ottawa.

Jordan looked around at the old posters and imagined young Alex growing up here in Halifax.

"So this is where you lost your virginity," grinned Jordan, hopping on the bed. It creaked.

"Haha, no." Bubba lost his virginity after he went away to university. "This is where I played video games and figured out what jerking off was."

They laughed.

Jordan took off his sweater and laid it on his backpack. Bubba's eyes flicked to the marks on Jordan's arm and back up to his face.

"I'm glad you're here with us," he said.

They went upstairs.

Holiday dinner at the Rose residence was joyous. Mr. Rose made a massive turkey with all the fixings and Mrs. Rose baked baskets of fresh bread. Grandma Rose baked enough pies and crumbles for twice as many people. Bubba's sisters and their partners were really nice. Everyone ate too much and after dinner they laid on couches and the floor in front of the fire and snoozed.

"I'm dying," groaned Jenny.

Her husband let out a massive fart.

"Daddy you dropped a Rose," said Jeremy, Jenny's son.

They all laughed.

"We're not fancy Jordan, I hope you don't mind," said Mrs. Rose.

"This is actually the best Christmas I've ever had," he said quietly.

They were all silent for a minute.

"We're so glad you could join us," said Mr. Rose finally.

Bubba gave his shoulder a comforting squeeze.

Jordan didn't know what his mother was doing right now and he didn't care. He blocked her number last year. The thought of Christmasses in his past filled him with deep pain. The days leading up to Christmas were more and more stressful, and Christmas Eve his mother and father invariably always had a massive screaming blowout. His brother Michael had made it bearable. If it got too bad, Michael would take him out to the ice rink by their house and they would slide around on their boots because they didn't have skates. After Michael died, Jordan spent every Christmas he could at a girlfriend's house.

"You're such a beautiful family," he said. "You guys are so lucky."

That night they all got dressed up in their snow gear and went out for a walk around the neighbourhood. The kids zoomed around the snowy street burning off Christmas dessert energy. Jordan joined them for a bit, chasing Jeremy and throwing snowballs at him. His body was so happy for the good meal and the exercise outside in the bracing cold.

Over the next few days they ate leftovers and relaxed. Bubba took Jordan on a tour of his old neighbourhood. They visited some of his old school friends and popped into the twenty-four-hour diner where they used to get poutine when they were stoned at four am. Alex had stayed in touch even after his family moved to Ottawa because they were always coming back to visit Grandma Rose. When his parents retired they planned to move back into the same house. Bubba took Jordan to the comic book shop, the old café that was newspapered over now, and the park where he used to hang out. Everyone around here called him 'Alex'.
"You guys gave me the nickname Bubba in Ottawa," he said.
"Really? I thought that was always your nickname," said Jordan.
"Nah."
Jordan let himself get lost in the slow rhythm of Halifax winter with the Roses.

*

Mercury Elmahdy walked up highway 6 to the railroad track. She intended to cross the American-Canadian border on foot over the tracks. There was no way she would be able to find her way through the forest in the snow, especially as night fell.
My freedom is waiting on the other side, she thought. She steeled herself and walked off the road and into the snow.
Mercury plunged up to her waist in the embankment. It was impossible to walk. She panicked, struggling to get out, but the snow held her in an icy squeeze. Finally she figured out that she could lie flat on top of the snow surface and roll. It was awkward but she was able to get to the railroad track.
That was a good lesson, she told herself. *Don't go off the train*

track, no matter what.

She was hungry from the effort. She pulled a granola bar out of her bag and polished it off quickly, setting out along the tracks. They were decently clear and she was able to walk.

She listened hard for the sound of the train but around her she heard only silence. The snow was bright and glowed even as the sun went down and the sky darkened into night. The moon rose high above her in the sky, surrounded by millions of stars as thick as milk.

It's beautiful, she thought.

She had never seen anything like this before in her life. The black evergreens towered above her on either side of the tracks, their branches bowed down with the weight of the snow. Everything was basked in blue light. It was like a dream.

She trudged on and on. Her feet were warm from walking but after an hour or so they started to hurt, and then they were numb. She wanted to walk faster but the snow made it difficult.

This is crazy, she thought.

She imagined National Geographic articles about the bodies of ancient Vikings buried in the tundra, their flesh perfectly preserved by the frozen environment.

She shivered and pulled her coat tighter around her. She was glad she bought the warm gloves. Even with them on over her little Washington gloves, her fingers were numb.

Suddenly, Mercury felt a vibration beneath her feet. She heard the sound of the wind picking up, but she knew that it wasn't the wind. A train was coming.

*

Baron searched for all the information he could about Valkyrie Snow's recent activity. He had access to her personal finances but there was nothing there to indicate that she was pregnant. He dug deeper.

A pregnancy test.

Baron looked at the date on the receipt and counted on his fingers. His hands shook with rage. She was pregnant for months and she never told him.

That bitch, he seethed. *That witch.*

He thought of all the time they spent trying to have a baby, how painful it was, how dark and difficult that time was. Their relationship never recovered.

And now here she is having our baby and not even telling me.

Baron went out to the Barn. He had preparations to make.

"Hi little dove," he said to Teresa, entering her room. He looked around.

Yes, this will do nicely.

"Hello," said Teresa, slipping her book down into the chair beside her.

"I have great news," he said. "I'm bringing you a roommate."

"Courtney?" said Teresa, her voice flat and lifeless.

"Oh no!" he laughed. "Good guess."

She stared at him with a blank expression.

"A baby, little dove. Valkyrie is having a baby."

Teresa said nothing.

"Could you share your room with Valkyrie and the baby?"

Teresa looked around at all the toys and pastel colours.

"It's a good room for a baby," she said.

Baron talked about Valkyrie a lot. That was his first wife.

"Thank you little dove. You girls will have so much fun."

Teresa wondered who the father was. She knew Baron was infertile.

"Yes," she said.

"Come help me move a new bed in here," said Baron.

Teresa followed him out to the hallway and into a room full of hospital supplies. There was a hospital gurney bed on wheels. Teresa and Baron pushed it into the baby room.

"There," said Baron softly. "Looks good."

It was a bit snug but it would do fine for the baby. Baron would have one of the hospital rooms converted into a living space like Teresa's. Eventually he would have to work on Courtney's room too.

So many responsibilities when you're a husband, he thought.

"Anything for my girls," he said, rubbing Teresa's shoulder.

She clenched her teeth.

"Thank you," said Teresa.

"You're such a good girl. Maybe for your next birthday I'll take you outside somewhere nice," he said.

"Thank you."

"Alright now, back in your room. I have some things to do. I'll be back."

He kissed her softly on the head and gave her bottom a soft smack into her room. The door clicked locked behind her.

Baron hummed with excitement as he went out to get supplies. He looked at cribs and fussed over diapers.

"How many of these do babies go through a day?" he asked the teenager at the store.

"I have no idea, let me look it up."

The teenager whipped out his phone.

"Apparently five to ten."

"A *day?*"

"Yea."

Baron filled his cart.

Taking care of this baby is going to be a lot of work, he realized. *Good thing I have three women in there.*

The sanitation was going to be an issue. He had people coming to take care of it now, but he didn't want too many employees poking around his warehouse. The less the better.

I have some planning to do... he thought.

As the afternoon went on, Baron decided to forgive Valkyrie.

Holding onto anger won't do me any good, he thought. *I can be the bigger person here. Valkyrie is probably crazy with hormones right now.*

He thought about the brain damage treatments.

Maybe she just isn't thinking clearly.

Suddenly Baron felt bad for her.

I left her all alone, he thought. *After the treatments, I just left her there to fend for herself.*

Valkyrie had told him to step off and she even changed the locks, but Baron just pushed that out of his mind.

It's the hormones, he thought. *I need to get her here as soon as possible.*

Baron stopped at the grocery store. He went to the pharmacy section and picked up some pregnancy vitamins.

I'm such a caring husband, he thought, heading to the checkout.

The tabloids were going on about some kind of cyber terrorist attack. He grabbed a newspaper.

"What's this about?" he asked the cashier. It was a cutesy little android.

"I hope you are having a beautiful day!"

It wasn't programmed for conversation that involved critical thinking.

Baron frowned and scanned the article. There was a picture of a punk-looking girl and a cellphone picture of the American White House building in Washington D.C.

"The terrorist infiltrated Georgetown University," reported the article. "Police report that she is now a fugitive in hiding. Sources believe she may be in or on her way to Ohio. The last activity on her phone was this picture she took while scouting the streets of Washington D.C. at night, planning her terrorist acts."

The barbarians sack Rome, thought Baron.

"Police are encouraging citizens to shoot to kill on spot."

Rome became barbarians, he amended.

He put the paper back on the rack.

CHAPTER THIRTEEN

Mercury Elmahdy stood on the railroad track between America and Canada looking down the rail bed into the darkness below. It was several metres down into deep snow. She started to realize how dangerous this idea was. She had trusted that everything would just work out fine but now the worst was happening. The sound grew louder and it was unmistakeable. A train really was coming. She felt nauseas.

Mercury turned around and she saw the train approaching fast. She had to make a decision. She crouched down low and tossed her bag off the rails. It rolled down and down. She swallowed hard. Now she would have to go after it. She lay as flat as she could and rolled off the side of the track into the shoulder. The incline was steep and she dropped faster than she thought. The train screamed by, showering her with snow. She felt the ground shake beneath her as it barreled along.

Soon it was silent again. The cold seeped into her body like knives. Her legs were frozen. She wished she was getting into her nice warm bed in Washington D.C. instead of lying in a northern forest.

Maybe everything would have been fine if I stayed put, she thought.

But she knew better.

Mercury steeled herself for the climb. She grabbed her bag and secured it firmly on her back.

No one is getting me out of this. It's up to me.

The thought was both terrifying and empowering.

She counted to three and then pushed up the embankment. The chunky snow fell away in her hands. She growled with frustration and packed it down hard as she moved up slowly. It was not yet January and the snow was still moist enough to manipulate. She inched her way up carefully, willing the snow below her to hold.

Finally, she reached the side of the track. It was icy and there was nothing to grab onto. She threw her body over the edge of the snow-covered railway bed, wriggling until she had enough traction to grab the iron bars with her hands and pull herself all the way up. She lay there on the tracks for a moment.

I did it, she thought.

The activity warmed her up briefly but as she laid there her body temperature quickly dropped again.

Time to move.

Mercury got up and kept walking.

In just a few minutes, she came to a bridge. Her heart beat faster. She walked onto the bridge and looked at the frozen river snaking away on either side of her.

Here we go, she thought.

Mercury passed over the bridge and into Canada.

She let out a huge sigh of relief and walked faster. She was halfway there.

I'm going to be okay, she thought.

*

After Christmas Jordan got a phone call. It was Prunella Stokes.
"Hey!"
"Hey."
"I miss you," said Pru.
"Oh yea?"
"Ya stupid. Don't you miss me too?"

Jordan was about to tell her that he missed her too but he swallowed and decided to be honest.

"Not really, I just spent a week with you."

"You bastard." Her tone was friendly.

Jordan laughed.

"What's up? How was your Christmas and all that?"

"The usual. I got drunk with my parents, my sister talked on and on about her divorce, and I ate so many dinners I had to make myself throw up two or three times a day."

"Groovy."

"What did you get up to?"

"Just chillin with Bubba's family on the east coast."

"What about your family?"

"I don't want to talk about that."

Prunella laughed.

"So you coming back up here for New Years?"

"I haven't planned that far ahead," said Jordan.

"Okay. Well the invitation's there."

"Cool, thanks. I'm probably sticking around here for a while longer. I need a rest from partying."

"But it's *New Years.*"

"Yea I don't really follow holidays," said Jordan.

"I can't believe you're spending New Years in *Nova Scotia* when you could be spending it in Toronto." She said the word 'Nova Scotia' like it was a hair in her salad.

Jordan laughed.

"If you miss me so much you should come up here."

"No thanks."

They chatted a while and then ended the call.

"Who was that?" asked Bubba.

"Pru. She wanted me to go to Toronto for New Years."

"And? You're not going are you?"

"Nah, I'm going to stay here if you guys don't mind me hanging around a bit longer."

"Of course man. New Years East Coast style."

Jordan grinned. He pictured frozen fingers picking songs on the mandolin around a blazing fire, with shitty fireworks going off at midnight and a lot of hugging and kissing.

"Sounds good to me." He paused. "Bubba, I can tell you don't like Prunella but she's a nice girl, really."

Bubba snorted.

"She's cool. She's my friend. Don't worry."

Bubba thought about the tracks on Jordan's arm. He didn't say anything.

"I'm fine. Don't worry about me," repeated Jordan, reading Bubba's mind. "I'm feeling really good."

"You look really good."

It was true. Jordan's colour came back over Christmas and the sparkle was back in his eyes.

*

Mercury crossed over the American-Canadian border. This region was the only area left without a wall blocking passage. She was lucky.

She walked on for another two hours and finally reached the small village of McAdam.

Am I safe now?

It was difficult to know. Guns were not allowed through the border so there was significantly less crime, but she was still close. There could be American police around. She decided to play it safe and not use her chip if she could help it. She walked through town, looking for somewhere to sit for the night. By now her feet were completely frozen and her whole body was shaking. She needed to get inside. She walked up the steps of a church. She tried to open the door. It was locked. She continued walking, exhausted.

Up ahead she saw a marquee. It appeared that something was open. It was a restaurant.

Tim Hortons.

Mercury opened the door and went inside.

"What can I get you?" said the woman at the counter.

"I'll have a coffee," said Mercury. "I just have to go to the bathroom."

"Sure."

Mercury went to the rest room and turned on the water, letting it run warm. She pulled off her boots and socks and ran her feet under the tap one at a time. She put on the hot air dryer and rubbed her hands together, warming them up.

When she was feeling a little better, she dried her feet with paper towel and put her socks and shoes back on.

A cup of hot coffee was waiting for her on the counter.

"My angel," she said, smiling at the attendant.

"That'll be a twoonie," laughed the cashier.

"I only have American change," said Merc. "Is that okay?"

"No worries, we get that a lot so close to the border," said the cashier.

Mercury paid and went to sit down in a comfy chair by the gas fire. She sipped her coffee and soaked in the heat of the fire. She fell asleep and the attendant didn't have the heart to wake her.

A few hours later Mercury woke up as the sun rose. She went to the rest room to wash her face and fill up her water bottle. She ate a granola bar and set off on the road with her thumb out. She walked about an hour before someone picked her up.

Mercury was exhausted. When she arrived at King's Landing she decided that she couldn't make it all day on the road and she broke and booked into a bed and breakfast.

I must be far enough into Canada now, she thought.

She collapsed exhausted on the bed and slept the rest of the afternoon and all night.

The next morning it felt good to have a shower. Her back ached from carrying so much in her backpack. She emptied it out intending to leave some things behind, but she couldn't bring herself to get rid of anything. All she had left of her old life was in that bag.

She charged her phone and was sorely tempted to risk logging onto wifi. She wanted to see if they'd figured out how to reverse her hacks yet. She smiled ruefully.

I, Mercury Elmahdy, changed all the pronouns on the English-speaking internet. It had not sunken in yet.

She resisted the temptation and packed her phone away. She would check when she got into the city. Even though the city had more eyes, she somehow felt safer and more anonymous there.

After her long sleep, Mercury felt refreshed and ready to face her day. She was even excited.

"How did you sleep?" asked the innkeeper.

"Marvelous," she said.

"Is that a London accent I hear?"

"Indeed! Have you been to London then?"

Mercury didn't feel the need to hide her accent anymore. She chatted with the innkeeper and ate a massive pile of pancakes and fruit with whipped cream.

"Want me to make more?"

"Oh no, I'm stuffed," she said. "But I could totally go for another espresso, that was lovely."

She paid for her stay with her chip and then headed to the highway to catch a lift into Fredericton.

When she reached the city she headed to the station to catch a Loop to Halifax.

Nice to be on the train instead of jumping out of its way, she thought.

Even though she was only here once before, Mercury felt relieved to be in a familiar place. Halifax was beautiful even in winter. The snow piled high and the day was bright. Mercury felt safe, and lucky that things were working out well. She booked into a motel and asked to use the computer.

"You'll have to sit in this room," said the clerk. "This computer is for guests who need to use the printer."

"No problem," said Mercury. She logged onto the internet.

What she found turned her blood cold.

There was a nationwide manhunt happening.

Shoot on sight.

Mercury shivered.

Two young women and a young man so far had been killed by people who thought they had spotted her. She felt sick.

Neena and Giddy must be out of their minds with worry.

Mercury thought of the bed and breakfast and this motel that she paid for by chip. She was sure that her bank was onto her location by now. Could the Americans access that information? Would she be safe here? She didn't know.

Why did I have to use my Allat avatar? she thought. She would never be able to use it again.

Halifax was decked out for the holidays. The ancient tradition of bright beautiful lights enculturated to allay the gloom of the darkest day of the year filled the snowy streets with whimsy. It reminded her of London at holiday time. Mercury walked the streets, popping into shops to enjoy hot cider and pastries, putting off making plans about what exactly she would do now.

She walked and walked and the snow began to fall. One by

one the shops closed down for the evening.

CHAPTER FOURTEEN

Jordan Barker was walking downtown. Large fluffy flakes of snow floated down softly from the sky and he loved the sound of the snow crunching under his feet. He loved winters in Ottawa but Halifax was beautiful too with its maritime moisture and precipitation. Something about walking in snowfall with his breath like a cloud in the frozen air, wrapped in warm clothes against a forbidding and deathly cold landscape made him feel powerful. Jordan crunched through the street feeling strong and carefree.

Suddenly he heard someone singing. He followed the sound to an unassuming hole-in-the-wall bar where a man was performing an acoustic set on his guitar. The song was unfamiliar.

He probably wrote this, thought Jordan. It wasn't bad.

A few people sat around with pitchers chatting quietly and listening to the music. The place had a good vibe. Jordan ordered a beer at the bar and settled into the back to relax.

*

Mercury Elmahdy was getting tired and cold but she wasn't ready to go home yet. When she reached the end of the street, she heard live music.

Perfect, she thought.

She followed the sound and she soon reached a bar where warm candlelight poured out the windows. Mercury went inside.

*

Jordan Barker saw a young woman walk into the bar. She was tall and graceful with a fuchsia coat. Her hood was pulled down over her face, but as she walked in she pushed it down and shook out the snow. She had fox-like features and she slinked toward him at the back, crouching down to avoid distracting from the music.

She sat at the table beside him and peeled off her coat. She sank back into the bench to enjoy the man making music.

After a few songs Jordan finished his drink. He got up to get another.

*

Mercury listened to the earnest and imperfect music of the man with the guitar. He was amateurish, but there were moments when his voice and the lyrics connected and drew her in.

Someone stirred in the darkness at the table beside her. He went up to the bar and came back with a beer. As he walked back toward her, they locked eyes. He looked strangely familiar. Something in his gaze felt like he knew her too.

Who is he? she thought.

She felt a bolt of fear.

What if he recognizes me from the news?

He smiled at her. A lock of hair fell down over his eye. The motion was uncannily familiar.

Is that... Jordan Barker? The musician? she thought. *It can't be!*

She couldn't look away.

The man hesitated, then came to her table.

"Can I join you? Just tell me to fuck off if you'd rather be alone." He laughed softly.

"Umm... sure yea it's fine."

*

She had a British accent. Jordan sat down, appreciating her outfit. There was something interesting about this girl...

"I'm Jordan."

"Mercury," she said, too stunned to say 'Anna' or some other name.

It is Jordan Barker. The singer. Jordan.

"Mercury? That's a cool name."

"My parents were raised on Queen."

"That's rad."

"So... I was at your concert here in the summer. I really like your music."

"Oh, cool."

"Do you live here in Halifax?"

"No, just visiting," he said. "Visiting family," he added.

"Oh right, Christmas and all that."

"How about you, are you from Halifax?"

"No, just a tourist."

"But you must like it here."

"What do you mean?"

"You're back again so soon."

"Oh. Yes I guess you could say that." The girl looked suddenly awkward.

"So... you sound British," said Jordan, recovering the conversation.

"Yea, grew up in London."

"Cool."

He sipped his drink.

"So are you a musician?" he asked. "You look... artsy."

"Not really. I'm a computer scientist," she said.

"I like your style."

"Thanks."

They chatted some more and then went back to watching the performance.

"He's not bad," said Jordan.

"That's serious praise coming from you."

Jordan laughed.

"Honestly I think half the battle is just getting your shit together and believing in your music. It transforms you."

"I could see that," said Mercury. "This guy's got confidence."

"Yea he does. Good for him." After a moment he added, "he needs a guitarist though."

"I can't tell," said Mercury with a laugh.

Jordan decided to take a video clip to post on his social.

It's just a little thing but it would be nice, he thought.

He pulled out his phone and took a quick snap and posted it.

On a whim, he turned to get a picture of Mercury.

She looked panicked and put her hands over her face.

"Please don't," she said.

Jordan put down the phone.

"Sorry, I should have asked first."

"You didn't post that anywhere, did you?"

"No, I'll delete it."

There was an awkward silence. Jordan wondered why this girl didn't want her picture taken.

"I hope you're not one of those beautiful girls who thinks she's ugly," he said.

Mercury rolled her eyes before she could stop herself.

"No, I just..."

She thought about making up a lie—*it's against my religion, my parents are looking for me and I need some time alone, my job doesn't want me posting pictures in bars*—and then she realized it was none of his business anyway.

"I just prefer if people don't take my picture without asking," she said.

"Sorry."

"It's all good."

They both smiled.

"So what brings you to Halifax for the holidays?" asked Jordan.

"It's a really long story..."

They chatted all night and when the set was over and the bar was closing, Jordan walked Mercury back to her motel.

"Hey I'm in town for a few more days, you want to hang out tomorrow, maybe grab lunch or something?" said Jordan.

"Yea, that would be fun. Swing by here and get me, I'll be around."

"Sounds good," said Jordan. "Goodnight."

"Goodnight."

Mercury went into her suite and went to bed. Jordan started the long walk home to the suburbs.

The next day Jordan came by the motel and he and Mercury went to a nice little oceanside fish and chip restaurant for lunch. They were both a little shy and a bit awkward but soon the conversation flowed easily between them. Mercury loved music and she could talk about it for hours. She was a little cagey about her personal life, but Jordan could relate to that so they got along fine. Mercury wore blue lipstick and she was just really *cool,* with a razor sharp edge and dry humour that kept Jordan laughing. Underneath it all though was a kind of naïve sweetness that was irresistible to be around. They were instant kindred spirits. When they were done eating they sat around drinking coffee all afternoon.

"So where are you off to next?" asked Mercury.

"Back to Ottawa. That's where I live," said Jordan.

He knew he shouldn't be telling people that but for some

reason he just trusted this girl.

"Where's that?"

"Oh. It's in Ontario."

"Sorry," she laughed, "I don't know where that is either."

"Ottawa is actually the capital city of Canada. It's a couple hours west by Loop."

"Okay, cool. I've never been anywhere in Canada but Halifax."

"No? Well you should come visit. It's the capital after all."

Mercury was quiet for a moment. She had the overwhelming urge to tell Jordan about what happened to her, but she knew that was stupid. She felt tears prick the corners of her eyes.

Jordan felt the energy shift.

"Are you okay?" he said quietly.

"I just have a lot going on," said Mercury.

Jordan looked at her. This was actually the nicest person he'd met in a long time. He hadn't laughed so much in one day in months.

"If you need to just get away for a few days, I'd be happy to put you up at my place in Ottawa. We can hang out and shoot the shit if that would help get your mind off things."

Jordan knew how sometimes when things got tough it was nice to just goof off and be distracted.

"That would be really great," said Mercury, her voice full of appreciation.

"Cool, no worries. You can stay as long as you need."

She smiled at him, but he could see worry in her eyes. He didn't press her for more information. If she wanted to talk about it she would.

*

Baron got the Barn ready for Valkyrie. He bought a crib and stroller and stocked up on baby supplies. Eventually he would have to create a new room for Val and the baby away from Teresa, not because Teresa was a danger to her but because Val would want luxuries that Teresa was not allowed to have.

My wife has expensive tastes, he thought with a chuckle, thinking about Valkyrie's apartment. She would want to drink espresso every day. Baron made a mental note to get something set up for when she arrived. These little things would make the transition to life in the Barn easier for everyone.

Baron had restraints ready to strap Valkyrie down if necessary, but he didn't think it would be a problem like it had been with Courtney. He saw pregnant women as weak and fragile, like beached whales struggling to get through the day. After she gave birth, Valkyrie would be ripped open and broken, and not in a position to react foolishly.

And the baby, thought Baron. *The baby will be a means to control all of the women.*

Baron knew that he should get a real doctor to deliver the baby, but he couldn't take the risk.

Women delivered babies at home for tens of thousands of years before hospitals, thought Baron. *Valkyrie will be fine. What's the worst that could happen?*

'Dr.' Hendricks would be there for Valkyrie's peace of mind. That would be enough.

Baron was annoyed that Valkyrie was having their baby before they could get remarried. He suffered from the antiquated preoccupation with the notion that a couple should be married before they got pregnant.

At least we've been married before, he thought. They would get remarried and it would be like the interim never happened.

Baron planned to consolidate their businesses. One of his brothers in the Fraternity was heavily involved with space mining and moon colonization with his company, Moon Incorporated, and he would be greatly interested in Valkyrie's Mars project.

Once we're married I'll own half of what she has, he thought. *Then I can take her little project and seriously monetize it. For us. For our family.*

The American space program was decommissioned in 2007 and sold to private investors. Now Canadian mining companies were using Cape Canaveral for launches. Baron's friend Rich was making billions of dollars from R&D contracts mining asteroids and the moon.

"Those buildings you see up there in the sky when you look at the moon at night are mine. I built them," announced Rich proudly at a Fraternity meeting. "When your children look up at the moon, they will see Moon Incorporated."

If we combine Rich's capitalist mind with Valkyrie's genius we can take over everything, thought Baron.

Suddenly, after years of stagnation, Baron was feeling on top of the world again. Valkyrie's baby breathed new life into him.

Everything happens for a reason, he thought. *Val and I needed our time apart for her to get this baby for us. Now we can continue where we left off and build the family we always dreamed of.*

Baron felt twenty years younger.

*

Jordan invited Bubba to hang out with him and Mercury. They spent the day playing board games at Bubba's house and in the evening they went out to catch some local music. Mercury loved to dance. She danced with an expression of pure joy, like dancing was a spell transporting her to someplace where she was blissed out.

Prunella loves to dance too, thought Jordan. *But she's a different kind of blissed out.*

"Are you sure you don't want something to drink?" asked Jordan.

"I'm not thirsty," said Mercury with a smile.

"But I mean, do you want alcohol..."

"I never do," she said.

"Seriously?"

"I'm having a good time right now without altering my consciousness," she said.

"Don't pressure her man," said Bubba. "Drinking all the time isn't normal." He looked at the drink in his own hand and he realized that if he really cared about Jordan's sobriety he should probably stop drinking around him too.

"Sorry," said Jordan. "I didn't mean to pressure you."

He felt anxious that Mercury was sober and he wasn't, and he didn't know why. The feeling sat uncomfortably with him.

"It's totally fine," said Mercury. "You don't need to ask if I want a drink because the answer will always be no." She smiled and he could see that everything was fine between them.

They danced all night and then Bubba and Jordan walked Mercury back to her motel.

"You're totally welcome to stay at my house tomorrow," said Bubba. "If you don't mind my crazy parents."

"His parents are lovely," said Jordan.

Mercury laughed.

"Thanks. I'll think about it."

They made plans to meet up again the next day and then Mercury went to bed.

Jordan and Bubba walked home.

"She's really cool," said Bubba.

"Yea, she's awesome."

"So... are you into her?"

"Into her? Like for dating? Why?" Jordan grinned.

Bubba blushed.

"You like her!" said Jordan.

"Maybe."

"But she's from London bro, that's not exactly relationship material."

"I know. Whatever."

They chatted as they walked home and went to bed.

The next evening Mercury came over to Bubba's house for dinner. For the first time since her journey from Washington she was able to forget how deep she was in trouble. She didn't know what her next move would be so she let herself avoid thinking about it for another day. Bubba's family was really nice and they had a cozy evening playing games and hanging out. It was the most human interaction Mercury had in a long time. Jordan told Bubba how he invited Mercury to come with them to Ottawa after New Year's.

That night, Bubba set up another mattress on his floor in the basement and although the three of them were grown adults they had a fun sleepover telling ghost stories and watching videos.

"Did you see this Gendergate thing? Even video streaming tags are gender-switched," said Bubba. "It's insane."

Mercury froze. What should she say? She didn't want to lie but she couldn't tell them the truth. She said nothing.

"Merc? You okay?"

"I'm fine." Her tone was tight and withdrawn.

Bubba pulled up an article about Gendergate.

"Police still searching for suspect Mercury Elmahdy in connection to the Allat terrorist ring..."

Jordan shot her a look.

"Hey, that's crazy, her name is Mercury too," laughed Bubba.

Jordan just stared at her. She stared back, silent.

Bubba looked at them. He looked back at the article.

"This... isn't you, is it?" he asked. He turned to Jordan. "You don't think this is her, do you?"

Jordan and Mercury said nothing.

Bubba went back to the article.

"Suspect has a British accent and was last seen wearing a bright purple coat. Holy shit, this is you!" he shouted.

Mercury wanted to say no, but she couldn't.

"I'm sorry," she whispered. She stood up quickly and started shoving her stuff in her backpack. "I shouldn't be here."

"Hey, hey, wait," said Jordan. "Wait a second. *You're* Gendergate?" he said, careful not to use the word 'terrorist'.

"Is that seriously you?" said Bubba.

"Hold on, Mercury, just relax for a second. You're safe, everything's fine. We're not going to call it in or anything."

He turned to Bubba.

Bubba shook his head.

"No, of course not. Just... what the fuck Mercury. Tell us what's going on."

Mercury paused and looked from one to the other. She thought about running right now, going straight to the Loop station and heading somewhere new. The thought was overwhelming and she knew it wouldn't solve her problems.

Jordan patted the mattress gently.

She sank back down slowly.

"I... am Allat. Yes."

Bubba let out a long whistle.

"You're... a terrorist?"

"No," she said crossly. "I just thought it would be sort of a fun experiment to mess around with the internet, that's all. I wasn't even sure if it would work."

"Well it worked."

"It *is* pretty awesome," said Bubba.

"Why are they calling you a terrorist?"

"I don't know."

Jordan thought about all the shootings in the US and the manhunt for Allat. He shivered.

"Are you safe?"

"I don't know."

"Why are you hiding out in Halifax?"

"Honestly I just thought I would be safer in Canada and this is the only place I've been before."

"Holy shit."

Jordan looked her up and down. He saw her in a new light. She wasn't just a sweet artsy kid; she was seriously brilliant and possibly dangerous. He couldn't help it though, he trusted her.

"So like, what's your plan?"

"Well first I thought I would get a flight from here back to London, but now I don't know..." she thought about the 'Egyptian' tag on her passport and how increasingly hawkish Britain had become since the Brexit crash of 2016. Despite her loyalty to Britain, they might not reciprocate her feelings and send her straight into American incarceration or death. "I was thinking of applying for refugee status in Canada."

"That sounds complicated..."

"The other option is to hide up here in a Canadian forest forever and ever," she said, trying to laugh but it came out hollow.

Suddenly an image of Valkyrie floated into Jordan's head. *Valkyrie and her interest in refugees.*

"I might know someone who could help you," he said quietly.

"Really?"

"Maybe."

Jordan thought about reaching out to Valkyrie.

It's been six months, he thought. *Is that enough time?*

The thought of seeing her tied him up in knots, but deep down he desperately wanted to see her. He still needed the closure.

Mercury leaned back against the bed. She was so relieved that they were speaking the truth now.

"Thank you," she said.

They talked late into the night and then finally went to sleep.

CHAPTER FIFTEEN

The next day Jordan got a phone call. It was Prunella.

"Hey handsome."

"Hey Pru. What's up?"

"I have a surprise for you."

Jordan had no idea what to expect. Prunella was a bit of a wild card.

"What is it?"

Prunella laughed softly on the other end.

"What? What is it?"

"I'm here," she said.

"What do you mean?"

"I'm in Halifax, for New Year's with you."

"What?"

Jordan was stunned.

"I'm sitting at a shitty little bar downtown right now."

"What about New Year's in Toronto?"

"I missed you. So I brought Toronto New Year's to you."

"What does that mean?"

But Jordan knew what she meant. Pills and juice.

Prunella laughed.

"So are you coming to get me or what?" she asked.

Jordan groaned.

"Pru this is not a good time, like I'm dealing with stuff with Bubba's family right now."

"Jordan just fucking come and get me. I came all this way for you."

"Why didn't you call and ask first?"

Jordan hated having this conversation. It was the last thing he felt like doing today.

"Because I knew you would be cool with it. Stop being an idiot and get over here."

Bubba came up beside him. He could see Jordan's dubious expression.

"Who is it?" he asked.

"Just a sec," said Jordan into the receiver.

"It's Prunella Stokes, man. She flew into Halifax for New Year's."

"Why?"

"I don't know."

Bubba lifted an eyebrow.

"She obviously thinks you're dating."

"It's not like that!"

"Dude."

"Well can she come here?"

"What?"

"Well she's waiting at a bar somewhere."

Bubba sighed.

"Yea sure. Give her my address, tell her to come after dinner."

Jordan came back onto the phone.

"Hey, Pru. Did you hear that?"

"Not really."

"Bubba's family is making us dinner, so drop by after, like in a couple hours. I'm not sure what our plans are for later but we'll figure something out."

"A couple hours? What am I supposed to do?"

"Go find a nice place to read, have dinner, I don't know."

"Jordan," she hissed. "Can't I just come now?"

"If we were in a hotel, sure. But we're with Bubba's family. So no."

"Fine."

Jordan gave her the address and then disconnected.

Bubba laughed.

"How do you get yourself into the most dramatic relationships my friend?"

"I don't know. And it's not a relationship, I told you."

"What's going on?" said Mercury, joining them.

"Jordan's not-girlfriend decided to surprise him for New Year's," laughed Bubba.

"Skyla Bright's here? Sweet," said Mercury.

"It's Prunella Stokes."

"What? What about Skyla Bright?"

"We're not together anymore," said Jordan quietly.

"Oh. I guess I missed that in the news."

Bubba grinned.

"Isn't it amazing that your love life is news for the masses?" he said.

"It's fucking terrible."

"So, wait," said Mercury. "Prunella Stokes... that's the vagina-camera sex tape bird, right?"

Bubba howled with laughter.

"Yes!"

Jordan glowered at him, and then broke. He had to smile a little.

"Well that'll be a fun evening," said Mercury.

Bubba laughed again, too hard.

They had dinner with the family and soon after Prunella showed up in a lift.

Bubba's mother looked her up and down and then let her in.

"Nice to meet you," she said. "Go on downstairs, that's where they are."

Prunella walked down the basement stairs.

"Hello?" she called.

"Hey," said Jordan, standing up and coming over. Prunella was dressed to kill in a black leather dress and pounds of makeup. She leaned in to kiss him and he turned and kissed her cheek.

"Pru, this is Bubba, I don't think you guys have actually met," said Jordan, bringing her over and doing the introductions.

"Hi Bubba," said Pru, batting her eyelashes. Her gaze turned to Mercury.

"And this is Mercury."

"Hey," said Pru.

"Hey, cool to meet you in person," said Mercury, holding out her hand for a shake.

Prunella shook Mercury's hand. The girl looked very familiar, but she couldn't think of who she was. She had a British accent. 'Mercury'... was she an up-and-coming British pop star? Prunella wasn't sure.

Prunella saw that Jordan and Bubba were wearing flannel pyjama pants.

"So what are you guys up to?" she asked, sitting down uncomfortably in her leather dress on the edge of the bed.

"Just hanging out."

"I see. Are we going out tonight?"

"A bit later we were going to go down to my friend's house to play some street hockey, and then maybe hit up a bar for the countdown, but nothing really solid."

"Street hockey is my new favourite thing," said Merc. She and

Jordan and Bubba grinned.

"Well I'm not really dressed for that," said Prunella. "When are we going out again?"

Jordan and Bubba looked at each other.

"Well we could get dressed and head out now I guess," said Jordan.

"Sure, yea."

"Great," said Pru. She pulled out her phone and put on some club beats. "Let's get this party started."

The boys got dressed.

"I like your outfit," said Prunella, looking at Mercury's bomber jacket and jewellery. She had a unique personal style.

"Thanks."

"Do you want me to do your makeup?"

"Oh, no thanks, I'm good," laughed Mercury.

"I'm good at it," said Prunella.

"Blue lipstick is all I need," said Merc.

She wore makeup as part of her personal fashion style, but not the kind that reproduced the 'cartoon femininity' look. She liked that her fox-like face was boyish and she wasn't interested in contouring it differently.

They chatted more as the boys got ready. Prunella was really nice, Mercury decided. She had some sharp edges to her, but she was really funny and she spoke her mind. Mercury liked that.

They got into their coats to head out to Bubba's friend's house.

"You're going to freeze to death," said Jordan, looking at Prunella's bare legs and cute little Toronto-winter jacket and booties.

"Nothing can kill me," said Pru with a wicked grin.

"Put on my mom's snow pants," said Bubba. He held them up.

Prunella eyed them skeptically.

"No thanks."

"Seriously, it's freezing outside," said Jordan. "We're walking there."

"Can't we take a lift?"

Bubba rolled his eyes.

"Fine," said Prunella.

She pulled on the snow pants begrudgingly.

They ran out into the night as the snow fell, hooting and pushing each other into snowbanks. There were other people out walking around too, enjoying the beautiful cold night and heading to evening gatherings to ring in the New Year.

"My feet are cold already," laughed Pru.

"Aren't you glad you've got the snow pants?" said Bubba.

They arrived at the party house. It was a clapboard place with an unfinished exterior with insulation sticking out along one wall.

"Not the rockstar party you're used to, huh?" grinned Bubba.

Prunella just shrugged. She had been to all kinds of parties.

There were beers and bottles of liquor plunged into the snow on the deck.

"Canadian fridge," laughed Bubba, letting himself into the house.

Bubba floated around introducing Prunella to people. They decided to call Mercury 'Anna' tonight, just to keep things easier. She avoided talking to people and mostly stuck to Jordan.

She's definitely a pop star, thought Prunella.

"Everyone's so nice here," said Mercury.

"Yea it's a friendly place," said Jordan. "Not the worst place ever to hole up and hide." He winked at her.

Prunella came over with a handful of drinks.

"Here's some moonshine," she said. "That guy over there made it!"

She gestured to a guy in a flannel button-up with a bushy beard. He waved with a grin.

Prunella handed Jordan and Mercury paper cups with a clear liquid inside.

"No thanks," said Mercury. "The last time I had moonshine it tasted like rubbish."

"More for us," said Pru, pouring Mercury's cup half in hers and half in Jordan's.

"Bottom's up," she said. She and Jordan tapped cups and drank the moonshine.

"Woo!" said Jordan. "That's intense."

"Mmm," said Prunella. "That's strong."

"It burns all the way down!" said Jordan.

Mercury laughed.

"Exactly."

"Let me get you a beer," said Prunella.

Jordan cut in.

"It's all good Pru, we're going to take it easy until we get to the bar I think."

We're. Prunella did not miss the way he phrased it.

Is he interested in her? She looked at them. It seemed pretty friendly. It was difficult to say.

Prunella hit the moonshine a few more times and it wasn't long before she was wasted and ready to move on.

Jordan went to find Bubba.

"Hey man, when you're ready, the girls want to go dance," he said.

"Okay yea let's take off soon."

Jordan called a lift to take them downtown.

They headed to the club. There was a small lineup. Prunella walked straight up to the front of the line.

"Wait," said Jordan, holding her arm. "Let's just be normal people tonight and wait in line."

She pulled away her arm roughly.

"Get the fuck off me," she said with a laugh.

Jordan had déja-vu of the day they met. Prunella pushed up the front of the line and talked to the bouncer. He opened the cord to let her in.

"Come on," she called.

Jordan shook his head. People pulled out their cameras to take pictures.

Mercury shrank back. This was the last thing she wanted right now. She grabbed Bubba's arm and went to huddle in line.

"Don't worry," said Bubba quietly, holding her arm. "I won't let anything happen to you."

Jordan walked up to Prunella.

"I'm waiting in line," he said quietly. "I'll see you in there."

Prunella rolled her eyes and went in. Jordan exhaled and walked slowly to the line. He saw Mercury turned into the wall chatting with Bubba.

Mercury, he thought. *She can't be in the news.*

He stood away from the line on the curb and smoked a cigarette. A few people came over to take their pictures with him and then everything settled down.

The line moved forward and Jordan went in with Mercury and Bubba.

Prunella Stokes was dancing on the stage. She was obviously drunk, but actually a great dancer. The crowd was cheering. Jordan couldn't help but smile.

Mercury relaxed. She started to dance. Bubba tried to dance with her, but he eventually gave up when it was obvious that Mercury was in her own world and needed her space on the dance floor.

Jordan wasn't big into dancing, but the way that Mercury just let her body flow to the music made him wish he could do the same.

Maybe I should take a dance class, he thought. Then he laughed at himself. He wanted to ask Mercury for some tips but she looked so happy that he didn't want to interrupt her.

Prunella came down from the stage and over to Jordan. The boys were trying to dance and Mercury was doing her own thing nearby. Prunella watched her movements. Mercury was graceful and strong. Something about her gave Prunella a sudden lesbian vibe.

Is she gay? thought Prunella. *Is that what I'm missing?*

She looked at Bubba and Jordan. They were both mesmerized by her. She laughed and stumbled over to them.

"Let's get a drink," she said. Then she reached in her purse and pulled out a bag of white powder. "Or something more..."

"I could use a drink," said Bubba. He turned to Mercury. "You want a drink?"

"No thanks." She kept dancing.

"You sure?"

"I told you... I don't drink alcohol. Go on ahead and just don't leave without me," she said.

"Of course not! We'll be right back."

They went to the bar and ordered.

Jordan wanted to tell Prunella she should slow down because she was already wasted, but he knew there was no point. Prunella Stokes did whatever the fuck she wanted, and if he tried to stop her it would just be a big fight.

"So she's not drinking?" slurred Pru. "What's that about? Is she in recovery?"

"Nah, she just doesn't drink."

An airhorn sounded. The crowd cheered. It was almost time for the countdown. Prunella got out her phone. She pulled Jordan in tight and kissed his cheek. She snapped a pic.

"This isn't Toronto but I'm having a good time," said Prunella.

"Great," said Jordan.

Prunella posted the picture on social with a dancing sticker that said "Happy New Years Baby!" The fan reactions flooded in.

Prunella put her arms around Jordan's neck and whispered in his ear. "Let's go to the bathroom."

Jordan knew why Pru wanted to go to the bathroom. He thought about his terrible plane ride in withdrawal and how he had to stay sharp to help Mercury. He was already drunk enough as it was.

"Not tonight Pru."

"Come on..."

"It's not happening."

Prunella heard the iron in his voice. She frowned.

"Seriously? You're such a buzzkill."

"Why are you pushing me? Do what you want. I'll do what I want."

"Fine. I'll go take my hit alone."

Prunella stalked off to the toilet.

Jordan watched her walk off.

Bubba came over and put his arm around Jordan's shoulder.

"Let her go man," he said.

"I did."

"I know. Good for you."

Bubba led Jordan over to where he and Mercury were dancing.

Suddenly the bartender got on a loudspeaker and called out the countdown. Everyone in the bar joined in.

"SEVEN! SIX! FIVE!"

Bubba reached over and pulled Mercury into his embrace with Jordan. They stood with their arms over one another's shoulders calling out the countdown.

"THREE! TWO! ONE!"

Someone shook a bag of confetti over the crowd from the balcony. Glittering bits of paper floated down from above.

"HAPPY NEW YEAR!"

The sound system played Auld Lang Syne and they hugged and

laughed.

"To a year of new adventures," said Bubba.

"To a year of new adventures!" repeated Mercury with a grin.

"Can we really reset our lives and start again?" said Jordan.

Bubba squeezed his neck.

"Every time," he said.

Prunella stumbled out of the bathroom. Her intensity and her heavy look were out of place in this light-hearted Halifax bar. She approached her friends, and from a distance she observed the expression on Mercury's face: puppy-like adoration of Jordan. Pru had convinced herself that Mercury was a lesbian but she didn't think so anymore.

"Come here," she said, pulling Jordan away and snuggling into his arms. She wasn't a jealous creature but a few subtle cues would nip a pointless crush in the bud.

"Hey," he said with a smile, still thinking about the spiritual possibilities of the New Year.

"Happy New Year."

"Happy New Year."

Prunella looked like she wanted to kiss him but he kept enough distance so she would know not to. The last thing he needed was paparazzi showing up and making something out of the time he was spending with her.

Bubba came closer to Mercury.

"You're really awesome," he said.

"You are too. I'm glad I ran into you guys."

"Yea," laughed Bubba. "I mean, you're like, really special."

Mercury looked in his eyes. His words were heavier with meaning than hers had been.

"Thank you," she said. She wanted to tell him that he was special too, but she wanted to be careful about communicating her feelings clearly.

"I can't wait to show you Ottawa when you come to our house," he said.

"That's going to be fun," she said. "Even though I haven't known you long, I know we're going to be friends for a long time."

Bubba nodded. She could see doubt swimming into him and

his opening heart retreat. She reached out and squeezed his hand.

"You're a lovely soul," she said. "I'm so glad to call you friend."

He smiled. He felt the warm glow of her platonic love, but he had to be sure.

"I... care about you," he said.

"I care about you too."

"But you just want to be friends."

"Yes Alex," she said, calling him by the name his mother used at their house. "I want to be friends who care about each other and have each other's backs."

Bubba nodded. He squeezed her hand back.

"Okay," he said. "That sounds good."

His heart was disappointed that he didn't get to connect on a romantic level, but this was still beautiful and really nice.

He wondered if Mercury had fallen for Jordan. He wouldn't blame her; Jordan was a handsome devil.

Handsome face, thought Bubba. *With a bit of ugliness inside...*

He loved Jordan but he would never set him up with a woman he cared about. He wanted to ask Mercury but it felt tacky in this moment so he said nothing.

It was last call at the bar.

"Two am? Seriously?" said Pru. She scoffed.

"I'm tired actually," laughed Mercury.

"I've got something for that," said Pru, pulling out a bag of coke.

"I'm tired too," said Bubba. "You want to head out?" He looked at Jordan. No matter how tired he was, there was no way he was leaving Jordan alone with Prunella and a bag of drugs tonight.

Jordan looked at the drugs and felt his heart jump with desire. He shook his head.

"I think I gotta hit the sack Pru," he said.

"No way. It's two am! If you go home you'll ruin my New Years!"

"We had a great New Years," said Bubba. "Now it's time to go home."

Prunella could see that she was outvoted by these goodies. Her influence over Jordan was weak against them.

"Fine, let's go home," she said.

"Where are you staying? We'll walk you to your hotel," said

Bubba. "Don't forget to get my mum's snow pants out of the coat check."

"I don't have a hotel," said Pru.

"What?" said Jordan. "You flew to Halifax without making any plans at all?"

"Because I knew you would take care of it, dumbass," she snapped.

Mercury's eyes went wide.

Such bad energy, she thought. She didn't say anything, she didn't need that kind of negativity in her life and she stayed out of it.

"Bubba's house is packed. It's completely full."

"Are you telling me that I can't come with you guys? You're going to leave me out on the streets of Halifax?" The shrillness level of her voice rose a decibel.

"No of course not," said Jordan quietly. "Just, you made a lot of assumptions when you came here."

"I don't know why you're being like this..." she said.

Jordan realized that he had to set some boundaries with Prunella if she was going to be in his life. She wasn't going to like it. She was the kind of person who hated boundaries. He looked at her. She was swaying slightly on her feet. She had raccoon-eyes mascara. She was fucked up. Tonight was definitely not the time to have a conversation about boundaries.

"I'm sorry man," he said to Bubba. "Can she stay at your family's place?"

"Yea man, it's okay."

They grabbed a lift and headed home.

"At least we can party at home," said Prunella, going down into the basement.

"You can't do drugs in my house," said Bubba. Prunella looked at him with a stormy expression. She wanted to snap at him— or more accurately, her craving for drugs made her want to snap at him—but she knew that if she fell out with Jordan's best friend then it could seriously damage her relationship with Jordan.

Mercury, Jordan and Bubba got ready for bed.

"Look at you in your cute pyjamas," laughed Pru.

"How about you get ready for bed?" said Jordan.

This was beginning to stress him out. Would he be managing Prunella all night? She was still fucked up on booze and drugs.

"Do you have something I can wear?" she asked Bubba.

He sighed. She came here with just the clothes on her back. He shot Jordan a glowering look.

"Let me go see what I can find."

He went upstairs to find some of his grandma's old clothes.

Mercury brushed her teeth and then curled up in her bed on the blow-up mattress.

"Goodnight all," she said.

"Night Merc," said Jordan.

He wanted to be cozying into his blow-up mattress beside her, but instead he was babysitting Prunella.

Bubba came back with a faded nightgown and a blanket.

"You want me to wear that thing?" Prunella laughed.

"Shhh, everyone's sleeping," said Bubba. "Put it on. You're sleeping in the bathtub."

"What the fuck," she said.

"I'm going to bed. Take care of your girlfriend," whispered Bubba to Jordan.

He went to bed.

"Put on the nightgown," said Jordan.

"I don't want to."

"Fine, sleep naked. Just get out of your tight dress."

Prunella laughed and peeled down her dress. When it was off Jordan pulled the nightgown onto her. She looked like a doll dressed in the wrong doll's clothes with her matted black hair and intense makeup on top and the lacy moomoo on the bottom.

"Where are you sleeping?" she asked.

"On the floor. There's no room for you. Come on."

He led her to the basement bathroom. There were spider nests in the corners of the shower. The tub was a pastel pink and the toilet was green. Jordan laid the blanket in the tub.

"There you go," he said.

Prunella climbed in.

"I've slept in worse places," she laughed.

"I don't doubt that," said Jordan. He turned to leave.

"Wait, kiss me goodnight," said Prunella.

Jordan came over and leaned down to kiss her goodnight. She pulled him down toward her, kissing him harder. He knew she wanted him to get in the tub with her.

"No way," he said. "I'm exhausted." He pulled up and away from her. "Good night Prunella."

She pouted. Jordan turned off the light and closed the door. He went to bed.

In the morning Bubba found Prunella in the bathtub. There was a used syringe on the floor. Bubba frowned. He wanted Jordan to deal with it but he didn't want Jordan to be triggered by touching the needle. He clenched his teeth and disposed of it.

She can't stay here ever again, thought Bubba.

He was worried about Jordan.

Mercury got up in the morning. She and Bubba had breakfast with his family. Jordan came up later. Prunella was still passed out.

"Happy New Year," said Mrs. Rose.

Prunella came upstairs in the afternoon.

"I'm starving," she called out.

Mrs. Rose came in and lifted the lid on the pan on the stove.

"You missed breakfast but I saved you some bacon. There's tomatoes in the fridge and fresh bread in the bin if you like BLTs."

"Sounds good," said Prunella, sitting at the table and waiting expectantly.

"Please help yourself to whatever you like," said Mrs. Rose. She went back out to the living room.

"It's been great having you for Christmas Jordan," said Mrs. Rose. "Come back any time." She turned to Mercury. "And it was nice to meet you."

Bubba's mother was observant. She could see the way that Bubba looked at Mercury yesterday, and how it had changed today. She could see how Mercury looked at Jordan.

"Nice to meet you too," said Mercury. "Thank you so much for your hospitality. It's been lovely. I'll never forget New Years in Halifax."

"Are you all packed up for Ottawa?" asked Mrs. Rose.

"Yep," said Merc.

Prunella came into the living room munching on bacon wrapped in bread.

"What's up," she said.

"I just have to pack up a few things," said Jordan.

"Where are we going?" asked Pru.

"Bubba and I are going home to Ottawa," said Jordan. "Mercury's coming with us."

"Oh cool. Sounds like fun," said Pru. "Maybe I'll come along."

Bubba frowned.

"Sure, if you want," said Jordan.

Mrs. Rose had tears in her eyes.

"I'll miss you baby," she said, giving Bubba a big hug and a wet kiss. "Christmas came and went so quickly."

"Love you mom," said Bubba.

Jordan looked away. He hated that he felt a tiny sting of jealousy. His own mother was a dead beat.

Bubba went downstairs to finish packing. Jordan got up to follow him.

"Hold up Jordan," said Mrs. Rose. "I need to show you something."

He followed her out to the kitchen. She shut the door on Mercury and Prunella.

"What is it?" he asked.

Mrs. Rose pulled out her tablet. Jordan looked at the screen. It was the picture Prunella snapped at the bar last night kissing Jordan's cheek. "Happy New Years Baby!" said the glittering lettering.

JORNELLA! IT'S OFFICIAL! blared the headline in the news.

He looked up at Mrs. Rose.

"We're not really dating, you know," he told her. "We're just good friends."

"Jordan, you've been my son's best friend for years. I know about all your ups and downs..."

Jordan looked alarmed. What had Bubba said about him?

"Now I know you don't have much in the way of family, and we don't need to talk about that. But now you've spent Christmas with us. You're like part of the family now, if you want to be."

"Thanks," he said quietly.

"I have to say this, because I don't know who else will. You gotta get your head straight on these women."

"It's not my fault..."

"Look here. Bubba told me you got your heart broken and I'm sorry for that. Then you dated that nice Skyla Brights girl. She seemed like a good girl even if she got her boobs done. No harm in that."

Jordan smiled.

"But this Stokes girl is trouble." Jordan started to protest but Mrs. Rose shushed him. "Don't you tell me you're not leading her on." She pointed to the picture. "You're a man now. It's time to grow up and take responsibility. You have healing to do. You do your healing, quit wasting your time playing around. Once your healing is done there are plenty of nice girls to catch your eye when you're ready."

Jordan was silent. He wanted to argue but she was right.

"You're a man now," repeated Mrs. Rose.

"Sometimes I don't feel like it," said Jordan quietly.

"I know. Your body is there already but you gotta get your head around it."

"I'll try."

"Any time you feel like talking you can always call me. Or Mr. Rose too. Neither of us is going to listen to any BS though, Jordan."

"What do you mean?"

"Well you're leading that girl on, aren't you."

Jordan sighed. "Yea. I guess I am." He knew he owed it to both himself and to Prunella to have that conversation about boundaries. Why hadn't he? He thought of Charlotte, the girl he strung along for months two years ago. Tears stung his eyes.

"I can't believe I'm back here doing this again," he said.

"You got a rough start in life Jordan, a slow start learning about how to have a real relationship. You gotta break that pattern. You gotta see it, and then break it. You can do it."

Jordan gave her a big hug. He closed his eyes and sunk into her warmth and let himself cry.

That afternoon, Jordan, Mercury, Bubba and Prunella took off for Ottawa.

PART THREE: THE EDGE OF THE WORLD

CHAPTER SIXTEEN

Valkyrie Snow was ready to pop. She felt the baby moving around inside her, getting restless.

Margarethe stopped by for a visit to check in on her. Margarethe and Mika were the only people allowed inside the stone house anymore.

"Not long now my beauty," she said.

She laid fresh bread and a jar of dried berries on the rough wooden table. The winter stores were running low on fresh produce, but they were well stocked with dried goods.

"Thank you Margarethe," said Val.

"Soon, soon," said the AI voice of the Oracle in both of their heads.

For the past few weeks the Oracle had been speaking Val's thoughts when she felt overwhelmed by verbal communication. Sometimes people in the village would knock on the one little window of Valkyrie's house asking for guidance. The Oracle would capture and synergize her scattered thoughts and answer for her. The people of the village renamed Valkyrie's house the Seer's Cottage.

"One moon away now," said Margarethe. Less than a month.

They were deep in the cold of winter, but Valkyrie's body was piping with heat. She kept the woodstove burning, but some nights she lay on top of the blankets wet with sweat.

Val felt hot, so she opened the door to let in a cold blast. She looked out over the land. Everything was white with snow. It was incredible. She imagined summer with its lush green trees and fields of flowers and food ready to be plucked from the vine. An icy wind blew up from the ocean and the powdery top layer of snow puffed in a cloud of white.

"Spring is always a surprise, hiding under there," she said softly. Margarethe chuckled.

"And hiding in you," she said, patting Valkyrie's massive stomach.

"How do seeds know to grow?"

The Mother knows," said Margarethe, knotting her shawl tight and going out into the snow.

"Sometimes it's as though I willed it to happen," said the Oracle. It pulsed with a faint green glow beneath her veil, hanging on a cord from her neck.

"What are we doing?" asked Val.

Margarethe turned to take a long look at the landscape.

"We are making deserts into gardens," she said.

Valkyrie smiled and closed the door. She pulled back her veil in the quiet darkness of the Seer's Cottage and sat down in her chair.

"I want to see the light," said the Oracle.

She shivered. Was the baby talking?

But Valkyrie realized that notion was silly. There was no difference between her thoughts and the baby's. The growing mass of flesh that would be a baby when it emerged and was cut from her was an organ that she was growing inside of her. It was part of her. Its flesh was her flesh. Its thoughts were her thoughts.

The baby has never seen light before, she thought. *Its senses are limited to the tight nest of flesh of my body. I must be projecting my own thoughts onto the baby.*

Valkyrie thought about what the baby would be like as it grew. Would it look like her? Or someone else? Maybe someone with green eyes?

Valkyrie sat on the floor to do her meditation.

Jordan, Mercury, Bubba and Prunella arrived in Ottawa and headed to Animal House, the co-op where Bubba and Jordan lived. Jordan felt relieved to be back in his own space.

"This is where you live?" laughed Prunella. His basement room was tiny.

"Yea. I love it here," he said.

It was true. This place represented financial freedom for him. The band was reaching a point where he could move somewhere nicer if he wanted, but this was home to him.

Prunella sat on the bed.

"Well I guess we can squeeze in tight," she said.

Mercury blushed.

Jordan was silent for a moment. He didn't want Prunella squeezing up against him for very long, but he wasn't sure how to bring it up. He thought of Mrs. Rose's pep talk. He owed it to himself and to Prunella.

"Sure, but it's a really small bed. How long are you planning on staying?"

"I don't know. I can get us a hotel though."

"I don't want to go stay in a hotel. I'm home now, Pru. Holiday is over. I have to get back to work on the next album."

"Okay no problem," she said.

Jordan felt relieved. He turned to Mercury.

"You can sleep on one of the couches," he said. "There's one that pulls out and it's pretty comfortable."

"Okay great."

They took her to the living room so she could check it out.

"There are events here in the evenings," said Bubba," so you'll have to pack up again every morning, but you can store your bag in my room if you want."

"Thank you."

They went to the grocery store on Rideau Street and Mercury bought food for the house.

"It's the least I can do for Animal House, for letting me stay."

Prunella looked confused. Why did Mercury need a place to stay? Why was Mercury here?

They ordered a pizza and sat in the upstairs hallway space that was a kind of makeshift living room.

"If you were a Greek god who would you be?" asked Prunella, taking a big bite of pizza.

"Dionysus," said Bubba straight away.

"You've thought about this," she laughed.

"Hell ya. Wine, pleasure, death and rebirth... Dionysus is my jam."

"Like Jesus Christ but more fun," said Pru.

Bubba laughed. "Yes!"

He smiled. Prunella was actually really nice when she was sober.

"How about you J?"

Jordan wrinkled his face, thinking.

"My ex called me Adonis once," he said. "I looked it up. Adonis was Aphrodite's mortal lover."

"Sounds like she was Aphrodite more than you were Adonis," said Mercury. "I see you as more of an Apollo."

"What about you Merc?" asked Prunella.

"Are you kidding?" Mercury grinned.

Prunella looked at her a beat and then realization dawned.

"Mercury," she laughed. "The Roman name for Hermes! God of communication, travelers, boundaries, the divine trickster."

Jordan and Bubba exchanged a look. It was eerie.

"What?" said Prunella. She felt the energy shift.

Mercury just laughed. "You just nailed it spot on," she said.

"Well not quite, Mercury's a boy," said Bubba.

"Not anymore," grinned Prunella. "Didn't you guys see that all the pronouns were changed on the internet?"

For as long as the pronouns were changed, kids growing up today and getting their information online had no idea what Hermes's gendering was before the switch.

Mercury wondered if the algorithm made the god female or other. She would have to check.

Intensity in the room crackled.

"What's going on?" said Prunella. "Just tell me." Her sharp psychic intuition was tingling.

Bubba looked uncomfortable. Jordan's expression was impassive.

"What is it?!"

Mercury cleared her throat.

"I trust Jordan," she said. "And he trusts you, so *I'm* going to trust you."

Prunella felt truth ringing. She was about to hear something incredible.

"I... am Allat."

Pru blinked. "Seriously?" She looked from face to face. "You're part of Femnonymous?"

"What?" Mercury looked confused.

"The hackers behind Gendergate..."

"I don't know about Femnonymous, but a week ago I was at George Washington University taking computer programming, and now I'm here in Canada because of a prank that spun seriously out of control..."

"You little Trickster." Prunella grinned.

"So what is Femnonymous?"

"It's like, the people who are taking credit for Gendergate."

"I haven't been online really," said Merc.

"Let's spin it up," said Jordan.

They grabbed his computer and looked up the latest news.

Mercury Elmahdy was being hunted and acclaimed online. The comment section on every article was a civil war of opinion about what she'd done.

Allat undoubtedly had her fans. Scores of people welcomed this disruption to business as usual online; some saw it as a prank, and others as a revolutionary act.

On the other hand, religious fundamentalist Testamenters were threatening to kill her for calling their prophets "She". Christians called it a Muslim conspiracy and Muslims called it a Christian conspiracy. Men threatened to rape her corpse because she undermined their supremacy. She shuddered thinking of all the men whose eyes she had looked into as she walked down the street who didn't know that she was the woman behind Allat. The young essentialists criticized her for not using enough pronouns. The Pop Philosophers, today's circuit rider evangelicals predicting the end of Western civilization, happily championed Mercury as the ideal constellation of scapegoats and tore her apart in scathing diatribes.

Mercury swallowed hard. She felt warmth rising in her body.

Too much heat... she thought. *All of this attention on me online is like millions of eyes condensed into one giant Eye of Sauron burning me when it looks my way...*

She looked at Jordan.

"How do you do it, Jordan Barker?"

Jordan smiled grimly. He knew exactly what she meant. It was the Rage Machine.

"At least they're not calling me a terrorist," he said.

It was like a giant unnatural beast built from human emotion and anxiety crammed into the internet and blaring its deafening wrath. Today Mercury Elmahdy was the target.

She felt the weight of it settle down onto her. The part that topped it all was that the pronouns were still scrambled, and newly uploaded content online was actively scrambling.

"It's still happening!" said Mercury.

"It is," said Prunella, her eyes twinkling with excitement.

"The hack was reversible," said Mercury. "I don't understand why it wasn't fixed yet. And I never made it so that new content would change."

Mercury realized that someone was keeping it going.

Mercury looked up Femnonymous. They had released a video online. She clicked on it.

"Oh yea, I've seen this," said Prunella.

People in head-to-toe black coverings and witch hats explained in the voice of Oracle that Gendergate would continue. They claimed to have a network of millions prepared to keep it going, and they were not stopping there. They were taking back the corporatized internet.

"Information will be free again," said a witch.

Femnonymous took up right where I left off, thought Mercury.

"Allat just got things started. We'll take it from here, Goddess."

They saluted the camera as the transmission ended.

Mercury sat back, stunned.

"Well at least the heat's off you," said Bubba.

"That's true," said Jordan.

"Or, now that Femnonymous is taking up the charge, the Americans will be just piling the wood higher around your effigy for when they get to burn you," said Prunella.

They all shuddered.

"I can hide you in Toronto," said Pru. "It's easy to get lost there."

"I don't know..."

I can't go with Prunella, thought Merc. *She means well, but I feel like she can't manage her own life, let alone mine too.*

They were all silent.

"Didn't you say you know someone who might able to help?" said Bubba gently to Jordan.

"Yea. I have to get in touch with her." He swallowed hard. The thought of contacting Valkyrie Snow filled him with all kinds of emotions.

"We'll figure out something," said Bubba. "Everything's gonna be okay."

"Thanks."

That night everyone else went out for a drink at a nearby pub but Mercury stayed home. She borrowed Jordan's computer to research what was happening online. It was incredible.

There were public marches for and against Allat. The Discordians ate a hotdog in Allat's honour. Mercury watched video after video of young women responding to Gendergate.

The American news reported that Mercury was the ringleader of a terrorist movement. Did they really believe that?

If that is their best guess then their online intel sucks and they have no hope of undoing the hacks, thought Mercury.

The digital libraries who blithely discarded their print books in the 2000s were bemoaning the insecurity of digital information; Christians could burn the books they didn't like in medieval Europe, but now hackers could erase them in the 21st century.

It was a global conversation; the world had finally caught up to the speed of the digital revolution.

The others came home.

Jordan came over to Mercury, her face glowing blue in the light of the laptop screen. She was deep in digital, her eyes scanning data on the screen.

"Hey," said Jordan softly.

Mercury looked up at him. Her expression was troubled. "What is it?"

"Was it wrong?" she asked quietly.

"You just engineered a completely nonviolent revolutionary movement," said Jordan. "You're a hero."

She tried to smile.

"Thanks..."

He came over and sat down beside her.

"Hey. This is intense, but we're going to get through it. We won't let anything happen to you," he said. He looked into her eyes. She felt reassured.

This was strange for Jordan. He was used to being the one getting taken care of, or the one pushing away. For some reason helping Mercury came naturally to him.

Mercury leaned on his shoulder. He put his arm around her.

"Thanks for being so cool about taking me in," she said. "I still can't believe it."

"It's pretty amazing that the last time you were in Halifax you were at my concert and then the next time we met."

"It is."

She snuggled into his arm. The human touch was so nice after so long. Jordan gave her a squeeze.

"I know you won't let anything bad happen to me," she said.

Jordan heard the beautiful naïve sincerity in her statement and he felt a flood of warmth. It felt great to have someone believe in you so completely. It didn't happen often.

More than anything Jordan did not want to let Mercury down.

That night Prunella bunked up in Jordan's little bed with him. They kissed, but Jordan wasn't into it.

"Got a lot on your mind?" asked Pru.

"Yea. Sorry. Just not into it tonight."

"That's okay." Prunella rolled over.

Jordan wrapped his arm around her and spooned her. It was nice not having to sleep alone.

The news stories about Jordan Barker and Prunella Stokes—Jordella—continued to spin. Jordan tried to ignore it as much as possible. He wondered what Skyla thought about it. She wasn't stupid, she would know it was fake news.

But is it fake news? thought Jordan. He was sleeping with Prunella at night. *What am I doing?*

The next night Prunella wanted to have a night out in Ottawa.

"Come on, prove to me that the rumours that your city's boring aren't true," she teased.

"Fine," said Bubba. "Let's do it."

Mercury elected to stay at home.

"You know I love to dance, but I'm going to take the time to call my family. They must be worried sick," she said.

"Be careful," said Prunella. "You never know who is listening in on your conversation. Convince them you're safe but don't give them any real information."

"Smart," said Mercury.

Bubba, Jordan and Pru went out.

"Should we take her to the Market?" asked Bubba.

Jordan thought about it.

"No. Let's take her the warehouse. Trust me, she's gritty enough for it."

The warehouse was a really grimy trance club in Vanier.

Prunella asked for an experience, and she would get it.

"Seriously, that's the worst place in Ottawa."

Jordan laughed. "Exactly, it's hilarious."

"Fine..."

When they got to the club Prunella shrieked with delight.

Bubba was confused.

"I guess you know what the woman likes..."

They grabbed a drink and went to dance.

Bubba pulled Jordan aside. "Honestly, I didn't like Prunella at first man, I gotta say. But she's growing on me. She's actually a lot of fun now that I know her better."

"I knew you just needed to get to know her a bit," said Jordan. "She's got rough edges but she's actually a cool chick."

They danced and danced.

After a few drinks, Prunella was junking for something harder. She was all out of drugs and she didn't have a dealer in the city so she pushed down the urge. She ordered a few shots, hoping that the booze would mellow her out.

She tried to focus on dancing. She was squeezing her fists and scratching her arm.

Finally she couldn't take it anymore.

"I gotta go to the bathroom," she said.

"You okay?" asked Jordan. He could see that she was agitated.

"Yea I'm fine."

Prunella went to the bathroom and checked the stalls for anyone doing drugs. No one. She washed her hands at the sink, waiting for someone to come in.

"Hey, you partying tonight?" she asked two girls who stumbled in laughing.

"Yea!" they cheered, wasted.

"I mean, do you have any drugs?"

"What?"

They laughed and peed all over themselves in the stall. They didn't have any.

Prunella looked at herself in the mirror.

Just chill the fuck out, she thought. She took a deep breath and went back out to the dance floor.

She tried to dance for a bit but the need creeped over her again.

"Ottawa sucks," she growled.

Bubba didn't say anything.

"Hey, you okay?" Jordan said. There was worry on his face.

"I'm fine, let's just go someplace else."

"You loved it here a minute ago," said Bubba.

"Did something happen to you in the bathroom?"

"No. I'm fine!"

They kept dancing but the mood shifted.

"Do you want to head home?" asked Jordan.

"No, I have to go to the bathroom again," said Pru.

She left.

"What's wrong with her?" asked Bubba.

She wants a fix, thought Jordan. He felt the ache for one too, but he wasn't as bad off as Prunella.

"She's not feeling well," he said.

Prunella went into the men's room. She asked around.

"I've got stuff," said a greasy man with a stained shirt.

"Perfect," purred Prunella, suddenly sweet again.

He wanted cash.

"I only have chip," she said.

He reached down and unbuttoned his pants. He looked at her

expectantly.

Pru looked at the drugs, then at his face, then at the drugs again.

She shrugged. It's not like it was something she hadn't done before.

Prunella came back to the dance floor high. Jordan could immediately see the difference in her. Part of him also wanted to be high, but he repressed it.

"Maybe we should head out soon," said Jordan.

"Nah I'm feeling a lot better now," said Prunella.

They danced a bit longer but soon she wanted some more, now that she knew where to get it.

"Do you have cash?" she hissed to Jordan. "There's a guy here who's holding."

Jordan shook his head.

"Let's go have a hit," she said.

"I don't want any."

"What's going on here?" asked Bubba.

"Want to try something fun?" asked Prunella.

Bubba looked at Jordan.

"She's fucked up, isn't she."

"Yea."

Bubba realized that Jordan was at risk.

"Let's go home."

"No!" shouted Prunella. "We can't leave yet!"

"We're going now."

"Fine, leave without me!"

"We're not leaving without you," said Jordan.

"Yes we fucking are," said Bubba. "Come on. She'll follow."

He grabbed Jordan's hand.

"We can't just leave her here."

"Brother, she's a grown-ass woman. She can do what she wants."

Jordan broke and followed.

Prunella raised her voice after them.

"Get back here!"

Bubba did not let go of Jordan's hand. He wove through the crowd with Prunella screaming after them.

The bouncer frowned and made his way over to her.

"I feel bad," said Jordan.

Bubba held his hand firmly and they watched as the bouncer dragged Prunella out of the bar.

"Come on Pru," shouted Bubba. "Let's go."

He remembered the needle at his parents' house and all the respect he had gained for Prunella Stokes was gone as his old feelings came back.

Prunella screamed at them in the street some more and then followed.

Bubba would have called a lift but he wanted Pru to walk it off a bit.

The air was frozen and their warm bodies emitted steam and they walked down the snowy street.

"Let's walk faster," said Bubba. It was really cold.

Finally they made it home.

Mercury was sitting in the living with tears streaming down her face.

"Aww, you okay?" asked Jordan, coming over to give her a hug.

"Yea. I just got off the phone with my grandparents. I miss them." Her voice cracked and she kept crying.

Prunella laughed.

"Sure, give *her* a hug, she deserves it," she said.

Mercury looked at her. It was like her body was talking but Prunella wasn't there.

"Are you okay?"

"I'm fine! Why does everyone keep asking me that!" she shrieked.

"Shut up, people are sleeping," said Bubba.

Prunella sat down on the floor and sulked.

"Maybe you should go have a hot shower," said Jordan. "That helps me sometimes."

Prunella ignored him.

They spent hours trying to get Prunella to bed.

The next day they all woke up slowly. They heard children playing at the school across the street. The holidays were over.

Jordan took Prunella out for breakfast.

"Just the two of us," he said. They had things to talk about.

"I'm sorry I was so annoying last night," she laughed as she sipped coffee in their booth. I'll make it up to you."

"Pru, I have to talk to you about something," said Jordan gently.

"Well I know what that fucking means," she said. "Just get on with it."

"It's not..." He trailed off. Then he thought of Mrs. Rose. He thought of Charlotte.

Be honest. Be clear.

He looked her straight in the eyes.

"You're a really cool person. You're smart, and lots of fun, and I love your style," he said. "I like everything about you." He took a breath and exhaled. "Except your addiction."

Prunella rolled her eyes and sat back hard in her seat, crossing her arms.

"New Years was fucking terrible. The last few days have been really nice. Then last night happened. I realized that it's not you, it's the addiction."

Prunella looked at him hard, her mouth in a line.

"There have been lots of things you've done, or we've done together that I was uncomfortable with, and they all have to do with your addiction. *You* are great. Your addiction... I can't handle it."

They finished breakfast in silence, contemplating the situation. Jordan couldn't tell what Prunella was thinking, but he could see that she wasn't angry.

"I get it," she said. "I'm just going to head back to Toronto."

"You're welcome to stay if want to try and get sober," said Jordan. "I'm ready to be there for that, if you need it."

"Just take me to the Loop station."

Jordan went with her to catch a ride back to her city.

In the leather dress and makeup she had been wearing for days, Prunella Stokes clambered onto the car.

They waved good bye to each other as the Loop swooshed away.

CHAPTER SEVENTEEN

Something was bothering Mika Nakamura. Ever since her last dinner with Valkyrie, a thought itched the back of her mind that wouldn't go away.

Valkyrie had brought her nightingale in his cage to Gray House last year from Glasshouse. Now she didn't remember it, and it triggered her brain injury migraine. Mika noticed that Valkyrie didn't remember Glasshouse either.

Last year Valkyrie had cancer and her chemotherapy was laced with a nanite system engineered to block certain memories through targeted pain. The migraines were causing long-term injuries to Valkyrie's brain. The brain specialist Dr. Thaila speculated that the nanite treatment was attacking specific memories.

Why?

The memories targeted seemed so random and innocuous.

Dr. Thaila believed that it could have been accidental, and Dr. Snow herself thought it might be experimental.

It couldn't be a business rival, because nothing crucial was forgotten. The treatment did not impact the building of the citadel, or the Mars expansion they were negotiating.

It must be personal, thought Mika. She shuddered. The feeling came straight out of her deep intuition and she knew it was true. It scared her.

Who could be so evil? she thought. Intentionally destroying someone's memories was a reprehensible violation.

As far as she knew, Dr. Snow had no enemies. All of her most beloved friends were here, living at Gray House. By this time, Mika trusted the sisters like family. They would never hurt Valkyrie.

Who did this?

Work on the citadel was slowing down in the depths of winter. It would not quicken until the spring thaw. Mika decided to take a trip to Ottawa to investigate further.

*

Mercury was settling into life in Ottawa. The city was beautiful in winter and Jordan and Bubba took her to the stereotypical Canadian capital tourist spots. Her favourite was skating for hours along the Rideau Canal, where a museum exhibit was curated beneath each bridge. She looked up as she glided by or sometimes skated closer to read the exhibit print. Beautiful wooded pagodas were installed along the canal to skate into and sit by a roaring fire and drink something warm and look at the stars. The canal once represented a piece of the greatest Canadian highway, carrying timber and pelts from the interior to the Ottawa River. Now it just sported small pleasure crafts and a tourist cruise. In the winter it came alive again, if only briefly, and the exhibits under the bridges illuminated by floodlights told the story of a past life.

Jordan and Mercury sat side by side on a bench, taking a break and enjoying the frosty night.

"I never imagined that people could survive outside in such cold," laughed Merc.

"It's not that bad," said Jordan with a grin.

"I don't mean it in a bad way. It's incredible."

"I know what you mean."

He smiled at her.

Mercury smiled back at Jordan with an expression of warm adoration. Since Prunella left, Jordan and Mercury had gotten closer. Even though she was so young, she was really fun to hang out with.

Jordan looked up at the stars.

Now would be a perfect romantic moment to go in for a kiss, he thought. Mercury trusted him. He was sure that if he wanted, he could make her fall in love with him.

He turned to look at her. She was a beautiful girl. She was smart too, about a lot of things, but she had a sweet gullible innocence about her. Jordan felt fiercely protective of her. He didn't want anything bad to happen to her.

Could I even treat her with the dignity she deserves? he thought. *I'm still so fucked up—I would probably just end up screwing her up.*

Suddenly he realized something that had never dawned on him before.

I don't need to seduce Mercury.

He frowned as the thoughts unfurled inside him like gems of wisdom.

Why should I use her respect and admiration just to sleep with her? Why corrupt her trust and her beautiful heart just to use her briefly and move on?

Jordan actually cared about Mercury's feelings, as a person.

I care about Mercury enough to be her friend.

Jordan had never really had a female friend before. He entertained the thought of loving Mercury the way he loved Bubba—

safely, and without ulterior motive. The thought settled gently into his mind and felt good.

Mercury downed the rest of her tea.

"You ready to keep going?" he asked.

"Yea! Let's go."

They skated off with their arms linked, laughing and telling jokes, and it just felt really nice.

*

Mika Nakamura went to the Hammer & Bone office in downtown Ottawa. Sukhwant Thaila would help her get to the bottom of this. Val's assistant had been the first person to notice that something was off with Valkyrie's memory.

The women sat down in Dr. Snow's office, looking out over the snow-covered city. Mika explained her concerns.

"So the question is, why Glasshouse,' said Sukhwant.

"Yes. What do you know that I don't about Glasshouse?"

"Nothing. I mean, you built it," said Sukhwant.

"What about the nightingale?"

"I'm sorry, I don't know anything about that."

"What was going on in her personal life last year?" asked Mika.

"Honestly, not much that I know of. She hosted her sister gathering—"

"Yes I attended that. At Glasshouse..."

"She went to the Ashemore Christmas party, but she goes to that every year."

"Okay," said Mika, "tell me more about that."

"They're Americans... they host a fancy party at Christmas time... that's really all I know."

Mika made a note to look into it further.

"Are there any records we can look at that might tell a story?"

Sukhwant thought on it.

"Perhaps her travel records."

She fired up the computer and opened Valkyrie's platinum travel account.

"Baron Toussaint," read Mika. "I feel like I should know that name. Who is that?"

"She shares the plan with her ex-husband," said Sukhwant.

"Really?"

"They kindled a friendship after the divorce," said Sukhwant. "They went to dinner together a few times last year, actually."

Mika frowned.

"I can give you his number if you like."

"Sure."

Mika would call him. If they were still in close contact then the man would want to know about Valkyrie's illness and her memory problems, certainly.

They scanned the records.

"There," said Sukhwant. "Her trip to Ashemore."

The records indicated that Baron Toussaint also went to Ashemore.

"They were still close," said Sukhwant.

"And who is that?" asked Mika.

"Jordan Barker..." said Sukhwant. "The name sounds familiar... but I don't know who that is."

"Well he flew with Valkyrie. His seat was next to hers on the plane," said Mika.

"Oracle," said Mika. "Who is Jordan Barker?"

"The lead singer of the Canadian band, the Waves," said the Oracle.

That didn't make any sense.

"Where did the nightingale come from?"

"Jordan Barker is the nightingale," said the Oracle.

Mika and Sukhwant looked at one another.

"What does that mean?"

"Initiating voice call playback," said the Oracle. Suddenly they heard Valkyrie's voice.

Valkyrie: "Call Nightingale."
Oracle: "Sorry, repeat?"
Valkyrie: "Call the young man who called today, Jordan Barker. He is Nightingale."
The phone trilled.

A man's voice: "Hey Val."
Valkyrie: "Hi Jordan. I'm ready for bed."
Man's voice: "It's kind of early, isn't it?"
Valkyrie: "I've had a busy day. Sing for me."

Man's voice: *laughter, and then singing*

A single bloom in a jar in the window
Pictures of all of the places you've been
A song for each memory, playing forever
Makes me come over again and again.

My heart song for you is a simple one
It's the stories I love that you tell
I still can't believe that you love me
When you know me so well.
When you know me so well.

I picture us happy, that's new for me
You're more than I deserve as I stumble through now
You're a lighthouse to tomorrow, if I make it out alive
This ship's still afloat anyhow.

My heart song for you is a simple one
It's the stories I love that you tell
I still can't believe that you love me
When you know me so well.
When you know me so well.

You glide into my life without warning
I forget how I got to this place with a smile
Like a nightingale song in the morning
I still don't know who you are...

My heart song for you is a simple one
It's the stories I love that you tell
I still can't believe that you love me
When you know me so well.
When you know me so well.

The transmission ended.
"Who was *that*?" asked Mika.
"Jordan Barker, apparently..."
"They sounded..." she trailed off. She didn't know how to

describe it.

"Familiar," finished Sukhwant.

"Yes. Close."

"How have we never heard of him?"

"Val was such a private woman when it came to her personal life," said Sukhwant. "She was never one to just chat idly about things like who she was dating. I only ever caught glimpses here and there."

"Such as?"

"Well she was calling someone from work with a beautiful smile on her face, so I thought maybe it was a lover. We never discussed it though."

"So you think this Jordan Barker was her lover."

"The way she called him nightingale... it was so tender. Do you think this man had something to do with Valkyrie's illness?"

"Something deep in my bones tells me they're connected."

Mika did some deep creeping on the internet and found a poster advertising a concert at Jordan's house.

Animal House, they called it. It was an informal event space. She got the address and hopped in a lift to pay Jordan Barker a visit.

*

Valkyrie sat at her wooden table alone eating a quiet meal. Mika was away on business and Val didn't realize how much she would miss the company. Margarethe dropped in occasionally, but most days the only person Valkyrie saw was Mika Nakamura or no one at all.

There was a knock at the door.

Valkyrie frowned and stood up.

"Strange," said the Oracle.

When people from the village sought the Seer's counsel, they would usually rap on the wooden shutters over Valkyrie's single window and she would speak to them through there. She was very reluctant to bring people into her cottage.

The knock was not the gentle sound of Margarethe, and Mika was away for another several days at least.

She pulled down her veil and went to the door. She opened it a crack.

The woman outside had a halo of white hair and she wore a faded dress. Her feet were shoved carelessly in untied winter boots and her trench coat hung open from her boney shoulders with a teddy bear peeking out from the pocket. Her face was lined with deep rivulets that traced a pattern of sadness and worry. She had no laugh lines.

Valkyrie's mind skipped along, trying to remember this woman who she could not recognize, but who looked deeply familiar.

"Valkyrie?" whispered the woman, staring at the veiled figure in the stone cottage.

"The voice..." said the Oracle.

"I came to see the baby," said the woman.

Something in the gentle timber of her voice *click-click-click* triggered recall for Val.

"Teresa," she said, opening the door a little more. It was Baron Toussaint's second wife.

The body was Teresa's. Valkyrie could barely detect this woman's soul.

Teresa took a step over the threshold.

"What happened to you?" asked Val.

"Your soul..." said the Oracle.

Teresa looked with wonder around the cottage, taking in the warm little woodstove, the simple handmade furniture, the carved wooden railing up to the loft.

"Your room is very nice," she said. "Can I see the baby?"

"I'm still growing it," said Valkyrie, rubbing her stomach.

Teresa sighed with disappointment.

"I so wanted to see it. Baron told me he would be here. The Saviour child."

"Baron?" Valkyrie felt a wave of nausea. She stumbled back into her chair. Something was wrong. Something was terribly wrong.

"You're right, there's an Oracle device in there," said a man into his headset. Teresa was bugged and he was monitoring her and reporting to Baron.

"Get the blocker on it," said Baron into the headset. "Don't let her see you until it's neutralized."

The man was standing beside a white van parked in the shadows under the overgrown cedars by the stone cottage. He grabbed a blocker box and crept to the house. The driver was poised at the wheel, ready for a quick getaway.

He listened close to his feed on Teresa's bug, waiting for his opportunity.

"Baron told me I was coming to see the baby," said Teresa.
"Where is he?" asked Val.
Suddenly a man dressed head to toe in black slithered into the cottage. He took a quick survey of the room, saw the glow of green under Valkyrie's veil, and leapt onto her.
"No no no no..." said the Oracle.
He ripped the necklace off of her and thrust it into the black box before the Oracle could broadcast a call for help.
He shackled Valkyrie in handcuffs and gagged her and dragged her out of the cottage.
"Follow me," he growled.
Teresa followed.

CHAPTER EIGHTEEN

Mika drove up to Animal House. It was a dilapidated two-story building with a paint-peeled porch and a chunk of siding missing. She went up to the door and knocked.
"Hi," said the young woman who came to the door with bright pink hair.
"Hello. I'm looking for Jordan Barker," said Mika.
"What for?" asked the woman. "Sorry, it's just that you're not the first person who's showed up here looking for him."
"I'm a friend of Valkyrie Snow," said Mika instinctively.
"V. Snow," said Sapphire. "Jordan's ex... Okay, come on in. If it were me I'd want to talk to you too." She held open the door and went to find Jordan.
Mika came inside and stood in the foyer. The house had beautiful bones, but it was left to fall apart with only hints of its former glory. There was old twentieth century wood moulding around the door frames and antique cast-iron heating vents in the scuffed walls and floor. The furniture was a collection of mismatched junk pickings and the walls were painted the most garish colours the revolving door of students who had lived there over the years could find. It looked like someone was sleeping on one of the couches in the living room.

A young man came up from the basement stairs and walked slowly toward her down the hall. He was wearing ripped jeans and a ratty old sweater zipped up halfway, his bare chest exposed. He had long silky hair that was not quite blond. Even though he was somewhat dishevelled looking, he emanated a pulsating creative and sexual energy. As he approached, Mika could see that he had beautiful green eyes framed in long lashes.

Green eyes, she thought. Valkyrie and the Oracle had mentioned green eyes before.

"Hello," he said. "I'm Jordan."

Mika was surprised at how young he was. She was instantly curious about how he and Valkyrie had met. They seemed to belong to different worlds. She thought about the longing in his voice when he sang to Val on the phone in the Oracle's recording. The tiniest blush reddened her cheeks.

"I'm Mika Nakamura," she said. "There are some things I need to talk to you about."

"Mika," said Jordan. "You built Glasshouse."

She nodded.

Jordan led her to the living room and they sat down.

Mika didn't know where to start. They sat there looking at each other, not knowing what to say.

"Can I get you something to drink maybe?" asked Jordan finally. "Water? Tea?"

"Tea would be great," said Mika.

Jordan wandered to the kitchen and put on the kettle.

He prepared the mugs.

Mika sat back in the couch. She didn't really know what to ask him, but she knew that this was an important conversation.

Jordan came back with two mugs of steaming liquid.

"You know I never had tea before I met Valkyrie?"

Jordan smiled and handed Mika her mug.

"She introduced me to a lot of things. Even though we're not together anymore, I'm trying to be thankful for the little things." Even though he was trying to suppress it, his voice was full of emotion.

Mika knew then, in that moment, that Jordan Barker did not have anything to do with poisoning Valkyrie with the nanite Trojan Horse.

"When did you break up?" asked Mika.

"Well she started getting distant when she bought the land out east and she was gone all the time. I mean, I thought everything was fine, but I can see now that it wasn't. Then she got back together with her ex-husband."

"What?" Mika frowned.

Did Valkyrie get back together with Baron Toussaint? How would I not know about that? Then she remembered that she didn't know about Jordan Barker either. Valkyrie kept a lot of secrets.

"She... sent me a message," said Jordan. He pulled out his phone and found it.

> Seeing you today really upset me. Please don't do that again. It would be best if you didn't contact me anymore either. My husband Baron and I have decided to get back together. He is the love of my life. The time that you and I shared was memorable but it is now over. Please respect my wishes.
>
> Valkyrie Snow.

His expression was pained as he showed it to Mika. She read it and looked at the date. It was right after Valkyrie's sickness.

"This doesn't sound like Valkyrie at all," she said.

Jordan looked at her.

"What do you mean? Why are you here?"

"Jordan... there are some things I need to tell you."

Mika gently explained how right before that message was sent, Valkyrie had cancer. Her chemotherapy treatment was contaminated with nanites engineered to tamper with her memory. She explained to him that Valkyrie had no memory of the year that they spent together, that it was blocked by a targeted pain delivery system.

Jordan could hardly breathe. The thin layers of healing that he built up over the last few months cracked open and his heart began to bleed as though the pain happened yesterday.

"Wait, wait," he said, trying to fully understand. "So you're saying that she didn't remember me when she sent this message?"

"Yes," said Mika.

"So that means..."

Mika saw where his train of thought was heading.

"That she must not have written that message, yes."

Jordan choked on a sob. He cried openly as he scrolled through his phone, retrieving the phone message he had listened to a thousand times that he was never able to erase.

"I'm sorry," he said, wiping his nose on his sleeve.

"It's alright."

Jordan enabled speaker phone and played the voicemail message.

"Hey Jordan, it's me. I'm just settling down for the night here at Gray House, that's what the girls are calling it. I'm thinking about you a lot. I miss you so much. I hate the way our last conversation ended. I can't wait to see you again, to be pressed up against you and make it all better. Anyway, I hope you're doing well and I know your show is going to be awesome. I can't wait to hear all about it. Goodnight."

"That's the last time I heard her voice," he said. "She left me that recording on my phone, and then I got the breakup message. She never even told me she had cancer."

He wept.

"I'm so sorry. I can't speak for her, but I think her memory loss has something to do with that."

"Do you think... if she saw me... she might remember me?" he asked, his cheeks wet with tears.

Mika thought on it. Seeing Jordan might trigger a serious bout of brain trauma.

Why would anyone want to erase this young man from Valkyrie's memory? Mika shook her head. It didn't make any sense.

"Honestly I'm worried about what the effect might be on her mind."

Jordan looked desperate.

"But I'm going to get to the bottom of this. I'm going to help Valkyrie," said Mika with iron in her voice.

Jordan trusted this woman's resolve. He remembered how Valkyrie spoke about her. Val trusted her.

"What can I do?" he asked. "I'll do anything."

"You spent a lot of time with her last year?" asked Mika.

"Every moment I could," he said.

"Then you certainly have information I need."

He nodded. His tears had stopped. His heart was full of hope. He ached to see Valkyrie again.

Mercury came upstairs from the basement. She sensed the intensity of the conversation earlier so she waited downstairs to give them space. Now she felt like she could come up.

"Hey," she said tentatively, peeking into the living room. Jordan was sitting with a small woman. She had a great outfit; Mercury recognized the intentionality of clean simple lines and high-quality fabrication.

Jordan turned to her. His face was wet with tears and his eyes were red from crying.

"Hey Merc."

"I'm sorry, I'll go back down," she said.

"No no, it's okay. Come on in."

She walked lightly into the room and sat in a chair. She eyed her bag on the floor by the couch, the thing she had come up to get.

Mika saw her eye movement.

This is who is sleeping on the couch, she thought.

She looked the young woman over. She was beautiful. Mika appreciated the long curve of her nose and chin, her bright eyes, and her long graceful limbs. She was like a lovely fox. Mika liked the way she looked comfortable, but her clothes were unforgettable unique pieces.

"I'm Mika," she said.

Mercury looked at Jordan questioningly.

"You can trust her," said Jordan.

Mercury nodded. "I'm Mercury."

Mika went back to the office to update Sukhwant on Jordan Barker. Mercury and Jordan went out for a late lunch.

"We don't have to talk about it if you don't want to," said Merc.

"Thanks. I'm okay."

Mercury tried to change the subject.

"So how is your new album coming?"

Jordan was quiet for a moment.

"Well this changes everything really. I have half the album totally written, but now it looks like I'm circling back for the next part..."

"Same lesson, deeper spiral?" said Merc.

"Yea. I like that."

"My Neena says that," said Mercury quietly.

"Neena?"

"My grandmother. I miss her."

"You're lucky to have her."

Mercury thought about it. She always felt unlucky that she lost her parents. In some ways she felt cheated by the universe out of something special that everyone had but she would never truly understand.

"My grandparents are wonderful. I have trouble feeling lucky sometimes though."

"At least someone in this world loves you," said Jordan. There was a raw edge to his voice.

"There are people who love you too, Jordan."

Mercury looked into his eyes across the table, reaching out to bridge the gap and hold his hand.

Jordan looked back at her and saw tenderness there. He felt guilty and pulled his hand away.

"Mercury..."

She looked at him expectantly.

"I don't know if this is a thing, but I'm just going to say it; my darkness eats everything. I don't want your bright soul ruined by it."

"I can take care of myself," she said.

"I know... but loving me is a waste of time, okay? If we hooked up it would only end badly."

Mercury looked at him a moment. Then she grinned.

"Hooked up with you? Never, my friend. Jordan I love you for more than your body, I actually like spending time with you."

Jordan's eyes widened with surprise. He really thought she was into him. Then he laughed. She laughed too.

He sighed with relief and reached out to take her hands again.

"Good talk," he said.

They finished their lunch and went home.

That night as he lay in bed, Jordan thought about his tumultuous day. His heart was full of careful joy, thinking about the day he could go and see Valkyrie.

Who poisoned her? he thought.

One name came to mind.

Baron.

Who else could it be? Valkyrie was kind to everyone. Baron hated Jordan, but would he go to such insane lengths to remove him from Val's life? It seemed unimaginable, but love made people do crazy things.

I can't tell Mika, he thought. *I have absolutely no evidence. It just sounds petty.*

He decided to try to gather some evidence himself to present to her.

He thought about the text message.

"My husband Baron and I have decided to get back together. He is the love of my life."

The more he thought about it, the more he felt like Baron must have written it.

All this time he thought that his mind was playing tricks on him and Valkyrie had never really loved him at all. But deep in his heart he knew that wasn't true. He knew that Valkyrie loved him with the same deep and unshakeable intensity with which he loved her.

Jordan Barker had such trouble trusting his heart.

CHAPTER NINETEEN

Valkyrie Snow woke up in a hospital bed. The lights burned her retinas and the pain in her head shot through her neck and shoulders. Her eyes were intensely sensitive to light. She moaned and lifted her arm to cover her face and found that she was strapped to the bed.

What's happening? She reached out with her mind to her Oracle.

Silence.

The door clicked open softly. Baron Toussaint came in.

"It was you," she moaned. "It was you."

I trusted you.

Valkyrie Snow realized that Baron Toussaint, the husband she gave twenty years of her life to, was the one who had poisoned her.

"Shh," he said coming close. "Shh, just relax."

He reached up and stroked her brow.

She shuddered, feeling disgust from head to toe.

"I'm going to take great care of you, don't worry."

Angry tears ran down the sides of Valkyrie's face. She was in hell. She was in actual hell.

Baron reached out and put his hand on her stomach, rubbing it gently. Valkyrie cried out like a wild animal in a snare. She writhed in her restraints.

Baron clucked his tongue.

"Come now, Val, I expected better behaviour from you."

She looked at him with dagger eyes.

Baron realized that this would not be as easy as he expected.

He pulled out a tranquilizer and buried the needle in the soft of her arm. Her fit relaxed until she passed out.

Her hormones are out of control, he thought. *Once the baby is born we can get drugs for that.*

The next time Valkyrie regained consciousness she kept her eyes closed. Realizations came tumbling over her like a waterfall. She tried not to cry.

Why? she thought. *Why did he do this to me?*

She couldn't understand it. When they were married, Baron had cheated on her with multiple women. He didn't seem that upset when they divorced. Why the sudden change of heart? Why now?

She felt the baby move inside her. She was due in less than a month. She felt a flood of emotion.

I could kill him for this, she thought.

Baron came back into the room.

"Hello Val. I know you're awake," he said softly.

He sat in the chair beside her bed. It was the same chair he sat in when he visited her while she was getting her 'cancer' treatments. Now she knew for sure, without a doubt that she never had cancer.

I trusted you, she thought again.

The betrayal made her want to throw up. She felt bile rise in her throat and gagged.

Baron ran to grab a bucket.

When he came back, she was vomiting all over herself. He unlatched one of her restraints so that she could turn on her side.

Hmmm, I forgot about pregnant women throwing up all the time, he thought. He needed to fast track his plan and get her settled in the nursery as soon as possible.

He went out to get Teresa.

"Come little dove. I have another job for you." He grabbed cleaning supplies from the storage room and led her to Valkyrie's room.

Valkyrie was spitting out the last of her throw-up. She looked up and saw Teresa. Memories of the night before came back to her. Teresa in the trench coat.

Teresa shuffled into the room.

Are they still together? thought Valkyrie. *What's going on?* None of this made any sense.

"Clean up the mess, Teresa," said Baron.

Teresa dropped to her knees and started cleaning the floor where Valkyrie barfed.

Baron sat in his chair and watched. He could see the expression of confusion on Valkyrie's face. He smiled.

She's jealous of Teresa, he thought. *That's good. A little rivalry between the wives is good.*

"What's going on here?" asked Valkyrie quietly.

"Don't be angry, Val. Teresa is doing you a favour."

Valkyrie frowned, still utterly confused.

"I don't understand."

"You will always be my first wife," he said. "Even with Teresa and Courtney. You will always be first wife."

She seemed calm now. Baron stood up and unbuckled her other restraint. Valkyrie sat up in bed and swung her legs over the edge.

Teresa stood up and wiped the vomit off Valkyrie's front. Val took a wad of paper towel and wiped her own face.

"There. That's what I like to see. My girls working together."

Teresa stared blankly at the wall.

"Right little dove?"

"Yes Baron."

She was brain dead. The sweet and kind Teresa that Valkyrie once knew was gone.

Is this what I would be like if Baron finished the treatments on me? thought Valkyrie. She looked at Teresa's face and realized how deeply she was in danger.

"Are you going to be good?" asked Baron, looking at Val.

She looked back at him. It was like looking at a stranger.

He took her silence as compliance.

"Show her your room," he said to Teresa.

She skittered out of the room and down the hall. Baron held Valkyrie's elbows in front of him and guided her down the hall.

Valkyrie took a quick inventory of the hallway. There were five doors. One at the end. That must be the exit to the hallway. It looked like a hospital but Valkyrie knew that it probably wasn't.

Teresa went into her room.

As Valkyrie looked inside panic rose in her as realization dawned. It was obvious that this was a bunker where Teresa lived. A cot and crib were set up in the corner. Valkyrie screamed.

Baron pushed her in and closed the door. It locked with a click.

*

Mika returned to Animal House.

"Would you be willing to come out East with me? I'd like to have you alongside to help me work out what happened last year."

"Yes," said Jordan quickly.

Mika noted his enthusiasm.

"You have to wait to confront her though," she said gently. "We don't want to hurt her."

"Like Orpheus," said Mercury, coming over. Jordan had explained everything to her about Valkyrie.

"Orpheus?" said Jordan.

Mika smiled. She got the reference right away.

"Orpheus, the Greek hero. His wife Eurydice died of a snake bite, and he travelled to the Underworld to beg her back from Hades and Persephone. His music was so beautiful that they agreed on one condition; he had to walk out of the Underworld with her walking behind him, and not look back," said Mercury.

"Let me guess; he looked back," said Jordan.

"Then she was gone forever."

"Yes," said Mika. "So you can't look back at her just yet. Not until she's out of the Underworld."

Jordan nodded. He didn't really understand what was going on with Val's memories, but he trusted Mika's assessment.

"So... would it be okay if I stayed here?" asked Mercury.

"Oh, Merc," said Jordan. "Can she come with us?"

Mika looked from one to the other. There was something here that was unspoken, she could tell.

"Are you going to tell me what's going on?" asked Mika. She wasn't one to mince words.

Jordan laughed. Mika missed nothing.

"That's up to you," he said to Mercury.

Mercury looked at Mika. She sighed.

Am I foolish to trust everyone? she thought. She couldn't help it.

"I'm here illegally," she said. "I'm British, I was studying in the United States, I ran into some trouble, and now I'm here."

Mika nodded.

"We have a lot of refugees at the arcology. You'll be in good company."

Mercury relaxed.

"Actually then, before we go I should take you by Valkyrie's office. There's some paperwork there it might be good to get a start on in this whole refugee process."

Jordan and Mercury looked at one another. Mercury wanted to cry with relief. She wanted to do things right. Jordan laughed.

"I'm so glad I ran into you," said Mercury.

"What is your field of study?" asked Mika. "If it's something useful to the company then the process can sometimes be easier."

"Computer engineering."

"Really." Mika was intrigued. She would ask her more about that later.

"Maybe I should just go ahead to Gray House," said Jordan. "While you guys deal with the paperwork." He was anxious to be closer to Valkyrie.

"I don't mind," said Mika. "If that's okay with you?"

Mercury shrugged. "I don't mind. You go do what you have to do Jordan."

We can't be long anyway, thought Mika.

She didn't tell them that Valkyrie Snow was due to give birth soon. One thing at a time.

*

Valkyrie paced the room like a caged animal.

Teresa sat in her rocking chair. Valkyrie's pacing was making her anxious and Teresa rocked hard back and forth.

"Baron lets you outside right? Like when you came to see me?"

"That was my first time outside," said Teresa. "To see the baby. The little Saviour child."

"What do you mean?"

"Baron says the child is a miracle that will bring heaven on earth," said Teresa. "The miracle is proof that he is a god among men."

"And how long have you lived here?" asked Valkyrie.

"Eight years."

Valkyrie rubbed her sore eyes. Her head was throbbing with pain. She needed to get out of here.

She went to the door and held her lips to the crack.

"Help!" she screamed. "Help us!"

Teresa was silent. She understood this need.

"Help!"

Suddenly she heard a noise outside. She listened.

"Help!" screamed a muffled voice back.

Valkyrie looked at Teresa.

"Her name is Courtney."

Of course. It was Baron's current wife Courtney.

"Valkyrie!" She shouted her own name. "Valkyrie!"

"Courtney!" the voice shouted back.

"How long has she been here?" asked Val. She tried to remember the last time she'd seen Courtney in person.

"The screams started eleven months ago," said Teresa.

"Baron's a busy man," she said.

"Husbands have many responsibilities," said Teresa.

Valkyrie looked her up and down. Teresa had sold her out and lured her into this doom. Obviously she had no choice in the matter, but did she know and understand her role in the deception in her current mental state? Had she lured Courtney the same way?

Teresa's expression was blank.

"Husband," muttered Valkyrie bitterly. "You mean monster."

Teresa's eyes flashed with fear. She stood up slowly.

"I have to use the toilet," she said.

She walked very close past Valkyrie.

"They see and they listen," she whispered as she passed, almost inaudible.

Val frowned for a moment and then realization dawned.

Security cameras. Bugs. Teresa was warning her.

Valkyrie shifted positions on the bed, the weight of her stomach uncomfortable.

Maybe the old Teresa is not completely gone, she thought.

She sat cross-legged and did her meditation, focussing with a laser-sharp intensity.

Heal my mind, nanites. Stop blocking my memories. Stop resisting my body. Heal my mind, nanites.

Green eyes floated into her mind. There was no pain. She looked into the eyes joyfully and continued her meditation.

Heal my mind, nanites. Stop blocking my memories. Stop resisting my body. Heal my mind, nanites.

Baron showed up the next day for a visit. He was humming with excitement. He unlocked the door and came into Teresa's room.

"Come with me, Valkyrie," he said.

She paused a moment and then followed. She decided not to resist. She would see as much as she could and gather all the information she could and wait for her moment.

He took her down the hall and let her into another room.

She looked around. It was her 'hospital' room when she had cancer. She felt anger rise in her chest but she pushed it down.

Anger is not helpful now, she thought. *I will use it when the time is right.*

She relaxed, breathing deep, and focused on remaining calm.

Baron went to a cabinet where he had set up a small espresso machine. He grinned at her, beckoning her over.

All the implements to make coffee were inside.

"Once your room is complete you can make your own espresso every day," he said. "You just can't have it in Teresa's room."

She nodded, adopting Teresa's blank expression.

Baron made them each a coffee. Val took stock of all the supplies in the cabinet before he closed it.

Baron sat in his chair. He gestured for Valkyrie to sit on the bed. She sat down gingerly, avoiding the leather straps with clenched teeth. He handed her the coffee and she sipped it with squinting eyes and a pained expression.

"What's wrong?" asked Baron.

The question was almost comical but Valkyrie knew what he meant.

"My headache," she rasped. "My eyes."

"I see."

Baron made a mental note to get some dim lights in here.

"I'll get you some painkillers," he said gently.

Why would he get me painkillers? thought Val. *If he is keeping me here to punish me, to torture me...*

They drank their coffees.

"Why am I here?" she asked, finally.

"I didn't like how much time you were spending out east," he said. "So far away from me. And with the baby coming."

The baby. Did he intend to steal the baby?

"You should have told me about the baby, Valkyrie," he said.

Why? It's none of your fucking business, she thought.

"I didn't know you had an interest," she said softly.

Baron laughed.

"Darling!" he cooed. "Of course I do! Of course! Silly girl..." He shook his head. "This is what we always wanted! I could never give up on you, Valkyrie..."

Give up on me? So he is still pretending that I was the one who was infertile. Even though this clearly proves the opposite. Delusions within delusions.

"Everything happens when it's supposed to," he said. "I see that now. It's all destiny."

His eyes glittered with madness.

"You mean... the Saviour child?" she said carefully. She wasn't sure if that was just something he said to control the brain-addled Teresa or if he was brain-addled himself.

"Yes. It's a miracle," he said.

He believes it then.

"I know," she whispered. "I feel it."

Baron felt a surge of excitement. Valkyrie felt it too! He looked at her face, searching for any sneer of ridicule. She just looked tired.

"I know it's been a tough few days my love, but this is all meant to be," he said eagerly.

Valkyrie smiled weakly at him and he continued.

"Teresa and Courtney are Rachel and Leah. You are my Virgin Mary."

In Baron's mind he was God. He had impregnated her with his thoughts.

He's completely lost his mind, thought Valkyrie.

"He is going to be a great leader. We will pave his path to success, and our legacy will reign forever," he said.

"Can I see Courtney?" asked Val.

"Why?" asked Baron, suspicious.

"Women need each other," said Val softly. "It's our nature."

She kept her head down and her eyes lowered. Would he buy it?

Baron chuckled.

"Yes of course. That's why I'm letting you stay with Teresa."

"Yes, Baron. But I would also like to visit Courtney, if I may."

He thought about it.

I suppose I could be magnanimous. She has been spending so much time out east with all those women. She's gotten used to it.

"I will allow it, just for you," said Baron.

"Thank you."

He led her out of the room and down the hall to Courtney's room. Val watched carefully as he unlocked the door.

Courtney was lying on her side on the bed. A pool of blood dripped down between her legs. The room smelled of iron. Courtney was menstruating. She lifted her head and saw Valkyrie Snow standing in the doorway with Baron looming behind her.

"He got you too," she said.

"Courtney," said Val, coming over. She put a gentle hand on Courtney's arm.

I'm so sorry, she said with her eyes. The women shared a look.

Val looked her over. She was hooked up to a nutrient drip and a colostomy bag. The back of her hospital gown was yellow and brown with dried puss and blood from the bed sores. Val frowned.

"She shouldn't be living like this," said Val softly.

Baron looked at Val's expression.

"This was a bad idea," he said, taking her arm firmly. "Time to go."

He pulled her out.

Courtney watched her go, and for the first time since she was captured, she had hope.

"I had to do it," said Baron crossly. "She was like a rabid dog when she first came here."

"But look at her now," said Valkyrie. "She looks fine."

"She does seem better," conceded Baron.

"I'm sure with my friendship she will cooperate," said Val. "At least get her off that colostomy bag."

It's probably too late, thought Baron. Courtney's own digestive system was probably ruined by now.

"Time to go to bed," he said. He let her into her room and closed the door.

*

Jordan Barker left the next day to go back to the east coast. Finally he was going to see the project site for Mother House that he had heard so much about. He spent so much time and energy blocking out this part of his life, and here he was, heading to see Valkyrie Snow's arcology. It was surreal.

He knew that it would take everything in him to avoid Valkyrie. He would do it though. Just being near her, knowing that they were working on a cure would be enough to fuel him until he could see her again.

*

Mika took Mercury downtown to Hammer & Bone. As Mercury entered the white marble fortress at Mika Nakamura's side she knew that she was in good hands. Mika showed her around the office and explained Dr. Snow's policy on refugees.

"Jordan's lover sounds like a formidable woman," said Mercury.

Mika still found it strange that Val had never mentioned Jordan.

"She certainly is," said Mika.

Mika took her to lunch at a sandwich shop in Gatineau.

"They have the best homemade bread," said Mika.

They sat inside and looked out the window. It was a bright snowy day.

"How long does winter last?" asked Mercury.

"Here? Until March or April," said Mika.

"That's a long time."

"The key is to get outside as much as possible. Staying inside can drive you crazy."

"I'd like my grandparents to be able to see this," said Merc quietly.

"Your grandparents?"

"They raised me. They were going to come to America for a visit... Before I got into my troubles."

Mika wanted to ask more about that but she knew Merc would reveal it when she was ready.

"My grandparents mostly raised me too. My parents worked all the time."

They looked at each other.

"What is it..." said Mika gently.

"It's just... I can't believe that I'm sitting here with you having lunch. My life is taking turns I never expected."

"Life does that."

"It all feels right somehow though," said Mercury. "I know that sounds silly."

Mercury had this feeling deep in her gut that the foundation of her destiny was being quickly woven in these moments.

"It doesn't sound silly." There was warmth and tenderness in the timbre of Mika's voice that was rare.

Mercury smiled.

They ate their sandwiches in amicable silence.

After lunch, they went back to the office to meet with Sukhwant.

"Mercury, this is Sukhwant Thaila. Sukh, this is Mercury..."

"Elmahdy," said Mercury.

"I know who you are," said Sukhwant.

Mercury tensed up.

"What do you mean?" asked Mika.

"This woman is all over the news, haven't you seen it?"

Mika looked at Mercury, whose cheeks flamed red.

"Gendergate?" said Sukhwant. "This woman is Allat."

Mika's mouth dropped open. She could tell by Mercury's expression that it was true. Then she grinned.

"That was you?" There was admiration in her tone.

"Yes..." said Mercury.

"I knew there was more to you," she said quietly. Mika was impressed.

"Aren't you worried that you just strolled in here with a wanted terrorist?" said Sukhwant.

"You're Allat," repeated Mika.

"I am... Allat," said Mercury.

"Computer engineering," laughed Mika. She turned to Sukhwant.

"Relax. This woman is a genius. And a hero."

Sukhwant frowned.

"We are going to protect her at all costs."

"What would Dr. Snow think about it?"

"Don't you see what this means? With Allat we can get access to any digital information we want." She turned to Mercury. "Unless I am overestimating your power?"

Mercury looked at her, allowing a sliver of pride out of her subconscious.

"You're not," she said with a rich voice that channeled the godd. Mika laughed.

"Let's get her paperwork started," said Mika.

Sukhwant nodded.

"You're one lucky terrorist," she said.

CHAPTER TWENTY

Jordan arrived in Halifax in the afternoon and he got a hotel for the night. He needed to get his thoughts in order. He walked the streets late into the night and the next day he hired a lift out to the arcology in Cape Breton. His heart was racing. As the car crunched up the long laneway, it reminded him of Glasshouse last year. He sighed.

To the left the trees thinned and a stone cottage emerged. His breath caught in his throat. He remembered Valkyrie mentioning it.

That's Val's house, he thought.

He turned away. It was imperative that she didn't see him. He didn't really understand why, but he didn't want to risk doing her any harm.

The car continued on to Gray House. It crunched to a stop. Jordan got out. He could see the base of the citadel rising up from the peninsula. It was magnificent. His heart burned with pride for Valkyrie.

He looked down the shore. Smoke rose through the trees in the distance.

Those must be the refugee houses, thought Jordan.

He turned back to the stone cottage. No smoke rose from that chimney.

She must not be home, he realized.

His breath made a white cloud as he walked up to the door of the summer kitchen and peered inside. He let himself in and knocked on the inner door. He heard scampering feet from within.

A small child opened the door. Another popped her head out behind him.

"Who are you?" said the boy.

A rasping voice from within spoke.

"Jordan Barker," she said. It was Margarethe.

The children blinked at him.

"Who is that granny?"

"The nightingale has returned," she laughed, opening the door and letting him in.

"Thanks," said Jordan.

"I'll make tea," said Margarethe. The kettle was already boiling.

Jordan went into the living room and sat down. Several women were working on a quilt at a large quilting frame. He saw the nightingale hanging in his cage above the piano.

Margarethe handed him his tea. When she touched his hand he shuddered with déjà vu of this moment.

"Sorry," he muttered.

Margarethe squeezed his hand tight and let go.

"It's all right. I was wondering when you would show up."

Jordan looked at her.

"You're Margarethe right? I know we've never met in person

but I feel like we have."

"Yes young man."

He breathed in his tea.

"What is this?" he asked. It didn't smell like any tea he'd ever had.

"Sumac and ginger," she said.

A large tuxedo cat jumped onto her lap and bumped her hand with his head. She scratched him under the chin.

"I've come to ask about Val," he said.

Margarethe was silent. Jordan continued.

"Mika came to find me. She told me about Val's memory problems. I want to do what I can to help."

"You still love her," said Margarethe.

"I do."

Margarethe leaned forward and inspected Jordan closely. Then she leaned back.

"She loves you too, you know. Even if she doesn't remember it with her mind. Her heart remembers."

Jordan swallowed back tears.

"You really think so?"

"Green eyes," said Margarethe, pointing at him. "It's you, I'm sure of it."

The cat purred loudly.

"Mika said that she is... different. Changed."

"She is. And still changing."

"Do you think... I could see her one day?"

Margarethe looked at him hard. Then she nodded.

"Let's go," she said, getting up from her seat.

"What? Where are we going?"

"To the Seer's Cottage," said Margarethe.

"But... Mika said..."

"It's all right," said Margarethe. "This feels right."

Jordan looked around the room. The quilting women ignored him.

"Come on," said Margarethe, already in the kitchen and on her way out the door. Jordan followed.

She hobbled out to the stone house and rapped on the window with her cane.

"Valkyrie," she called. "Valkyrie..." She turned to Jordan.

"You must not be alarmed. She is different indeed."

Jordan was nervous. Mika would be angry at him. But surely she knew of the persuasive powers of Margarethe...

Margarethe went around to the door. It was open a crack. She frowned and pushed it open all the way.

An unfinished plate of dinner sat on the table. Valkyrie's white veil lay crumpled on the floor. The room was stone cold.

"Something's wrong," said Margarethe. "Quick, check upstairs."

Jordan jumped and ran up to the loft. It was empty. He frowned and shook his head at Margarethe.

She hobbled to check the bathroom. Empty.

"Where is she?" asked Jordan.

"I don't know."

Margarethe opened the woodstove and touched the coals.

She's been gone more than a day," she said.

They returned quickly to the house.

"Get Mika on the phone," said Margarethe to the sisters.

*

That night, Mika invited Mercury to stay at her apartment.

"I don't mind staying in a hotel," said Mercury. "I don't want to impose."

"You really want to stay in a hotel?"

"...no, not really," laughed Merc.

"That's what I thought."

Mika's apartment was a corner unit in a new build in Hintonburg. Her living room was white on white and sparkled with glass.

Mercury gasped when she walked in.

"This is incredible," she said.

Mika threw her purse on the couch.

"Perks of being an architect," she said, proud of her work. She was involved in designing the building and got a great price on the unit.

Mercury went over to the windows.

"Great view," she said. There was a tree-lined bicycle and pedestrian boulevard below. It used to be an old fossil bus transit-way.

"I love this neighbourhood. I can bike straight downtown

there," said Mika.

Mercury lingered, enjoying the sunset. In the distance she could see a massive river.

"Can I get you a drink?" asked Mika, heading to the kitchen.

"Sure. A sugar-free pop would be good if you have it."

Mika poured her guest soda water in a tall glass and a nip of scotch in a tumbler for herself. She brought the glasses over to the window.

"Valkyrie taught me about good scotch," she said, sipping hers.

"Thanks," said Mercury, taking her drink. "I'm looking forward to meeting this Valkyrie."

They watched the sun go down and then sat on the couch.

"So why did you do it?" asked Mika.

Mercury knew exactly what she was talking about.

"I just wanted to show people that they don't need to hold onto things so hard," she said. "We have to be fluid to advance as a human race as we expand out beyond our planet into the universe. We need to see beyond labels."

Mercury had stars in her eyes.

"These boxes we trap ourselves in."

"Exactly."

"Well you certainly did that," grinned Mika. "Even government databases are gender switched."

"That wasn't me directly... I never expected it to blow up so big."

Mercury thought of Femnonymous. She felt a frisson of delight.

"It's incredible," said Mika. "The world will never be the same. In one act you did what decades of theorizing were not able to do. You brought the revolution straight to the masses. There is no way to undo all the pronoun scramble. You did it."

"I did it."

Mercury could still hardly believe it. It was such a simple thing. In some languages gender was irrelevant. In English, 'he' and 'she' became silos of restrictive meaning.

"Let me throw your dirty clothes in the wash," said Mika.

"Do I stink?" said Mercury with a grin.

"No, no," laughed Mika. "You just probably haven't had a chance while traveling."

"Thank you, that would be lovely."

Mercury peeled down to her underwear and emptied her backpack of clothing.

Mika opened a closet where the apartment-sized washing machine was and tossed in Mercury's crumpled clothes.

"How did you think of it?" continued Mika. "Gendergate, I mean. It's so simple and brilliant..."

"I can't draw or make music or anything to save my life, but in some ways I'm an artist," said Merc.

Mika could see it in the way she dressed herself. She nodded.

"So the saying goes, artists are the most dangerous people because they mix with all levels of society. I think that's true. The artist in me has mixed around a lot and I see the world in a different way than my fellow cyber security peers, or my rave friends. It was just my One Small Great Act."

"What do you mean?"

"I called the pronoun project my One Small Great Act because I believe that everyone has one in them, one brave act that makes their life worthwhile. One act that is their little part in changing the world."

"I see."

"So what's your One Small Great Act, Mika?"

Mika thought about it.

"I don't think I have one. For me it is making a good choice every day."

"A good choice?"

"Yes. One thing every day. It could be picking up a piece of trash, or helping a refugee," she grinned, "or choosing a local food instead of an imported one. One thing, doesn't matter how small. Not all of us are genius hackers," she laughed.

"I love your laugh," said Mercury.

"I don't laugh a lot," said Mika. "So thank you for bringing it out of me."

They relaxed comfortably in the cushions.

"So why Allat?" asked Mika softly.

Mercury sighed.

"That I kind of regret, I must admit," she said.

"Why?"

"The association with Islam twisted thing whole thing into some of kind of terrorist thing."

"Mercury *Elmahdy*? You think it wouldn't have gotten twisted this way no matter what?"

"I just... my heart breaks every day when I hear about Muslims getting shot in the United States."

"That was happening long before Gendergate."

"Right... but the people getting shot who... look like me..." she struggled not to cry.

"You can't take responsibility for that," said Mika, reaching out and holding her hand. "You can't hold that on your own. It's not fair."

Mercury knew she was right but it still weighed heavy on her mind.

"I just wish that there were a way that I could make it right, but there isn't and there never will be."

Mika wanted to hold her and comfort her, but she felt suddenly shy. She pulled her hand away.

"I'm so glad I met you," said Mercury.

"I'll help you any way I can."

"I know. But I also feel like we've known each other for years. This is going to sound stupid, but I feel more comfortable with you than I've ever felt with anyone."

Mika looked at her earnest fox-like face, her silky hair, her beautiful brown eyes. She felt a flood of warmth.

She coughed. She was suddenly hyper aware of Mercury's bareness so lose to her on the couch.

"I feel really comfortable with you too," she said softly. Her hand pulsed where she had held Mercury's. She withdrew it further, subconsciously. She felt warm and light-headed.

Mercury smiled at her.

Mika stood up. "Well I guess it's time for bed," she said.

"You want to go to bed?"

"Uh, yes. Well *I* need to. You can do whatever you like," said Mika. Her cheeks were red.

Why is she so flustered all of a sudden? wondered Mercury.

"Okay, sure."

"I insist you take the bed though," said Mika, remembering her manners. "I can sleep on the couch."

"Absolutely not, I wouldn't dream of kicking you out of your bed."

"I insist Mercury. Please sleep in my bed."

Her cheeks grew red again.

"Okay fine, I don't want to upset you," laughed Mercury.

Mika made up the couch while Mercury got ready for bed.

"Is there anything I can get you?"

"I've been sleeping on the couch at Animal House," said Mercury. "Your beautiful bed is absolutely fine."

Mercury sat down in the chair beside the couch. She wasn't ready to go to sleep yet.

"Do you think things are going to get better?" she asked. The world felt precarious, like the dream that children have of world peace was in danger.

Mika thought about the children running free on the beach by the Mother House citadel.

"I think they already are."

They chatted more.

"You still never told me why Allat," said Mika, lying back in the blankets on the couch with a smile.

"Oh. Allat is the feminine form of Allah, the Muslim god," said Mercury.

Mika waited for her to continue.

"Well, not the feminine form exactly... Allat was the ancient Arabian goddess who was worshipped before Allah was invented."

"Really? Interesting..."

"Basically men started declaring themselves gods, or prophets, or the only true messengers of a supreme male god, and they made war on indigenous traditions with many godds. All the Testamenters did it. But the temples and sacred spaces devoted to the goddess Allat were converted to spaces for worshipping Allah. If you go back in the history of any land that is Christian or Muslim now, it once had many godds and the people were connected to the earth and her spirits."

"That's like Japan. We don't have man's religion there. My grandparents taught me to respect nature and the land."

"Yes!" said Mercury, excited to talk about this with someone who could understand. "The oasis in the desert was sacred—the trees, the water, the growing season—Priestesses called Dreamers would sleep beneath the sacred trees to receive messages from Allat." She paused. "To me, she symbolizes a time when people were more connected to the world's beauty."

Mercury and Mika talked late into the night. Eventually Mika fell asleep on the couch with Mercury beside her in the chair.

CHAPTER TWENTY ONE

Valkyrie woke with intense pain in her abdomen.

No, she thought. *No, no, no, no...*

She willed the pain to pass. She could not give birth here, in this place.

Not yet, little one, she thought.

The pain passed, but she was due soon. The baby could come any day now.

Baron stopped by in the morning for coffee.

"Let me make it," said Valkyrie.

She opened the cupboard and prepared their cups while Baron ranted and raved.

He called himself the father of the baby. He fantasized that he was having a boy.

"How will I give birth?" asked Valkyrie. "Do you have a doctor on call?"

"Women have been giving birth forever," he boomed. "Nothing to worry about."

"Giving birth and dying," said Val. "Especially old ones like me."

"Everything will be fine. I'm sure of it."

Valkyrie was not sure. She was worried. This psychopath could get her—and the baby—killed.

Valkyrie slipped the metal spoon from the cabinet into her shirt. She brought Baron his coffee.

"Here dear," she said.

Val worked on Baron to get Courtney off of the colostomy bag. At least then she would be helpful in an escape. In her current condition she was a helpless creature.

Like me, thought Valkyrie, holding her massive stomach. She hadn't run in months.

When their coffee was done Baron kissed her cheek and sent her back to Teresa's room.

Valkyrie could not figure Teresa out. She spent all day reading fairy tales. Sometimes she seemed alert, and other times she was completely vacant.

"What happened to you?" Valkyrie asked.

Teresa just looked at her with her ghostly sadness-lined face.

Valkyrie spent the day filing the spoon handle against the strip of sand tape running along the floor under the door frame. After about an hour she relaxed into a rhythm and continued with her meditation as she filed. Teresa looked up at her occasionally with a blank expression.

That evening Baron came by with dinner. He wheeled Courtney into Teresa's room.

"Hello my beauties," he said.

Courtney barked a single terse laugh. Valkyrie was squinting and sweating and dishevelled, Teresa looked like she had the life sucked out of her, and Courtney herself was a wreck.

Valkyrie laughed too. She squeezed the spoon hard in her hand, waiting for her moment. The handle wasn't as sharp as it could be, but it was sharp enough.

"I thought we could all have a nice dinner together," he said.

The gurney Courtney was on was propping open the door. It was perfect.

Baron reached into his bag to pull out the takeout boxes.

As he bent down Valkyrie seized the moment. She channeled all her anger inside of her and with one enraged thrust she plunged the sharpened edge of the spoon into Baron's neck with a scream.

Baron shot up, swinging a fist and catching Valkyrie directly in the face. She stumbled back and fell on the floor.

He scrambled backwards into Courtney's gurney. She raked the claws of her free hand along his face. He pushed her down the hall and slammed the door to Teresa's room shut. He ran down the hall to the exit with the spoon sticking out of his neck and flew out the door with the sound of Courtney laughing crazily echoing in the hall behind him.

*

Mika woke in the stillness of morning, the winter sun shining in onto her face.

She looked over at Mercury who had spent the night in the chair. She smiled. Thinking about their conversation last night warmed her. Something about Mercury was special. She was a treasure. She snored softly with her head rolled to the side.

Mika rose slowly, careful not to wake her guest. She put Mercury's clothes from the wash into the dryer and then went to the kitchen to make coffee.

Mercury woke soon after.

"Coffee?" asked Mika.

"Mmm, thank you," said Mercury.

They enjoyed their cups together to the soft hum of the dryer.

"I wonder how Jordan is getting on in Nova Scotia," said Merc.

"He's in good hands," said Mika, thinking of Margarethe. "The sisters will know what to do with him."

"Sisters?"

"The arcology, the community... it's a long story."

Mika explained the project that Valkyrie was working on, that she herself was working on.

I am a sister too, realized Mika. The thought was comforting, like discovering a long-lost family.

"I've heard of it," said Merc excitedly. "I saw a video on YouTube about it. The way you describe it sounds more... spiritual."

"Whatever that means," said Mika. "Yes. We did a little promotional video to encourage investors when we needed more start-up capital. We're well-endowed now. Valkyrie is quite a visionary..."

They went out for lunch and spent the afternoon chatting.

That evening Mika's phone rang.

She answered.

"Hello?"

"You need to get home right away."

It was Margarethe.

"What is it?"

"Valkyrie's gone."

*

Margarethe hung up the phone with a clatter. She was frowning.

"Could she be out shopping or something?" asked Jordan.

"No. Something is wrong. I can feel it."

Jordan looked around this slow and mystical place. He felt

shadows of all he missed in the last months away from Valkyrie. This journey he was on was taking him in strange and unexpected directions.

"What should we do next?" he asked.

"Wait for Mika. She will know what to do."

By Loop and then lift she would be here in a few short hours. Margarethe paced back and forth.

"Hey, I'm sure everything will be okay," he said.

"You don't understand. She is in no condition to be gone like this."

"Mika said she only lost memories of last year, that she still has her faculties," said Jordan.

"No young man, that's not what I'm talking about. Valkyrie is heavily pregnant."

Jordan's jaw dropped.

"What? Are you serious?"

Margarethe eyed him and chuckled.

"So Mika didn't tell you?"

"No."

"Ah well, she knew you would find out soon enough. Yes. Last year Valkyrie became pregnant."

Jordan looked devastated.

"Don't worry, there is no other man in the picture," cackled Margarethe.

"How..."

"A miracle," said Margarethe.

I hope not Baron's, thought Jordan darkly.

"What are you glowering about? A baby is cause for celebration."

"I just... hope it's not Baron's," he mumbled. No use hiding his thoughts from Margarethe.

"It's not," said Margarethe. "Valkyrie told me so herself."

Jordan sighed with relief. He imagined Valkyrie large with child. She was probably a beautiful pregnant woman. He missed her more than ever.

*

When Baron returned that evening he was livid. His neck was bandaged up and he'd cleaned up his bloody face where Courtney scratched him. He looked a fright.

He shoved Courtney on her gurney back into her room. He shackled her as tight as her restraints would allow.

"I'm never letting you free again you filthy bitch," he spat in her ear, slamming the door behind him.

I might do away with her yet, he thought. His hope for her recovery was dashed when she clawed him.

He took a deep breath and opened the door to Teresa's room.

"Valkyrie," he said, stepping into the room.

Teresa whimpered quietly in the corner facing the floor.

"Shut up," he snarled.

She was silent.

Valkyrie was sitting on the bed. A huge bruise puffed out on her swollen face. Her arms were wrapped around her stomach and her eyes were closed.

Baron closed and locked the door behind him.

He pulled a charged-up Taser out of his pocket.

"Don't push me girls," he said. "Why did you do this to me?"

Valkyrie said nothing.

Baron grabbed her arm and squeezed.

"Why?" he shouted.

"Don't hurt the Saviour baby," cried Teresa from the corner.

Baron shot her with the Taser. Her entire body went rigid and her face looked terrified as she crumpled to the floor, her hands twisted into claws. When Baron released her, she shrieked with pain.

"Shut up!" he screamed.

She sobbed as softly as she could.

Baron pulled Valkyrie roughly up.

"Into your own room," he said. He took her down the hall.

He shoved her into her room, holding the stun gun ready. He grabbed the espresso machine and ripped it out of the wall, throwing it into the hallway. He opened the cupboard doors and slammed everything inside onto the floor.

"Sit down," he commanded. Valkyrie sat on the bed.

"Why are you fighting the prophecy?" he hissed.

He pulled a small Bible out of his pocket and opened it to a well-worn page.

The angel went to her and said,

'Greetings, you who are highly favoured! The Lord is with you...

---

blessed art thou among women, and blessed is the fruit of thy womb...
You will give birth to a king.'

'How will this be,' Mary asked the angel, 'since I am a virgin?'

'The Holy Spirit will come on you, and the power of the Most
High will overshadow you.'

And Mary said, 'I am the bondslave of the Lord. Do unto me
according to thy will.'

Baron shut the book and put it back in his pocket.

"The God in me is becoming man through your body Valkyrie.
How do you not see that?" he roared.

Valkyrie said nothing. Hot tears ran down her cheeks. Her
bruise throbbed.

"You have been chosen as the vessel of salvation, you ungrateful
wretch!"

He paced back and forth.

Valkyrie willed him to leave.

Finally, Baron stopped pacing. He took a few deep breaths.
Then he pulled out a needle.

"I think it's best for our family if we continue your treatments,"
he said.

Valkyrie felt instantly sick.

"No," she murmured. "Please, no."

He took a step toward her. She felt bile rising in her throat and
she vomited all over him.

He leapt back in disgust as she puked her guts out.

When she was done he grabbed her roughly.

"Stay still," he snarled.

"What will it do to the baby?" she shrieked.

Baron wavered. He looked hard at her for several long beats,
the muscles popping out in his clenched jaw. Then he lowered the
needle.

Valkyrie relaxed.

Baron plunged the needle into her arm. She sank into
unconsciousness.

CHAPTER TWENTY TWO

Mika and Mercury rode in the lift from the Loop station out to the arcology.

"What is the community like?" asked Merc.

"It's a beautiful place, sure," said Mika. "But the people make it what it is. We work together. We trust each other. It's like nothing I've ever experienced before."

Mercury thought of Allat and her ancient followers. She couldn't explain it, but as they drove along the unfamiliar highway into the desolate, snowy unknown, Mercury Elmahdy felt like she was going home.

Mika arrived at Gray House with Mercury by her side.

"Tell me what's happened," she asked.

"Come," said Margarethe, taking her out to the Seer's Cottage.

"It looks like she left in a hurry."

"And the door was slightly open," said Margarethe. "She must have."

"Could she have gone into labour?" asked Mika.

"Perhaps."

Margarethe held the veil close to her heart. She and Mika exchanged worried looks.

"I'll go straight into town to check the hospitals," said Mika.

"Can you check online?" she asked Mercury. "Maybe she's registered somewhere."

"I'll get right on it," said Mercury, glad to help. She pulled her laptop out of her backpack.

Margarethe cast a glance at her.

"Who is this?"

"Allat," said Mika.

Mercury blushed red. She was still not ready to fully own her power.

"Allat," said Margarethe. "We welcome your wisdom in the Order."

Mercury felt dizzy with the spiritual weight of the moment. She nodded, saying nothing. Her eyes said everything.

This was the community she was waiting to find.

She swallowed hard and sat at the table, getting to work on finding Valkyrie Snow.

*

Mika took off for the city. She checked every major hospital looking for Valkyrie. She found nothing.

Jordan was beside himself with worry. He was pulling on his hair, wishing there were something that he could do to help. He pulled out his own laptop and started researching.

"What's this?" asked Mercury, coming up beside him.

Jordan tilted his screen down, embarrassed. He looked at Merc shamefaced.

"What is it?"

Jordan tilted the screen back up. Mercury wouldn't judge him.

"It's Valkyrie's ex-husband," he said. "I just don't trust him. Every time I try to imagine what happened to Valkyrie, all I can think of is Baron Toussaint."

Mercury came closer with interest.

"Did you tell Mika?"

"No... it seems petty. To suspect her ex."

"It's not unreasonable," said Mercury quietly. "Most women who are murdered are killed by their exes."

Jordan swallowed hard, feeling a spike of panic at the word 'murdered'.

"Not that anything bad happened to her at all," said Merc quickly. "Just if there were foul play it could logically be him."

Jordan showed her the news article about the legal trouble Baron's company was in.

"He looks stressed," she said. "Were they on bad terms?"

"No. I have no proof at all," said Jordan.

Mercury went back to her research.

Mika returned late that evening to Gray House.

"Nothing," she said grimly.

"Me too," said Mercury. "She's not registered at any hospitals in the province that I could find."

Jordan felt ill.

"Where can she be?" he moaned.

"You should tell her your suspicions," said Mercury.

Jordan looked momentarily embarrassed.

"I feel like her ex-husband Baron Toussaint might have something to do with this," he said.

"Why?"

"I don't know."

"Can you look into that?" she asked Merc.

"I did a bit. I can look deeper."

That night, Farrah set Mercury up in one of the small wooden cabins in the village that had been left vacant for the winter.

"It's not insulated, but with a fire in the woodstove you'll be plenty warm to sleep."

It was nice to have a private space to spend the night.

Mercury got up at the crack of dawn to get to work investigating Baron Toussaint.

What she found was that he was a slimy creature. Employees in his company were caught up in the child sex industry. Baron was violently anti-union and hired guns to put down attempts by workers in his foreign operations to demand a living wage.

Mercury found out that Baron was an active member of the Friday Club. It was an upper-class branch of the Fraternity. The Fraternity was one of the unfortunate by-products of the crumbling American government. Where the federal legislature receded, pseudo-governmental forces rose up. The Mormon Church took back the lands it governed in the theocratic rule of Utah Territory in the nineteenth century. Gangs took over poor neighbourhoods across the United States and regional autonomies emerged. What made the Fraternity particularly dangerous was their far-reaching solidarity across state lines.

The Friday Club that Baron was part of was largely based out of the New England region of the United States. He appeared to have joined up at the end of his marriage to Valkyrie Snow. Mercury trawled deep into the internet looking for more connections. Nothing.

She read a manifest of members.

...Hiram Switzer.

John Decker.

She paused. Why did that name sound familiar?

She looked up John Decker.

There was nothing in the conventional channels but the usual business scandals. Then she found something creepy.

John Decker was involved in some kind of organ harvest racket.

He was supposedly dealing some kind of Cadillac drug derived from human tissues.

Mercury scanned the information feeling her pulse quicken.

Her eyes caught a headline: *Missing University Students.*

Her heart skipped a beat. She thought of Anastasia, her missing friend from a lifetime ago.

John Decker. Jensen Decker. The President of the Alpha Alpha Delta fraternity.

She found Jensen Decker's resume on the Georgetown website for Alpha Alpha Delta. He did an internship at John Decker's company. They were probably related.

Mercury's blood cooled at the connection.

Poor Ana, she thought.

Mercury was sure now that Baron had something to do with Valkyrie's disappearance. She couldn't prove it, but there were too many eerie coincidences for it not to be so. She dug deeper with a vengeance.

After hours of searching, Mercury hit a wall. Barring actually infiltrating Baron's personal finances, she couldn't find a direct link between Baron, the missing women, and Valkyrie Snow. She considered going down that path. The thought made her nervous. She wanted to lay low for a while and that would be highly illegal. Messing with the bank was probably more difficult and dangerous than anything she had ever done in the past.

She decided that it was time to reach out to Femnonymous.

*

Mika was desperate and she resorted to driving around the countryside looking for Valkyrie. After several hours she accepted that it was a waste of her time.

Could this all have something to do with Baron Toussaint?

She headed home. She would call the hospitals in the Ottawa area.

And then I may just take a trip to Ottawa myself, she thought.

*

Mercury received a message on her phone.

Let's meet in virtual, A11+.

Mercury shivered. Femnonymous used Leet/1337 to avoid bots sweeping for her name. These were her people. She sent her Virtual information.

Not Virtual Reality Connect. It's not safe. Use Virtuous.

But isn't that less safe? Hackable?

We control the medium, typed the FemAnon.

Mercury realized that was true. The hack networks were permeable but chaotic. They would be almost impossible to trace if you didn't know where to look.

See you in ten.

Mercury trudged out of the village to the Seer's Cottage. She'd seen snowshoes hanging on the wall and she knew she would need them in the deep snow off the beaten path. Mercury's Crossing had taught her a great many lessons, one of which was to be prepared.

She strapped on the shoes—an incredible gift from the Onamag—and headed out to the arcology on the peninsula. The area was bare of trees and she would be able to cast a 3D construct against the snow with her Augmented Reality phone, like a projector.

She turned on Virtuous and held the phone in the air.

Two mythic figures walked into the construct from a distance.

One was dressed in white with massive wings and the other had a black veil and witch hat like the Femnonymous video.

"Hi," she said.

"Greetings Allat," said the witch. "It is an honour to meet you."

"Thanks," said Mercury.

"I'm a cyber angel," said the other. "I don't interfere, I do nothing illegal. I merely observe. I bear witness."

These people could be anyone in the world. Mercury wondered what their bio lives looked like.

"I need to know what happened to Valkyrie Snow," she said.

"Valkyrie Snow," echoed the two voices.

"Give us a moment Allat," said the cyber witch, her avatar going still.

Mercury waited. The angel watched her closely.

"You're really shivering... that's not a construct. You show your bio face and your bio reality," she said.

"I have nothing left to hide," said Mercury.

The cyber witch returned.

"We hacked her Oracle," she said. "It was last connected almost a week ago. Here is the last recovered data."

A drive-in theatre appeared in Virtual and the Oracle transmission appeared on the screen like a trippy gif. Mercury saw a white-haired woman in a faded dress at the door of the Seer's Cottage. She looked helter-skelter and she was talking about a baby. The image was broken and unclear, recovered from Valkyrie's own processing of the visual data.

"No no no no..." shouted the Oracle and the image went black.

"Who is that woman?" asked Mercury.

The cyber witch went still again and the image of the woman appeared back on the screen. Thousands of images streamed by for comparison. Several top matches floated in the sky.

Mercury scanned them, frowning.

Then she saw him.

Baron Toussaint.

There was a picture of the woman smiling up at him. She looked much younger.

"There," said Merc. "That one."

"Teresa Bernard," said the witch. There was a pause. "Missing since 2027."

"Where is the picture from?" she asked.

"Toussaint International twentieth anniversary party," said the witch. "With her husband, Baron Toussaint."

"Valkyrie Snow's ex-husband," said Mercury.

"Indeed. Teresa married him next."

"And they are both missing," said the angel.

The angel went still. Then she returned. "Courtney Grant, Baron's current wife, is also missing," she said.

All roads led to Baron. And things did not look good for Valkyrie Snow.

"What else can we do Allat?"

Mercury thought on it.

"Jensen Decker. John Decker. The Friday Club," she said. "Something terrible is going on. Please find out what it is."

"A pleasure, for you," said the witch, passing along the information at electric speed.

"And my friend. Anastasia Simon," said Mercury. "She disappeared. Please find her."

"Are you safe?" asked the angel softly.

"I'm safe," she said.

There was silence. The meeting was coming to a close.

"Do you have a message, Allat?"

"Yes," she said. "Keep going."

So much for lying low.

The transmission was over. Mercury was back to reality, standing in the darkness on the edge of the ocean in snowshoes in Canadian winter. It was as surreal as virtual.

Mercury hiked back to Gray House and her laptop computer. Now that she was certain that Baron Toussaint was the keystone in her troubles, she was ready to take him down.

CHAPTER TWENTY THREE

Mercury shamelessly hacked Baron's every move online.

If it turns out that he had something to do with Anastasia's disappearance, I'll do more than violate his digital privacy, she thought.

At this point she was certain that if Valkyrie Snow was alive, she was in Ottawa. According to her research, Baron took a lift out to a location on the outskirts of town fairly frequently. It wasn't his office. Closer investigation revealed that one of his companies was leasing the building from one of his other companies.

His visits to the building had been going on for years. He used to change up his patterns and use different companies, but in the last five months or so he wasn't hiding his activity at all.

Got you, thought Mercury with grim satisfaction.

Either he got too busy in the last few months to take care of things or he is getting cocky.

Mercury filled everyone in on what she discovered.

"See?" said Mercury pointing to a graph she spun up of Baron's lift activity. "When Courtney went missing there was a spike in activity. And when Valkyrie went missing it spiked again."

Jordan's face looked ashen.

"You seriously think she's in there?" he asked, but in his heart he knew it was true.

"Yes."

"Should we call the police?" he asked.

"The problem is that they don't have enough evidence to go in, and she could die in childbirth by then," said Mercury.

Jordan gulped.

"To be brutally honest."

"So you know exactly where she is?" said Margarethe.

"Yes."

"I'll go," said Margarethe.

"No," said Mika.

"Absolutely not," said Chanda.

"I'll go," she said, more firmly. "Don't argue with me." Her tone was imperious.

"It should be pretty straightforward actually," said Mercury. "He uses this trackable service to get to and from the warehouse. I can tap right in and see what he's doing."

"Unless tomorrow he decides to take a different car," said Mika.

"But judging by this behaviour pattern, that isn't going to happen," said Mercury.

"Piece of cake," said Margarethe.

Mika frowned.

"I can work from anywhere," said Mercury. "If we get chatterbugs I can talk directly to Margarethe from a headset and we can all tap in and listen."

"I want to go," said Jordan.

"You can't," said Mika. "We still don't know what will happen to her mind when she sees you. I'll go."

"You will not," said Margarethe. "The arcology needs you."

"I'm going," snapped Mika.

"And what if she's dead already?" said Margarethe. "If something happens to you, what will the community do then? All of Valkyrie's dreams will die with her."

"You can't go," said Farrah gently. "We need you here. The community needs you."

Margarethe grabbed her chin with a firm hand and looked into her eyes. "I may be old but I'm not dead yet, *oy blin!*"

"Sorry grandmother," muttered Mika.

It was decided. Margarethe would go to Baron's warehouse.

Mika, Jordan, Mercury and Margarethe went into the city and hired a hotel room to monitor Margarethe's progress from. They got chatterbugs and showed Margarethe how to use hers. Then she left for Ottawa.

"I still can't believe I agreed to this," muttered Mika.

"I hear you now," said Margarethe.

"I know."

*

The next time Valkyrie woke up it was just like when she 'had cancer'. She was strapped to the bed in the room styled as a hospital and she was hooked up to a bag pumping green fluid into her body through an IV. She groaned. Her head felt like it was splitting open. She tried to meditate but her thoughts were a mess.

There was no night or day in the bunker and in her current state Valkyrie completely lost track of time. She drifted in and out of tortured consciousness for what could have been weeks or merely hours.

In a moment of clarity she wondered what was happening at Gray House.

Have they even realized that I'm gone yet? she thought through the pain. *Please... please help me...*

*

Margarethe arrived in Ottawa by Loop and took a lift straight to the area of the warehouse. The car waited in the parking lot of a nearby restaurant.

"We'll wait until he leaves for the night and then you can go in," said Mercury.

"You are a powerful witch, Allat," said Margarethe.

Mercury laughed.

Mika frowned and shook her head. She wished she was there.

Jordan was pacing the hotel room.

Finally Baron took the car to the warehouse.

"We have movement," said Mercury into the earpiece.

"Can I go now?" asked Margarethe.

"No. he's heading to the warehouse now. I'll tell you when he leaves."

They waited over an hour.

"What's he doing in there?" asked Jordan. He felt sick.

"It's a good sign. It means she's probably alive."

Then the car left the warehouse. Mercury could hardly believe the power of information at her fingertips.

"Wait for thirty minutes," said Mercury. "Just in case he comes back."

They all waited.

When enough time had passed, Margarethe took the car out to the warehouse. It was a dull concrete building that looked abandoned. Margarethe felt her heart beat faster.

My shotse is in there, she thought. It made her sick just thinking about it.

The car circled the building twice. The door at the back had a tiny green light in a panel on the wall. It was the only sign of life in the place.

That must be where the devil goes in, thought Margarethe.

She got out of the car, crowbar in hand.

"Stay close," she told the robot driver.

She crept to the door.

"You're sure he's not here?" she whispered.

"We know he isn't there right now," said Mercury into the earpiece. "But be careful."

"Please be careful," said Mika. Her voice was tense with worry.

"You don't know how many times I snuck between East Berlin and West Berlin in the eighties," said Margarethe. "If the Stasi couldn't find me, this devil won't."

Mika felt oddly comforted.

Margarethe looked at the panel on the door.

"There is a security box here," she said. She raised the crowbar.

"I thought there might be," said Merc. "Just a sec."

"What are you doing?" asked Mika.

"Since I discovered this building I've been monitoring all networked activity I can there. It turns out that the security system broadcasts and it was a pretty easy hack actually." Mercury grinned.

"So you know the code," said Jordan.

"I think so, yes," she said. "Margarethe, try this." She explained the two sets of numbers.

Margarethe followed her instructions. The door clicked open.

"I am in, Allat," cackled Margarethe.

It was dark inside. Margarethe stepped into the hallway. The motion-sensored lights flicked on one by one as she walked. She tried the first door. It was locked. She squinted at the locking mechanism. She walked to the next door. It opened beneath her hand. Inside there were shelves and shelves of food and medical supplies. Her eye was drawn up to a shiny black box on the shelf. She walked over to it and ran her hand over it. It was seamless. She slipped it into her knitting bag and left the room, searching.

"Valkyrie!" she shouted.

*

Val heard her name. It was a woman's voice. She sounded familiar. Val shook her head lethargically and sat up as straight as she could in her restraints.

The IV machine hummed softly beside her, dripping green poison into her veins.

"Valkie!" she heard the voice again.

It was Margarethe.

"I'm here!" she screamed. "I'm here!"

She railed against the leather straps, cutting her own skin trying to pull out her hands.

She heard footsteps approach.

The door rattled.

Valkyrie closed her eyes and tried to focus her swimming thoughts. She tried her best to remember and then explain how to disengage the lock mechanism. In moments the door swung open.

"Hello darling," said Margarethe.

Val shrieked with emotion. Tears burned a familiar trail down her cheeks.

"Guhhhh...get me out NOW," she struggled to say. Speech was difficult. White foam dripped down the side of her mouth.

Margarethe unlatched the restraints and helped her off the bed. She ripped out the IV. Blood sprayed across the wall.

"Sorry shotse," said Margarethe.

She grabbed Valkyrie under the arm with a surprisingly strong grip.

Val found her feet and they hobbled out to the hall.

Valkyrie stopped at Teresa's door, swatting it with her arm.

"Another," she said.

Margarethe disengaged the lock. Teresa stood on the other side pressed up against the wall.

"Come now!" said Margarethe. Teresa stepped forward.

"Baron just called the lift," said Mercury into the earpiece. "He may be on his way. Get out of there."

"They say Baron is coming back," said Margarethe. "Quickly, we must go."

Teresa panicked and jumped backwards.

"You must make your own choices," said Margarethe.

They walked away and the door swung shut.

Valkyrie paused a moment outside Courtney's door.

"Get moving!" shouted Merc. "He's coming!"

"He will be here any moment," said Margarethe.

Val thought about the colostomy contraption connected to Courtney. She frowned and ran as best she could, holding Margarethe's arm.

They burst out of the building. A car was waiting for them.

"This is our ride," said Margarethe. They tumbled in and rode away.

Valkyrie broke down and cried in the back seat of the car. She squeezed her arms around herself and rocked back and forth wailing.

"Shhh," said Margarethe, stroking her hair. "You are safe now, shotse... shh..."

"Little doves, little doves, little doves..." said Valkyrie over and over, rocking back and forth.

"Take us straight to Cape Breton," said Margarethe to the driver. Valkyrie was in no condition to catch a Loop.

"What's going on?" asked Jordan.

"I have her. She is safe." Margarethe held her tight, willing her to relax. "We will meet you at Gray House."

Eventually Val stopped rocking. She shivered in Margarethe's arms, her head throbbing.

"What has the devil done to you," murmured Margarethe, pulling a handkerchief out of her knitting bag and wiping Val's brow.

Her face was half swollen and bruised. Her arms were bleeding and raw from the restraints.

Valkyrie just whimpered. She couldn't speak.

CHAPTER TWENTY FOUR

Margarethe gave Valkyrie a bath and put her to bed in her room upstairs at Gray House. The next evening they moved her to a room in the Mother House arcology. No one unwelcome would be able to get inside the thick walls of the citadel; even partially built it was a fortress. Valkyrie was on bed rest for several days.

The community was on high alert. Women patrolled the property perimeter in groups of four or more, on the lookout for any goons who might try to get Valkyrie back.

Mika sat at Valkyrie's side day after day, holding her hand.

"He won't get away with this," she said, bathing Valkyrie's arms with salve and changing the compress on her bruised face.

The energy at the arcology was heavy. Everyone watched their leaders going back and forth from the convalescence room, waiting to hear a report on the Seer's condition.

*

Jordan ached to see how Valkyrie was doing. He prowled the edges of the property all night. Baron was rich and powerful and there was no telling what he would do to get Valkyrie back. Jordan sang, his voice echoing into the crisp darkness like the nightingale singing for his lost love.

*

After several days, Valkyrie was feeling much better. The bruise darkened to purple and and it yellowed around the edges. The swelling went down.

Valkyrie's thoughts were a jumble. It was difficult to keep things straight. She spent every waking moment meditating and willing the nanites to heal instead of harm her brain.

Margarethe came to visit.

"I stole something from the devil," she said.

She pulled out the shiny black box she had taken from Baron's supply room.

"Do you know what it is?"

Valkyrie took it in her hand, testing the weight, stroking the material.

"I'm not sure," she said.

She ran hers hands over it as she and Margarethe visited.

"I must go tell the children their bedtime story," said Margarethe after a long chat, kissing her on the forehead.

"I would like to hear that," said Valkyrie quietly.

Margarethe brought her down to the large room where the heart of the arcology pulsed and hummed. While construction was ongoing, the children had made this room into a fort. There were pillows and quilts all over the cool floor. Margarethe arranged Valkyrie comfortably in an old chair. She continued playing with the black box, touching it and applying pressure in different places; she was sure it would open. The children of the arcology gathered around on the floor and Margarethe told them a story about a demon who stole a beautiful baby from a village by the ocean.

"Where do babies come from?" asked a little one, laid out on the pillows with her arms curled around her friends on each side of her.

"They grow like flowers in mommy," said another. The children giggled.

Valkyrie heard a soft *click* as the box opened. She looked down at the glowing green orb inside.

"Well that is another story," said Margarethe. "But since the Seer is with us tonight I will tell you about the babies who were brought by the stork."

Margarethe regaled them with ancient stories of the bird of life, death and rebirth accompanying souls from the great garden at the edge of the world back into new reincarnations on earth.

"Like our garden, Baba?"

Margarethe chuckled. "Is this the garden at the edge of the world?"

"Yes," said the Oracle into all of their minds.

"Yes," echoed Valkyrie, sitting with the children, her eyes starry and far away.

The Oracle pulsed back to life. Valkyrie relaxed as it absorbed the new analog data from her memories.

Mercury received a message from Femnonymous.

We have a report on the Friday Club, A11+.

Mercury cast a construct and met with a group of cyber witches. A cyber angel hovered nearby, keeping watch.

"We thank you for uncovering this evil, Allat," said a witch. "We are working to destroy it."

"What have you found?" asked Mercury.

"This human treachery runs deeper than we could have ever imagined."

They explained what Baron Toussaint, John Decker, the Friday Club, and the entire the Fraternity were up to.

It was unspeakably evil.

"And Anastasia Simon?" she asked.

"I'm sorry Allat. She is dead."

Valkyrie woke suddenly in the night. Her legs itched to walk in the cool outside. She climbed carefully out of bed. For once her mind felt strangely clear.

She slipped her bare feet into boots and padded softly down the circular hall to the exit. She walked out into the night, her nightgown flapping in the icy wind around her massive stomach.

Jordan sat in the Seer's Cottage. He felt Valkyrie's energy here in every carefully crafted detail. He let himself think of Glasshouse. Those were his life's best memories. In the last few months he blocked them from his mind because it hurt so bad to remember what he lost, but now, with the love of his life so close by recovering slowly, he let himself dream and go back to those cherished shining moments. He imagined that he was curled up with Valkyrie in the floating bed that hung from wooden chains from the ceiling, suspended beneath crystal windows in the green and golden glow of filtered light in the forest. Holding her in his arms, their hearts' energy made one, singing their love in waves of rapturous pleasure, he felt like his life was complete. All the hard days of life were made worthwhile for those moments of wondrous joy. Love bathed him

clean and renewed his spirit like he never imagined possible. He
didn't even realize that he was singing, his heart pouring out his
memories in song.

*

Valkyrie walked in the night along the cleared path toward the
warm glow of Gray House and the shadows of trees beyond.

Suddenly she heard beautiful sound. It was like the song of a
bird. Clouds of feeling moved quickly into her head, both physical
and emotional. She felt the spike of a headache, but even stronger,
her third eye tingled. Her mind and body were indiscernible as she
moved uncontrollably toward the sound. It was sweet and mournful,
and she felt in the pit of her womb that it was calling to her and her
alone. A flood of warmth dampened between her thighs as a flood of
memories pricked every nerve in her body. Her third eye itched with
memories that only her body remembered.

She arrived at the door of her stone cottage, her dear little
beloved house. She reached out and caressed the rough wood of the
door. Every nerve in her body heightened, singing in harmony with
the beautiful instrument inside. Her hands shook, the tips blue with
cold in the wintry night. She took a deep breath and pushed open the
door.

A young man sat at the table in the dark inside. As moonlight
flooded the room and outlined her silhouette against the snow, he
jumped up. His song stuttered to a halt and the chair clattered to the
floor behind him.

She stepped inside and closed the door behind her.

"Valkyrie," he said, his voice raw with emotion.

She felt the word deep in her heart and it whispered over and
over in the memories pushed just out of reach, gasped in her ear in
the throes of passion, murmured lovingly wrapped in his arms.

She wavered on her feet, dizzy with overwhelm, her body
fighting to break through the pain searing in her head.

Jordan leapt forward, holding her steady.

"Val," he said, his voice breaking with longing.

She collapsed in his arms, closing her eyes. Her body reacted
instantly to the warmth of his embrace. She felt desire rip through her
even though she didn't know who he was. She held him tight.

Jordan let out a sob.

"I love you," he said. "I love you so much..."

He squeezed her in his arms. She kissed his neck. His lips found hers and their sweetness was so familiar. She kissed him, her mind tumbling trying to remember. They kissed and kissed.

He ran his hands over her hair, down her back, every touch healing him with tender joy. He stroked her round belly with shaking hands.

Valkyrie laughed. Jordan laughed too. They kissed more.

Valkyrie shuddered with cold.

"Hey, you're freezing," he said. He kissed her forehead and went over to the woodstove. He put wood inside, not sure what he was doing. Valkyrie came over and helped him light it. The kindling caught fire and she smiled at him in the glow of the firelight. He looked at her and suddenly she caught a glimpse of his eyes.

Green eyes.

Her smile faltered and the pain jabbed her intensely. She sank down slowly on the floor.

"Val," said Jordan, sitting cross-legged on the floor and pulling her onto his lap.

"Valkyrie," he moaned, thinking of the story of Orpheus and the journey back from the Underworld.

Green eyes... The memories burst through the veil of her consciousness, flooding her with their rich detail. The smell of the wood-burning stove, the cool fingers of the pond as they swam, the sweet taste of the first berry bursting in her mouth. Heartsong. Jordan Barker's hair falling softly in his beautiful green eyes.

Jordan Barker, she thought. *Jordan...*

Suddenly she felt a tremor from within.

"Jordan," she murmured.

He pressed a hand to her head.

"What do I do?" he asked.

Valkyrie moaned. She put a hand on her stomach.

Another wave of pain shuddered through her, but this time from below. She grabbed her stomach with both hands.

Realization came over Jordan. He wrapped his arms around her and held her tight from behind.

Valkyrie laughed. It was all she could do. Her mind was overwhelmed but her body knew exactly what to do. She had no choice; the baby was coming.

"Should I go get help?" said Jordan.

Valkyrie just moaned, willing the birth to be smooth.

"I can't leave you like this," he said.

The thought of pushing her out of his lap and leaving, even for a few minutes, filled him with panic. He couldn't imagine ever letting go.

He remembered his phone. He called Mika.

"Jordan?" she said, answering.

"I'm in the Seer's Cottage with Valkyrie. She's giving birth."

There was a full second of pause.

"On my way."

Mika hung up.

In moments Margarethe was at the door.

"Mika is getting the doctor," she said. "Stay where you are."

Margarethe busied herself boiling water on the woodstove and digging around for towels.

It was not long before Mika arrived with a woman from the village. They had several doctors in the community.

Valkyrie was in labour all night.

Finally, as the dawn broke on the horizon, so did the baby.

She separated from Valkyrie's body into the welcoming arms of many smiling women. Margarethe seared the umbilical cord with a burning coal from the woodstove.

Octavia Dawn was born.

Margarethe cleaned the baby and wrapped her in Valkyrie's veil. She nestled the babe into Valkyrie's waiting arms.

Valkyrie was exhausted but overjoyed.

Jordan and the women helped to carry Valkyrie to the bathroom and into the tub. She and Jordan were drenched in Valkyrie's childbirth blood and juices.

That night, Valkyrie, Jordan and Octavia Dawn slept nestled in the cozy loft of the Seer's Cottage.

I'm going to be a better father than mine ever was, thought Jordan fiercely, falling asleep touching the tiny pink hand.

Over the next few days Jordan brought Valkyrie everything she needed while she recovered.

The childbirth blood soaked into the floor of the cottage; he tried to scrub it away but the crimson flower would not be removed.

"No matter," said Margarethe. "The first of many childbirth stains on this floor."

Valkyrie recovered quickly. The hormone aftermath of birthgiving flooded her body with strength. Her bruises went down, her headaches subsided and her womb was restored. She kissed Jordan for hours, and the endorphins of their connection coursed through her body, shooting into every fibre of her being and healing her.

More than that, she felt a change within her. The memories did not completely return, but she felt as though the battle inside her was over. It was as though the nanites stopped fighting her and were helping her heal.

CHAPTER TWENTY FIVE

Mika came by Mercury's little cabin. She knocked on the door.

"Hey," said Mercury, glad to see her.

Mika came inside. There wasn't much room so she came and sat beside her on the bed.

"How are you getting on here?" asked Mika. "Are you warm enough?"

"Oh yes. It's cold if I don't wake up to put wood on the fire in the night, but I'm getting pretty good at it," she laughed.

"Good, good."

They looked at each other.

"What is it?" asked Merc.

"Do you think you'll stay?" There was hope in Mika's voice.

"I love it here. I could definitely see myself making a life here. Sometimes I miss home though."

Mika nodded.

"I miss Neena and Giddy."

"Your grandparents?"

"Yea. I was thinking that maybe they could come live here

when the arcology is built," she said. "That might be wishful thinking though."

"You never know," said Mika.

They looked into each other's eyes. Warmth and admiration passed between them.

"So how is Jordan doing?" asked Mercury. "And Valkyrie? I want to go properly meet her when she's feeling better."

"They're good. They're happy."

"Is that an Oracle I see around her neck on a chain?"

"Yes."

"Cool, I've only heard about those online, I've never really seen one. I'd like to talk to her about that too."

"I was wondering if you might want to come check out the arcology with me?" said Mika. "It would be great to get your digital genius input on our architectural plans."

"Really?" Mercury grinned.

"Yea."

Mika gave her a tour around the base of the citadel that was built so far. She showed her where her room was, and she showed her the heart chamber where the molecular disassociator machine was housed.

"Pretty cool," said Merc.

"Valkyrie invented it," said Mika.

She showed her the plans for the finished building.

"This is incredible."

"Unbelievable, right?"

Mercury felt her pulse quicken with excitement. This was definitely a project she could lend her expertise to. Ideas bubbled up from her creative fountain.

They spent the rest of the afternoon pouring over schematics and planning the citadel's future.

*

March came, and the community prepared to celebrate the beginning of spring in their feast of Eostara. Eostara was the ancient godd of the dawn, and so Valkyrie was combining the feast day with a ritual blessing for Octavia Dawn.

A dancing floor was stomped out in the snow on the peninsula by the arcology. It was still winter, but the drip of water from the eaves and the occasional chirp of returning birds whispered the coming of spring. A series of fire pits were prepared and boughs of last year's dried flowers were tied to poles. They would dance spring into existence out of the fires of winter.

Jordan prepared a set of vows to sing to Valkyrie and Octavia Dawn at the festival. The women kept the surprise.

The last of the winter food was hauled out of the corners of the cellars. They would make a great feast and then observe a light fast until the first crops. The seeds were already germinating in the greenhouses, ready to creep out of the soil any day now.

Food was set out in mounds on low handmade tables as the sun sank lower in the sky. It was an odd assortment of last season's leftovers; potatoes cooked up by the children on sticks over the fire, sundried tomatoes soaked in sunflower oil, dried seeds and fruit pastes, popcorn, and chewy jerky.

Women lit the fires, and the stones heated up slowly to cook up bowls of grain-pounded Viking-style bread dough. There was plenty of butter and milk from the cows to enrich the meal.

A group of visitors arrived. The community had invited the neighbouring First Nations to join in the feast. Some wore their community regalia and they went down to the village to meet the people there.

The festival planning committee donned their festival dresses woven of dried grass and shredded fabric and walked through the village with torches and sceptres, inviting the community to the dancing floor. The children squealed with excitement, stepping in line with the growing procession and joining in the dance.

Their last stop was the arcology. They anointed the building with an offering of fresh eggs in Eostara's tradition.

Circling the dance floor drummers began to lay out an enticing beat.

Then the dancing began.

Mercury was overwhelmed with joy. She danced ecstatically by the fire, thoroughly in her element.

She's beautiful when she dances, thought Mika.

Mercury noticed her looking and beckoned with a smile.

Mika usually hated dancing but she was powerless to resist. She danced close, letting the music guide her movement.

"You are so graceful," breathed Mercury.

Mika was a martial artist and her gestures reflected her training. She laughed. They danced and danced.

The drummers slowed on Margarethe's signal. It was time for the ritual.

Valkyrie brought Octavia Dawn forward.

"We welcome you to the world," she called out to the gathered women. The community murmured their assent.

"By the honour of Eostara, we welcome Octavia Dawn," shouted Farrah. The gathered people cheered.

Margarethe anointed the baby with a cracked egg. Then she rubbed the rest of the egg on Valkyrie's stomach.

"We honour the sacred womb of Eostara, giving birth to spring," she said. Valkyrie closed her eyes, channeling the godd. She started to dance.

Margarethe signalled the drummers and the beat leapt with happiness as the dance resumed.

Several hours later, the dancing lulled again. The drummers guided the dancers to a hum, and people broke away to enjoy the food and drinks laid out on the feast tables. Storytellers came forward to share and entertain.

Jordan Barker stepped forward.

"I have an offering," he said. "To honour this woman, the heart of my heart, and this little gem."

Valkyrie's eyes shone with happiness. Octavia Dawn snoozed in her baby wrap around Valkyrie's front.

Jordan's sweet voice lifted in song.

Little gem shines out of the darkness
Bringing light to the cold of winter
She's a diamond girl like her momma
Little light of my life.

Who can say what little gems can do?
I have such beautiful hopes for you
Your little heart is oh so true
Little light of my life.

Her pearly hair shines in the sun

Her tiger's eyes laugh at my jokes
Her sapphire smile heals like her momma's
Little light of my life.

Who can say what little gems can do?
I have such beautiful hopes for you
Your little heart is oh so true
Little light of my life.

I vow to love you as long as my heart beats
I vow to love you as long as the stars shine in the sky
I swear on the moon I vow to love you two lights of my life.

The song finished and the crowd cheered. Jordan's heart was bursting with love. He held Valkyrie and Octavia Dawn tenderly.

"I love you," said Valkyrie.

"I love you," said Jordan.

"That was beautiful," breathed Mercury.

Mika smiled, standing beside her.

"It's good to see them so happy."

Jordan and Valkyrie were kissing each other softly, caressing one another with gentle hands.

Mercury caught Mika's eye and they looked at one another. Mika's cheeks blushed red and she looked away.

Mercury took her hand.

"Let's dance," she said.

They found a spot and joined the revelry, falling into rhythm with the drums.

They danced all night filled with the joyful energy of the coming spring.

The sky began to hint of dawn. The fires burned low and the dancing slowed. Women stood in pockets dreaming of spring and chatting about what they planned for the coming season. This year the community was getting horses; it was a major undertaking. They also planned an ambitious corn crop. There were many things to look forward to and celebrate.

Several people still danced. Mercury and Mika were holding one another with eyes closed, moving in time to the music. Mercury squeezed tight.

Mika felt happier than she ever had in her life. Her arms were encircled around Mercury's waist and her head was resting gently on Merc's breast. She felt safe, and completely at peace.

Mercury kissed the top of her head gently. Her heart beat faster.

Mercury's emotions and energy were tumbling around inside of her. She was dizzy with feeling. She was imagining how soft Mika's lips must be. The warmth of Mika's thighs pressed up against hers was wonderful.

What is happening? she thought.

She decided to enjoy the moment and not overthink it. She and Mika had lots of time to explore this and figure out what it was. She sighed and relaxed, pressing her cheek to Mika's head and holding her tighter.

Mika held tighter too, and their energies reached gently into one another, budding with soft pleasure.

A child walked to the main fire pit. She sobbed quietly.

The women turned at the sound, watching her approach. Her eyes were wide with worry.

"What is it?" asked her mother, running forward and kneeling in front of her.

The child sniffled. She took her mother by the hand and led her down the long laneway. The other women followed. Mika and Mercury held hands as they walked down the lane.

The child led them to an old wooden cart blocking the drive. Blood was splashed around it in the snow. A sharpened cross was plunged in the centre of the cart through the body of a large brown rabbit, the symbol of Eostara.

Valkyrie frowned, holding Octavia Dawn close to her breast.

There was a note pinned to the rabbit.

SHE IS MINE, it read.

"Baron Toussaint," said Mercury.

All the women looked to Valkyrie. Her grey eyes burned.

"Baron has to die."

Valkyrie was surprised by the words as they slipped out, but she felt the truth of them like winter melting into spring. Baron had to die for them to live.

CHAPTER TWENTY SIX

The community leaders held a council meeting in the heart chamber of the arcology.

"I'll do it," said Mika.

Margarethe frowned but said nothing.

"No Mika, I'll go. He's my ex-husband," said Valkyrie quietly.

"Could you really kill him?" asked Jordan.

Valkyrie's expression was impassive.

"Yes."

"I could too," said Mika.

"He's a garbage human but I don't know if I could actually kill him, when it came right down to it..." said Mercury. "How would you do it?"

"Well I already tried stabbing his neck," said Valkyrie grimly. "So I'll have to think of something else."

"I don't want you to go," said Jordan quietly, sliding an arm around her waist. Valkyrie kissed his cheek.

"I could do it," said Margarethe. "But Baron will be expecting us. We don't know what we might find at the butcher's place, but it won't be so easy for an old one like me to get inside this time."

"I'll go," said Jordan.

Valkyrie frowned.

"You're a lover, not a fighter," she said.

"I know. But I want to protect you and Octavia."

Mercury had an idea.

"We trap him inside," she said. "We trap him inside his own little torture prison."

There was silence. Nods.

"I like it," said Mika.

"It's easy enough," said Mercury.

"But the other women," said Valkyrie quietly. "The ones I left behind. We can't leave them in there with him."

"No. We can't," said Margarethe.

"That's going to be a little more complicated," said Mercury.

They all thought on it.

"I could lure him in," said Valkyrie. "I could ask him to meet me for dinner while you rescue the others."

"And then we wait inside for him to bring you back," said Mika.

"I don't like it," said Margarethe. "He could beat you to death this time. No." she shook her head.

Jordan looked worried.

"What do you suggest, Margarethe?"

"I don't know. I think Allat should come up with a plan where no one needs to get into his devil hands."

"Remote..." said Mercury, thinking hard. "Yes. We've got to do it remote."

"Allat?" said Valkyrie.

Mika filled her in.

Suddenly Mercury was struck by an idea. Her hands dropped to her keyboard and raced across the keys. She needed to look into something. She searched the web, looking for it...

The others gave her space and continued brainstorming.

Mercury contacted Femnonymous.

Need your help, she said.

The coven awaits A11+.

"I'll be right back," she said, taking her phone outside to cast a construct.

Mercury met with a cyber witch and they formulated a plan. For this to work, she would need extra help.

Mercury filled the others in on her plan and they got to work setting it in motion. Margarethe took care of Octavia Dawn.

"I have the most important job of all," she cooed, holding the baby.

*

Valkyrie and Mercury went to a hotel in Ottawa near the St. Laurent warehouse.

"Are you ready?" asked Mercury.

"Yes," said the Oracle, throbbing green around Valkyrie's neck.

Valkyrie's Oracle was being pushed to the edges of its

technological limits. The Oracle was connected to the worlds' digital data suppository; its powers stopped just short of critical thinking, but the connection to Valkyrie's human will bridged the gap. The Oracle was essential to their plan.

"Go ahead. Wake him up."

With the help of her FemAnons, Mercury hacked the Oracle. She was fascinated to find that she needed Valkyrie's help. Her Oracle was fine-tuned to the analog data collected from her experiences: images, sensations, sounds. The Oracle was reformatted by long-term connection to Valkyrie's mind. The data was almost indiscernible without Valkyrie's analysis. Even stranger, Mercury realized that Valkyrie herself could hack the Oracle with her mind.

Together, Valkyrie's will and the Oracle's nanite fog were re-engineering the nanites in Valkyrie's body. The possibilities for medical research and the human body's potential were astounding.

Far away in a golf course manor in New England, HiramBot's eyes flicked open. He stretched out his arms as he was programmed to.

The Oracle was tapping into HiramBot, Hiram Switzer's ImmortaBot. Valkyrie Snow's body went slack. She closed her eyes. Usually the Oracle worked overtime to see through Valkyrie's senses, but now the situation was reversed. Valkyrie tried to 'see' through the sensors of HiramBot's body through her connection to the Oracle. It was a careful balance of control and letting the Oracle do its thing. HiramBot was programmed to pass as a human with self-navigation and fine motor skills so all they had to do was get him here.

Get up, thought Valkyrie.

HiramBot stood up and slammed his head into the back of the box. Valkyrie realized that she was exerting too much specific control. She relaxed, letting herself slip into a deeper meditative state.

Go outside, willed Valkyrie.

HiramBot wandered the house until he found the exit himself.

Mercury was casting a construct with the cyber witches, who watched Valkyrie's recall on the drive-in screen in the sky.

"I don't like this," murmured the cyber angel. "It's illegal."

"No need to hack Switzer's security," said a witch. "We're breaking out, not in."

The other witches cackled.

Mercury hailed a lift. The car drove up and HiramBot boarded.

"Hiram Switzer," said HiramBot. "Take me to Ottawa please."

"Right-o," said the driver robot in the car. It took off down the lane.

The most difficult part was over: getting HiramBot out of the house.

Robots like the driver connected to the global Oracle network were not capable of violence against humans. It was Principle One on the United Nations Conventions of Artificial Intelligence set out in 2025. HiramBot was a whole new generation of robot and Mercury doubted that Hiram Switzer cared about the UN conventions, but still, they couldn't rely on him for violence.

"This bio-drag is unreal," said Mercury, pulling up another screen with security camera footage from inside the car. HiramBot looked exactly like bio-Hiram. No wonder the driving bot couldn't tell the difference.

The drive was four hours. The next hurdle would be getting through the border.

"Don't worry," said a witch. "We've done border work before."

Mercury was glad she had the FemAnons on board. She knew she couldn't have done it without their help.

The border crossing was nerve-wracking but fairly straightforward. Bio-Hiram had a Nexus pass and a note on his file for expedited passage. One glance at the file and the lower-than-average-looking white middle aged man in the back of the car, and the border agents waved him along.

They hummed over the border into Canada and HiramBot headed to Ottawa.

Jordan and Mika were camped out in the restaurant near the warehouse.

Finally, HiramBot joined them.

Mercury pulled up her monitor on Baron's lift activity. It looked like Baron had never left the warehouse since their last incursion. Mercury knew that wasn't the case; Baron had figured out their hack.

"We need to be extra cautious this time," she warned into the chatterbugs. "He will have his guard up this time. You have to be prepared for anything."

Mika dropped her hand to the sword at her side.

"We're ready," she said.

The two cars drove over to the warehouse. Mika and Jordan parked in the darkness of the adjoining parking lot. HiramBot parked outside the warehouse.

In the darkness of the hotel room, Valkyrie steeled herself and relaxed, focussing on guiding Hirambot but not too intensely. It was time.

HiramBot got out of the car. He stood in the parking lot, ready.

Jordan and Mika slipped out of their car and crept through the shadows to the back of the warehouse.

"He changed the password," said Mercury. "But it's not a problem." She overrode the security system and fed them the new digits.

Mika let HiramBot into the building. She and Jordan crouched down in the ditch nearby under the cover of trees.

Valkyrie shuddered. She wanted to get in and out as soon as possible. HiramBot twitched. She forced herself to be calm.

HiramBot stalked down the hall of the Barn. The overhead lights were already on. Baron was here.

"Baron is here," whispered Valkyrie in the hotel room with her eyes closed.

"Val says that Baron is in the building," said Mercury into the chatterbugs.

"What's happening?" whispered Jordan.

"Nothing yet," said Merc.

What should I do? thought Valkyrie.

HiramBot stood in the hall, waiting for instruction.

A door down the hall opened. A man came out.

"Baron?" he said.

It was 'Dr.' Hendricks, Valkyrie's 'cancer specialist'. Baron was not here after all.

"I'm Hiram Switzer," said HiramBot. "A friend of Baron's."

'Dr.' Hendricks tensed up. He was anxious.

"Does Baron know you're here?" he asked.

HiramBot took a step forward.

"Of course," he said with a smile.

Hendricks was not convinced. He took a step back.

Valkyrie decided to take the offensive. HiramBot lunged forward, swinging out toward Hendricks. His fist made contact with the man's face, tearing off the tender flesh. Blood splattered everywhere. Hendricks fell backward into the room he came out of. He slammed the door closed with his feet.

Looks like Hiram Switzer doesn't care about the UN conventions, thought Valkyrie.

HiramBot left him and went to Teresa's room. HiramBot disengaged the lock and slammed open the door.

"Come out," he ordered.

Teresa, mad-eyed, did as she was told.

"Get out of here," he said, pointing down to the exit. She ran off.

HiramBot went to Courtney's room. Valkyrie's adrenaline was raging and she couldn't focus on communicating the lock mechanism through the Oracle. HiramBot slammed it with his fist. He slammed it again. And again. The door popped open. His hand was mangled.

Courtney looked at him in horror.

"Hiram?" she asked, incredulous.

She looked at his mecca hand, the rubber skin shredded away exposing circuitry.

"It's Valkyrie," said HiramBot, ripping off the leather straps and grabbing the gurney and pushing it out of the room and down the hall.

Baron was standing at the end of the hall with a gun to Teresa's head.

"Stop right there," he boomed.

HiramBot stopped. "What are you going to do?" he said calmly.

Baron was amazed at the facial animation. It was just like Hiram.

"Who's in there?" he asked. "I know it's not Hiram."

"Who the fuck do you think?"

Courtney laughed.

Baron pointed the gun at her.

"Shut up, bitch," he said.

Suddenly the door behind him opened. Mika burst in, slashing him across the back with her sword. He whirled around and unloaded his gun on her, spraying bullets everywhere. One caught her and she fell to the floor.

HiramBot slammed the gurney with Courtney on it and it clattered over Baron, knocking him down. Courtney was thrown off. The colostomy needle ripped out of her and blood and feces spewed everywhere.

She howled with pain and grabbed the sword from Mika on the floor. She raised it, ready to finish Baron. She looked down at him. He looked up at her from under the gurney and she faltered. She couldn't do it.

"Kill him!" screamed Mika.

Baron slithered out from under the gurney and grabbed the sword out of her hands.

Teresa raised her fist. Something glinted silver in her hand. It was a sharpened spoon.

She sank it deep into Baron's eye with a wail.

HiramBot tumbled over the gurney and slammed a hand onto the spoon, driving it all the way in.

The car screeched up outside.

Jordan dragged Mika and Courtney into the backseat with him. Teresa jumped in the front and they took off to the hospital.

"What's happening?" shouted Mercury into the chatterbugs.

Valkyrie withdrew from meditation, disengaging from HiramBot.

"Mika..." said Jordan. "I think Mika is dead."

The backseat of the car was pooled with blood.

Mercury gasped. She and Valkyrie grabbed a ride and met them at the hospital.

Emergency staff grabbed Mika's limp body and took her away.

CHAPTER TWENTY SEVEN

After a week in critical care, Mika finally opened her eyes. She lost almost half of her blood from her gunshot wound, but with multiple transfusions, her condition stabilized.

"Mika," whispered Mercury, holding her hand.

Mercury had spent every day at Mika's side.

Mika moaned softly. Her whole body ached.

"Hospital," she rasped, taking in her surroundings. Her throat was bone dry.

"Yes. You're safe. You're going to be okay." Mercury's voice broke with emotion. Tears rolled down her cheeks.

"Sorry, I'm happy," she laughed.

Mika smiled. She squeezed Mercury's hand and looked up at her face. It was the most beautiful thing she'd ever seen.

Jordan was also in the hospital. He was committed to being a good father to Octavia Dawn and Valkyrie was supporting him in his journey to recovery. He was seeing a therapist and trying out different medications to manage his depression.

I think I will make it past twenty-seven after all, he thought.

EPILOGUE

Octavia Dawn was growing like a weed. Her short legs carried her across the beach into her mother's open arms.

"Hi little gem," said Jordan, kissing her nose. She giggled. Jordan felt his heart swell with a happiness that burned deep in his soul.

"You're going to have a brother and sister soon," said Valkyrie. She turned.

Mika and Mercury walked toward them on the beach. They both held their baby bumps in one hand. Their other hands were wrapped around one another. Neena and Giddy Elmahdy walked not far behind, holding hands, their bare feet joyously kicking the sand.

The completed arcology rose up behind them, a massive green citadel at the edge of the world, touching the clouds.

ABOUT THE AUTHOR

Cameron Dreamshare is a Canadian author, artist, and feminist anarchist unicorn.

Subscribe at **www.CameronDreamshare.com** for updates like the release of the next book in the series.

www.ingramcontent.com/pod-product-compliance
Lightning Source LLC
Chambersburg PA
CBHW021004120726
47905CB00009B/2849